The Italian Affair

By the same author

True Deception
Ultimate Betrayal

The Italian Affair

Loren Teague

ROBERT HALE · LONDON

© Loren Teague 2010
First published in Great Britain 2010

ISBN 978-0-7090-8995-7

Robert Hale Limited
Clerkenwell House
Clerkenwell Green
London EC1R 0HT

www.halebooks.com

2 4 6 8 10 9 7 5 3 1

Typeset in 10¾/15pt Sabon
by Derek Doyle & Associates, Shaw Heath
Printed in Great Britain by the MPG Books Group,
Bodmin and King's Lynn

Acknowledgements

Writing a novel is a huge challenge and I couldn't have completed this story without help from Kaye Kelly and Andrew Grant, my long time friends and writing partners. Also thanks to Eileen Street and Lisa Buonocore for reading through the manuscript and giving me valuable feedback on Nelson and the Italians.

I feel very fortunate to have my own personal adviser on police procedure, Senior Constable Dave Colville of the New Zealand Police. Thanks, Dave. The Club Italia does exist (established in 1931). Special thanks to them for letting me include the club in the story.

PROLOGUE

Once he had been part of *them*. The elite. The wealthy. The accepted.

He backed away from the hotel window and turned to the black canvas bag lying on the bed. Inside the bag was the rifle, a Remington Model 7. He unzipped it. Then, lifting the rifle out, ran his finger lightly over the barrel. The metal was cold, smooth to touch. It gave him a sense of power as he cradled the weapon in his arms. He loaded it.

Taking several steps back to the open window, the watcher concentrated on the scene below. The guests arriving for the wedding were from the upper echelons of society; a mix of lawyers, doctors and businessmen with a few well-known artists thrown in for good measure. Most were dressed in formal lightweight suits, their starched white shirts a startling contrast against their tanned skin. As for the women, their expensive silk and linen gowns added vibrant colour to the crowd of people. Money was no object. Diamond necklaces sparkled as emeralds flashed coldly in the afternoon sun.

His gaze wandered, eventually settling on the red roses climbing up a wooden trellis alongside the entrance to the hotel gardens. Their velvety petals were as red as the blood soon to be spilled.

The watcher waited. Five minutes passed. Then ten. Sweat started to pour down his temples. But still he did not move, nor take his gaze off the scene below.

A white limousine pulled up at the black wrought-iron gates. An usher moved forward to meet the vehicle. The rear door opened.

Two women in their early thirties alighted, smiling brightly. Both women were dark-haired, of Italian descent, with high cheekbones and olive skin. They were identical twins. One wore bridal white, the shade of a winter's moon, and the other wore lemon-yellow, fresh and tart-like.

His gaze lingered on one of the women. She was so beautiful. So beautiful that she made his heart ache. But what was beauty, he reminded himself bitterly? Her beauty had been poisoned, consumed by lies. Then she'd deserted him when he really needed her.

Betrayal, his mind screamed.

How dare she.

Pushing the window further open, he rested the rifle on the window ledge. He took aim, counting slowly. One ... two ... three.

CHAPTER ONE

Marriage could be heaven or hell, thought Gina Rosselini. She ought to know, she'd been there. She smoothed her hand over the silky material of her gown and said, 'What is it about weddings? They always seem to make people cry.'

Her twin sister, Maria, turned to face her. 'I'm not crying and I'm the one who's getting married.'

Gina gave a smile. 'Hmm . . . don't I know it? If only our mother and father could see you. They would have been so proud.'

'Please . . . please . . . don't talk about them. It makes me feel sad. And I don't want to feel sad on today of all days.'

Gina gave her sister a quick hug. 'I'm sorry, I didn't mean—'

'I know you didn't. But right now, all I can think of is walking up that aisle.' Maria raised her eyebrows. 'There are two hundred guests sitting there, waiting for me. I only hope I can get through it.'

'You sound nervous,' said Gina quickly. She didn't blame her sister if she was. Who wouldn't be on a day like today?

'Actually, I'm terrified.' Maria bit her lip. 'Don't tell me I look it. For God's sake tell me I don't.'

Gina shook her head, injecting a soothing note into her voice. 'No, you don't. And your dress is stunning. It's worth every effort we put into it.' Gina angled her chin. 'You look like an angel.'

Gina meant every word. Maria had an ethereal quality about her, today of all days. It wasn't just the wedding dress, made of French lace and creamy silk, designed and sewn by the top designers in the country, it was the innocence in her sister's green eyes.

Maria giggled. 'Me? An angel? That's the first time you've ever said anything like that to me.'

Gina fell silent. There was so much more she *wanted* to say to Maria on her wedding day, but somehow she couldn't. The words were locked inside of her. Perhaps they always would be.

A lump swelled in Gina's throat. She tried to swallow, hoping to stem the tears starting to prick at her eyes. She gazed downwards, smoothing her fingers over her gown again as if that would provide a distraction, but she should have known better. Even as children, Maria had always sensed any change of mood within her.

Maria lightly touched her arm. 'Please . . . please . . . don't cry, Gina. If you start, that will definitely set me off. And then where will I be?' She gave a smile. 'I'll have red eyes in the wedding photos. Not to mention what it will do to my mascara.'

Maria was right. Gina tried to get a grip on her emotions. But it was so hard. 'I'm so sorry . . . forgive me,' she said huskily. 'Perhaps if we could wait a few more minutes?' She just needed time to compose herself; to prepare for the ceremony that would mean she would lose Maria to a man she disliked intensely.

Maria shook her head firmly, surprising Gina. 'No, Sis, I don't want to be late. You know how Anthony hates to be kept waiting.'

Gina forced a smile. 'It's the bride's privilege, don't forget? This is one time he won't mind you being late.'

'No,' repeated Maria, sharply. 'It's now or never.'

Now or never, repeated Gina in her mind. Finally, she replied softly, 'OK. I'm with you all the way.' Today and forever, she added silently. Through good times and bad times.

Lifting her gown so as not to trip, Maria descended the stone steps leading to the hotel gardens. Gina followed. The usher, hovering nearby, gave the signal for the violinist to begin playing. Gina recognized the tune immediately as 'Summer's Day'. It was a haunting tune somehow reaching deep inside her, churning out memories she had hoped to forget, especially on today, of all days. She gave a small sigh. Why had she made such a mess of her own life while Maria had done everything right and was marrying a respectable wealthy lawyer?

Go figure.

Sucking in a deep breath, Gina took the bouquet of fragrant white roses handed to her, and stretched out her hand to guide her sister along the paved flagstones. Gina could see their grandfather, Luigi, waiting nearby. Somehow he seemed so solid and comforting with his broad shoulders and large build. He was a man used to being in charge. After all, he had built an empire in the New Zealand fishing industry. Rosselini Fisheries.

He fell into step beside Maria. Neither of them spoke, but he gave them both an encouraging smile. To Gina, the warmth in his eyes showed how much he loved them.

Gina heard gasps of delight from the seated guests rippling along the rows as the bride passed. Everyone knew this was no ordinary wedding. One of the Rosselini sisters was getting married and being Italian New Zealanders, they did it in style.

Cameras flashed. How was Maria going to cope with the attention, Gina wondered? But she needn't have worried. All the hours of practice they'd put in beforehand had paid off. Maria smiled warmly, not a trace of nervousness to be seen as she glided towards the altar and her waiting bridegroom, her arm firmly tucked into her grandfather's.

Just like a lamb to the slaughter, Gina thought silently. Immediately, she chided herself. She *had* to stop thinking that way.

The priest stood in a white flowing robe. He looked at them all benignly, his words sombre as he spoke into the microphone. 'We are gathered here today . . .'

As Gina listened, honeysuckle, the fragrance sweet and sickly, drifted around her, along with the drone of bees. A tui, its ebony wings fluttering wildly amongst the nearby palms, burst into song like an invisible blessing from above. The moment was poignant and

Gina felt it strongly.

Her glance settled on the best man, Rick Caruso. Taller than average, he was lean looking, wiry even, with olive skin. His black hair was tied back in a pony-tail. She'd met him a couple of times but only briefly. Last night he had called around to see Maria and Anthony to discuss last minute wedding details. He'd been polite to her, though something about him made her wary. Whether it was because he was a private investigator, Gina wasn't sure. She had a feeling he was an expert at ferreting things out of people. Secrets, confidences, mysteries.

Then, as if he knew what she was thinking, he turned and looked straight at her. His eyes were a deep striking blue reflecting the intensity of the ocean nearby. She stared mesmerized for a moment, unable to look away. Then he winked at her. It was so subtle, for one moment she thought she had imagined it. But she hadn't.

Of all the nerve, she thought furiously. And in front of all these people too. Someone might have even have caught them on camera. She saw his mouth lift slightly at the corners. Gina averted her gaze, pretending to ignore him.

She heard the priest say, 'Do you take this man to be your lawful husband?'

Gina felt her shoulders tense, her eyes close briefly. This was it. The part where the bride vows to love the man for eternity. The part where Maria would sign her life away.

Don't do it, Gina screamed inside.

Her breath caught in her throat as she waited for Maria's answer. Gina found herself clutching the roses tighter and tighter. So tight, a thorn pricked her finger.

The bride's words in response to the priest were uttered softly and with complete sincerity. 'Yes, I do . . . for ever . . . and ever. Until death do us part . . .'

Gina watched Anthony slip the gold ring delicately onto Maria's slim finger.

Letting her breath out slowly, Gina tried to steady the emotions rushing through her. The ceremony was almost finished. Her sister was now bound to Anthony Monopoli by a simple band of gold and her wedding vows.

She wasn't jealous. But she was worried about her sister. If only Anthony would treat her well. That he will always love her as she deserved to be loved.

Gina said a silent prayer. For both of them.

Maria turned slightly and gave Gina a reassuring smile as if to say, 'Didn't I tell you? Everything will work out just fine.'

Gina almost believed that smile . . . and the strength of the message in her sister's eyes. Her heart rose with joy.

A sharp crack rang out like a small explosion. Gina started, nearly dropping her bouquet of roses. She looked at Maria, seeing her stiffen.

'Maria . . .' murmured Gina, uncertainly. Something was wrong.

Gina watched as Maria's body suddenly went limp and she fell sideways against Anthony. He caught her in his arms and staggered a couple of steps, before crashing into the marble pedestal standing in front of them.

A scream tore through the air.

Gina dropped her bouquet and rushed forward, screaming. '*Maria . . .*' Her heart slammed into her throat as she knelt down beside her sister. A red stain flowered unevenly across the front of her sister's wedding gown.

'Oh my God . . . she's bleeding. She's hurt,' uttered Gina.

'She's been shot . . .' added Rick Caruso grimacing.

Gina gasped, horrified. 'Shot? But I don't understand . . .'

Rick took off his jacket and placed it gently over her sister. 'Keep her still. If there's a bullet in her, we don't want it moving.'

Gina glanced at Anthony. He hadn't said a word though she could see his eyes wide with shock.

'An ambulance is on its way,' someone shouted from within the crowd.

'Thank God,' murmured Gina, her whole body starting to shake.

She bent closer, smoothed her hand over her sister's forehead, noticing how pale she was. 'Just hang on, Maria. Please . . . hang on. Help will be here soon,' she said softly. She touched her sister's cheek tenderly. She didn't know what else to do.

The guests circled. A man with grey hair appeared, pushing his way through. 'I'm a doctor . . . please . . . let me see if I can help.'

Gina moved back to let the doctor in.

'Her pulse is weak . . . very weak,' he said, shaking his head.

The flash of a camera went off. Before Gina could say anything, Rick had already chased the photographer away. When he returned, she felt his hand on her shoulder squeezing reassuringly.

'Just keep calm. The ambulance will be here soon,' he said.

Her voice came out like a whisper. 'Thank you.'

Within minutes, flashing lights and sirens sounded. A white ambulance drew up close, scattering guests widely across the expanse of lawn.

Rick shouted, 'Come on, everyone, step back, please. Let the medics through.'

The soft sound of weeping drifted around them as if it had turned into a funeral. Gina heard a voice whisper behind her saying, 'It's a vendetta. I'm telling you, it has to be.' Bewildered, Gina looked up but she couldn't see who had spoken.

Her gaze returned to Maria. Her wedding veil had fallen off. It was torn, soaked with blood. Gina lifted the veil aside. A fragrant smell of perfume drifted around Gina, reminding her that the woman who had worn it was still living and breathing . . . but only just.

The medics worked fast. Within minutes, Maria was in the ambulance. Gina intended to follow but she couldn't put one foot in front of another. Her head started to spin. She couldn't seem to get her breath. She was sure she was going to faint. She leaned up against the arch to steady herself, then, before she knew it, the ambulance doors had closed.

'Wait,' murmured Gina, trying to take a step forward. But she was too late. The ambulance had already started moving away. Her heart sank.

Rick Caruso came up to her. 'Come on, I'll take you to the hospital,' he offered gently.

'But my grandparents . . .' she trailed off, looking around for them.

'They've gone on ahead.'

'Oh . . .' What was she to do? Feeling numb, she followed him to a station wagon. To her surprise a surf board was tied onto a rack on the roof. The car had obviously seen better days and it looked like it needed a good clean. He held the door open for her while she climbed in, then slammed it shut. Her gown caught. She wrenched it, ripping the material but she didn't care. All she could think about was her sister lying injured in the ambulance. She tried to fasten her seatbelt but her hands were shaking so badly.

'Here . . . let me do that for you,' Rick offered, taking the seatbelt from her and clipping it in sharply. Then, he revved the engine hard and put it into gear, backing quickly out of the parking lot.

'I can't believe this is happening,' she said. 'I mean . . . one minute Maria is getting married, the next she . . .' Gina shook her head. 'Why on earth would anyone want to hurt Maria? It has to be an accident.'

Caruso frowned. 'It seems to me a strange type of accident. She was shot right in the middle of the hotel gardens on her wedding day.' He paused slightly. 'Think about it. There aren't any forests around. We're in a built up area in town. So it's not as if a hunter could have let off a shot if he was chasing a deer.' He accelerated. 'Any idea who might be responsible?'

She shook her head. 'No.' Her hand moved to her temple where a headache was beginning. 'I keep seeing her lying in front of me. All that blood. Dear God . . . it was terrible.' Gina's stomach lurched. Nausea swept over her. 'I feel sick,' she gasped, turning to face him.

He gave her a sympathetic glance. 'It's delayed reaction. You're in shock. I can stop if you want.'

'No, no . . . please don't. We mustn't waste any time.'

'Open your window. That should help.'

Her fingers pressed the button to wind down the window. She gulped in the fresh air, her hair whipping around her face. 'I have to reach the hospital quickly. I need to be there. Just in case . . .' Her voice trailed off. She wasn't going to say, just in case Maria died because she couldn't even bear to think that way.

Understanding crossed his face. 'Just hold on tight. We'll be there in a few minutes.' He accelerated. There were no cops on the highway and minutes later he began to weave expertly through the traffic. Before she knew it, they pulled up outside the emergency department of the hospital.

'You go in. I'll park the car and be with you as soon as I can,' said Rick.

Gina nodded and climbed out of the car and walked steadily toward the double glass doors. The doors hissed open and she passed through. A nurse was standing there, near reception. Gina made her way forward. She glanced at the nurse's name tag. Yvonne. She had a warm smile.

'Can I help you?' the nurse asked.

'Yes, my sister, Maria . . .'

The nurse spoke calmly. 'She's already been taken to theatre. Come through to the waiting area. The doctor will be with you as soon as he can.'

'My grandparents. Are they here? I have to find them,' added Gina urgently.

'They're waiting for you.'

Gina followed. As soon as she walked in, it suddenly hit her how old her grandparents looked. Maybe she had just been so wrapped up with her own life these past few months, she had never noticed.

Her grandmother lapsed into Italian as soon as she saw Gina. '*Non capisco . . . ma perché* . . . why did this happen to our Maria . . . our *bambina*? She didn't deserve this . . . no . . . no . . . it is so terrible.'

She dabbed at her eyes with her embroidered handkerchief.

Gina put her arms around her grandmother. 'Nonna, shh now . . . she's going to be fine.'

Gina glanced at her grandfather standing there, in front of them, tight lipped. At eighty years old, he was still a big man towering over everyone. Well known for his determined streak, whether in business or personally, he also had a true Latin temperament. Gina was used to it although it had resulted in both of them being at loggerheads at times. Her grandmother, Rosa, had often told her she was more like him than she realized and that's why they always fought.

'Nonno,' said Gina gently, meeting his gaze. He slipped his arm around her shoulders, but said nothing.

The nurse came back into the room. 'You may have a long wait. She's in surgery now. The doctors are doing their best.' The nurse's face was sympathetic but professional. 'Can I get you something to drink . . . a hot cup of tea, perhaps?'

Gina nodded. 'Yes, please.' She guided her distressed grandmother over to the nearest chair. 'Just rest there, Nonna. I'll give the nurse a hand with the tea.'

Rick stopped her at the doorway. 'Gina, I'm going back to the hotel to see what's happening. The police will have cordoned the area off and will be asking questions. I'd like to be around when they do.'

She nodded. 'Thanks for what you did to help back there. And also for the lift.'

Rick flashed a brief but strained smile. 'It was the least I could do.'

Gina's throat tightened, but she couldn't afford to cry. She had to see to her grandmother first. Be strong for her. Her heart heavy, she followed the nurse down the hallway to the kitchen.

Rick hovered. He needed to speak to Anthony. He saw him sitting there, a dazed expression on his face. 'Are you all right, mate?' asked Rick.

17

Anthony didn't answer but inclined his head, distress etched across his face. He cleared his throat before he spoke. 'I don't know. Any minute I think I'm going to wake up and find this didn't really happen. If I lose Maria, I . . . I . . .' He closed his eyes, then opened them as if he was having difficulty seeing. 'Why would someone want to shoot her? She's done nothing to hurt anyone.'

'I don't know.' Rick shook his head, his expression thoughtful. 'But it's one hell of a thing to happen on your wedding day.'

CHAPTER TWO

Gina didn't know if Maria would live or die. The bullet had been removed from her chest and she was in intensive care.

The surgeon said, 'Your sister is critical but stable.' He advised Gina and her grandparents to go home and rest and he would be in contact if her condition changed. But Gina wasn't ready to leave. She wanted to stay a little while longer to be with her sister. Eventually though, she had to admit there was nothing else she could do and decided to return home. The nurse called a cab for her. It was waiting when she walked out of the hospital.

As she sat there, flashes of the wedding reeled before her eyes. She put her hands to her face as if she could shut the images out. It didn't work. She could almost hear the sound of the shot as the bullet had slammed into Maria's chest.

Taking a deep breath, she focused on the journey home. The cab drove through the wrought-iron gates and up the driveway, pulling up outside her apartment. Situated in an area nicknamed Millionaire's Row, the double-storey apartment overlooked the harbour of Nelson. Millionaire's Row wasn't a name Gina particularly liked. It sounded snobbish. And that was something she was not. All through her life she had never been comfortable with her family's wealth though she was honest enough to admit it enabled her to buy the things she loved like a piece of art, or clothes from a designer boutique. She'd always maintained that spending

19

money locally was money well spent, simply because it would benefit others somewhere down the line.

She got out of the cab and paid her fare adding a generous tip.

'Thanks, ma'am,' said the driver appreciatively.

She forced a smile then walked towards the building. Gina lived in the apartment below and, until recently, shared it with Maria while their grandparents lived above them. Each apartment had its own entrance and was completely separate. It was a suitable arrangement enabling her and Maria to be independent and, at the same time, they could respect their grandparents' privacy. It also gave them a sense of family unity knowing each other was only a moment away if needed.

Living at Millionaire's Row had its benefits, Gina had decided long ago. It was also safe; a haven from the turmoil in her life the past three years.

Gina started to go down the stone steps. A motion-sensitive security light at the corner of the building flashed on. Shadows jumped out in front of her; dancing silhouettes from the branches of the kowhai tree as it swayed in the sea breeze. A morepork hooted suddenly, making her jump. By the time she got to the last step, there were tight ripples of tension in her neck.

She slid the key into the door and stepped inside. The chiming clock struck midnight as she closed the door behind her. 'Sanctuary at last', she murmured gratefully, kicking off her high-heeled shoes.

In the living room, she switched on the lamp. An amber glow spilled into the room easing her sense of aloneness. She caught a glance of herself in the Venetian gold-framed mirror hanging above the mantel. Her face looked so pale, her eyes haunted. She felt so exhausted and drained. No wonder, she thought. She still couldn't believe what had happened to her sister.

Gina looked at the cream, linen-covered sofa and wanted to curl up into it and close her eyes, but she had a feeling sleep wouldn't come easy. On the glass coffee table, several books were scattered; a mixture of romantic novels she'd bought a couple of weeks ago from a local fair but hadn't had time to read. Maria had taken one of the books intending to read it on her honeymoon. Gina could remember them both sitting on the sofa a few nights ago, drinking a glass of white wine together. She had teased Maria saying, 'You won't get time to read. You'll be too busy having fun with your husband.'

Maria had laughed. 'You think so? I bet Anthony will take some work with him. You know what he's like.'

A pang shot through Gina at the sound of Maria's voice echoing in her mind. Maria had to make it. She just had to. Tomorrow she'd go to church to pray for her.

With a heartfelt sigh, she made her way to the French windows to close the striped burgundy curtains. Since a child she'd had a fear of the windows at night time. They made her feel vulnerable, as if someone could be watching her but she couldn't see them.

Just to reassure herself that no one was there, a habit she had never been able to rid herself of, she glanced through the window. No figure loomed up. Instead, under the moonlight, she could see Tahunanui beach; a long stretch of golden sand curving like a half-horseshoe. White surf lapped onto the shore in a rhythmic sound like the soft beat of a heart. Across the bay, lights enticed and blinked, while a flashing red light of a plane slowly but steadily made its way across the deep blackness of the sky. She stepped back, her fingers curling around the edge of the curtain. It was then she noticed something move in the garden. She stared. Someone was out there.

The door bell buzzed. She jolted. Who on earth could be calling at this hour?

The bell buzzed again.

Carefully, she looked through the peephole in the door and recognized him straight away. Rick Caruso. The private investigator. Anthony's best man. He stood there, outlined against a shaft of moonlight, dressed in denim jeans and a black leather jacket emphasizing his leanness and masculinity.

She opened the door.

'Hello,' he said, his blue eyes looking at her speculatively. As he moved forward, he threw an even deeper shadow across her path.

'I wasn't expecting anyone,' she replied. Her hand moved to the edge of the door, holding it ajar but not far enough for him to come in. 'If you're looking for Anthony, he's not here.'

His tone was casual. 'I'm not looking for Anthony.' One dark eyebrow shot up enquiringly. 'Aren't you going to invite me in?'

Before she had time to answer, he pushed the open door wider, so Gina had no choice but to step back further into the hallway.

'Your security isn't very good, you should have a deadlock fixed on to the door,' he added, as he moved past.

His dictatorial attitude infuriated her and reminded her of Anthony. She pushed her hair back from her face. 'Thanks for the advice, but there are more important things on my mind,' she replied coolly. 'The last thing I need right now is a discussion on my security arrangements.'

He inclined his head and flashed a grin, obviously not in the least put out by her reply.

'We'll see . . .' he drawled, strolling through to the living room as if he owned the place. When he took off his leather jacket and threw it over the back of the chair, Gina nearly choked. 'Hey, what do you think you're doing?'

His gaze skimmed her face thoughtfully. 'I'm here to offer my services.'

'Services?' she repeated blankly.

'Yeah, that's right. It means I'm staying the night.' He lifted up a delicate Murano glass vase nearby and examined it closely.

'You're . . . you're what?' she stammered. She took a couple of steps towards him. 'You must be joking.' She wrenched the vase out of his hands and placed it back on the antique dresser.

He shrugged carelessly, his muscles flexing briefly. 'I don't see anyone laughing.' He moved closer, so close she could smell the fragrance of after shave and with it something else. Brandy, she thought, her mouth firming. It was a potent combination and yet one not altogether unpleasant.

She stepped back quickly, feeling she had to put some distance between them. 'You've been drinking,' she said, in an accusing tone.

His mouth twitched. 'Yeah, well, so what? I'm sure I deserve a drink or two after what happened today.' His voice dropped an octave, making it sound even deeper and sexier in the dim light of the room. 'Besides, Anthony's in a bad way. He needed to talk. So we went to the Club Italia.' His gaze swept over her briefly, before he added, 'but then again, I'm sure you realized that he's upset.'

'We're all upset,' she replied sharply. She looked at Rick trying to weigh him up but it was impossible. 'Please go, I have no intention of letting you stay,' she said firmly. 'As you can see, I'm fine. I don't need your help. And I'm sure you've got your own bed to go to.' She lifted her shoulders and added, 'Or some girlfriend's, maybe?'

She picked up his black leather jacket and handed it to him.

'Ah, my reputation precedes me,' he said, drily. He took two steps closer. 'I can assure you I'd rather stay here.' He flashed a quick smile.

'If you don't go, I'll call my grandfather,' she threatened.

His laugh took her aback. 'Well, you go right ahead.'

Frowning, she went over to the white phone on the table and punched in the number. Within seconds, she slammed down the phone and turned to face him. She could only gaze at him furiously.

'Well?' he asked. His mouth twitched again.

She put her hands on her hips, her chest rising slightly. 'Why didn't you tell me my grandfather had hired you as a bodyguard?'

Rick smiled a slow easy smile. 'You never gave me time – you were too busy trying to throw me out.' He paused momentarily. 'You're not too happy about me staying the night, I take it?'

Gina's hands clenched by her side. 'No, I'm not. I don't need anyone to watch over me. I can take care of myself,' she replied tightly.

'I'm sure you can,' he drawled.

She bristled. 'And what exactly do you mean by that?'

'I hear you're divorced.'

Gina took a short, sharp breath. 'That is none of your business.'

His gave her a serious look. 'It might be.'

Gina shifted uncomfortably but couldn't help being curious. 'What exactly do you mean?'

'Your ex-husband has been released from rehab, hasn't he?'

Gina made herself take some slow breaths. 'That has nothing to do with you. You might be a friend of Anthony's, but you've no right to pry into my personal affairs. So please . . . just keep out.'

Unexpectedly, his voice gentled. 'I'm sorry. I really didn't mean to upset you. It was your grandfather who told me what happened, not Anthony.'

That cut her to the core. 'Nonno? He had no right, absolutely, no right at all.' The pain of her failed marriage was still with her in spite of her divorce. The truth was she hadn't been able to erase it, no matter how hard she had tried. To think her grandfather had betrayed her private life to this stranger made it even worse. She'd heard Rick Caruso was a known womanizer and probably hadn't an ounce of sympathy in him.

'Don't take it so hard, your grandfather had every right to tell me,' Rick said quietly. 'He's worried about you. Can't you see that? Your sister's been shot and he wants me to protect you.'

She gulped. 'Protect me?' She tried to take an even breath but couldn't. 'I don't understand. Surely, you don't think someone wants to hurt me as well?'

He shrugged. 'Who knows what to think? But maybe the police might come up with something.'

Feeling drained at the turn of events, Gina reached out for the back of the chair to steady herself. Everything seemed to crowd in on her in a most disturbing way.

'Oh my God,' she murmured. 'I just can't believe this.'

Rick moved forward as she swayed slightly. 'Gina, are you all right?' As quick as a flash he was beside her, his hand on her arm, supporting her.

No . . . no, she wasn't all right. She felt like her whole world had exploded into tiny fragmented pieces and no matter how she tried, it couldn't be put together again. How could she tell him that since her parents had died there had been a special bond between her and Maria. They had always been close, inseparable as children. Even more so as identical twins. If Maria died, she couldn't bear to think what would happen.

Her voice came out shaky. 'Of course, I'm all right.'

He inclined his head thoughtfully, his eyes enigmatic. 'For a minute I thought—'

She whirled on him. 'You thought what? That I'd need a man to take care of me? Wrong, on the first count, Mr Private Investigator. Sorry to disappoint you, but I don't need you at all.' Taking another deep breath, she added, 'Look, I really am grateful at what you've done to help, but now, I'm too tired to argue. Since my grandfather employed you for one night, I'll honour that promise. Quite honestly, I simply can't be bothered to throw you out. So, please, just stay out of my way, OK?'

Then she promptly walked out to the hallway cupboard to find some clean sheets. He could have the spare room, though the bed wasn't made up.

Gina swallowed hard. She was too near the edge. It wouldn't take much for her to break down, dissolve into tears. All she wanted to do was sob her heart out in private. But not in front of him, of all people. All evening she had kept control, but talking about her ex-husband had pierced the barrier.

The last thing she needed was a man living with her. She'd had enough of that when she was married. There was no way her freedom was going to be curtailed. She wouldn't allow it.

'First thing tomorrow, I want you to leave,' she threw at him along with the sheets.

His mouth tightened. 'I wouldn't count on it.' He hesitated. 'Any chance of a coffee? It's been a long day.'

25

She shrugged, her voice still cool. 'Kitchen is on the right. Help yourself.'

'Thanks,' he said drily. Then he muttered under his breath, 'For the welcome.'

A few minutes later, Gina went to bed. She didn't know that during the night, Rick had come into her room concerned because he had heard her call out. When he entered the bedroom, he wasn't prepared for the sight of her lying on the bed, her silk nightdress slipped to reveal the curve of one breast. But it was her serene face Rick had noticed most of all. Those dark eyelashes closed tight, emphasized golden skin smooth as a flax leaf. Was it true what they said about her, he wondered? Was she a spoilt rich girl who didn't give a damn about others? In spite of her confidence, he sensed an underlying vulnerability. Common sense told him never to believe all he heard on the social grapevine and he preferred to reserve judgement for himself. He stared at her for a few seconds before pulling the sheet up around her and returning to his own room.

A sense of guilt shot through her at how badly she had treated Rick Caruso the night before. After all, like he had said, he had only been trying to help and he had been kind enough to give her a lift to the hospital.

Determined to be a bit friendlier, she approached him with a smile. 'I see you're up early.' She noticed he had already pulled up the Roman blinds in the kitchen. Bright sunshine beamed through the leaded light windows.

Gina took him in quickly. He was sitting at the pine kitchen table, eating eggs and toast. He had already showered, his hair wet but not tied back in a pony-tail. He wore a black T-shirt stretched tight over his chest, emphasizing hard-earned muscles. Gina tried averting her gaze but didn't quite succeed. The picture wasn't entirely repulsive to her. Somehow she couldn't ignore the warm flush it brought to her cheeks. She swallowed, trying to appear calm and uninterested. Not easy when her system had just gone into overdrive.

Then she noticed her kitchen. She stared in dismay at the collection of pots littering the sink. Her kitchen had never been in such a mess. He'd even managed to figure out the espresso coffee machine, so she hadn't mistaken the tantalizing aroma of coffee when she had woken first thing.

'You've obviously already made yourself at home,' she said, unable to prevent the sarcastic note in her voice from slipping out. 'Did you find everything to your satisfaction?'

Rick's eyes narrowed. 'Not everything: you've run out of sugar and you've no jam.'

'Jam's in the top right hand cupboard,' she said tightly, 'so maybe you didn't look hard enough?'

His eyes skimmed her speculatively. 'Oh, I looked all right.' He paused as he took a bite of his toast and swallowed. 'What about you? Did you have a good night?'

Gina reached for a cup, sighing. 'Not really, I couldn't sleep. How could I after what happened yesterday?'

'You looked pretty well out of it when I saw you.'

Gina froze. 'You what? Are you telling me you came into my room?'

He leaned back casually. 'Yeah, I did. You must have had a nightmare and I came in to check you were all right,' he explained. 'I was concerned.'

'I'm sure that wasn't necessary,' she replied, realizing she sounded ungrateful again but unable to help it. Having him so close was unnerving. Even more so, having him eat breakfast and using her things was more than she could handle.

'Would you like a hot drink?' he asked, ignoring her furious look and giving her a smile as if he was enjoying himself. Now he was asking if she wanted a drink in her own home. She shook her head. 'Thanks, but I can get it myself,' she replied, through gritted teeth.

'Don't you know breakfast is the most important meal of the day?' he told her, as he reached up to the cupboard to find the jar of jam. 'That's when your energy is at its lowest.' A sound of jars clinked and then Rick produced the jam, placing it beside her on the table.

Gina stared at the red jam which suddenly reminded her of her sister lying in a pool of blood. Maria was in hospital and here she was discussing what to have for breakfast. Suddenly she got up and rushed over to the phone. Rick was there before her, his hands on top of hers.

'I've already phoned the hospital and she's still stable; she hasn't come around yet,' he said, his face full of concern.

'Are you sure?' she said, conscious of his blue eyes as deep and as unfathomable as the sea outside.

'I'm sure,' he replied quietly. 'So why don't you sit down and relax? Then we'll discuss what you're going to do today. When you're ready to go to the hospital, I'll take you.'

His words took a few seconds to sink in. She untangled her fingers from his and dropped her arms stiffly to her side. Conscious of his close proximity, she took two steps back.

'I . . . I'm just going to take a shower first,' she murmured, feeling an overwhelming desire to be on her own. She hurried back into the bedroom and sat down on the bed to think. It would be a good idea to talk to her grandfather. Make him understand she didn't need Rick Caruso.

Quietly, slipping out of the French doors, she made her way up the stone steps to her grandparents' apartment. Halfway up, Gina paused to look at the sea. Several large fishing boats belonging to Rosselini Fisheries were heading out to deeper waters. They'd be away for a few weeks then would return filled to the brim with orange roughy, hoki, tuna, tarakihi and other fish destined for the local and international market. It always gave her a thrill to see her grandfather's fleet on the sea. Some of the vessels he owned, others were contracted out to him by their skippers. Shading her eyes, a black silhouette caught her eye: an oil tanker, stalking them. A marine horn sounded. It was the tanker marking its territory, sending out a warning not to come too close. Even the sea had its hierarchy, she thought.

Her thoughts returned to her grandfather. He had originally come from a small coastal village in Massa Lubrense in Italy and had once told her that when he'd sailed from Naples as a young man, he'd made a vow that when he got to Nelson in New Zealand and made his fortune, he'd build a house overlooking the Tasman Sea so he wouldn't forget his roots. He'd done just that.

She admired her grandfather because of what he'd achieved. He'd arrived penniless in New Zealand, leaving Italy after the Second World War and had built up Rosselini Fisheries through hard work and determination. And, as he often had told her, 'Luck.'

Gina reached the top apartment and entered through the back door to the kitchen. Maggie, the housekeeper, was busy frying bacon. Saying a polite 'Good morning,' Gina passed quickly through the steam-filled kitchen until she reached a conservatory. Her bare feet made no noise on the cool terracotta tiles. Large potted palms and fragrant flowers in terracotta tubs grew everywhere giving an exotic feel to the room. Her grandparents would be having breakfast at the table, near the far end of the conservatory, just as they had done every morning for the past fifty years.

'Gina, my darling,' said her grandmother warmly. 'Come and have breakfast with us.'

Gina noticed her grandmother's face was pale and drawn as if she hadn't slept much either.

Gina smiled affectionately. 'I'm not hungry, really, Nonna. Just a cup of coffee will do.'

Her grandmother tutted. 'You must eat more. You've lost too much weight already.'

It was true, Gina thought. She had lost a few kilos. Stress had played havoc with her system over the past three years. Even so, she replied, 'I'm fine, honestly I am. And I'm not thin. I've seen photos of my mother and she looked exactly the same at this age.'

Her grandmother sighed sadly. '*Sí* . . . you look more like your mother every day.'

Gina loved hearing about her mother, but right at the moment, her mind was elsewhere. She had to sort out this business with Rick Caruso before anything else. She sat down at the table opposite Anthony. She noticed he hadn't even greeted her had just given her a brief smile.

'You've arrived early,' she said to him. 'I thought you might have been at the hospital.'

'I dropped in earlier on. And I'm going back shortly after I've seen your grandfather. We've got a few urgent things to discuss.' He pointed his fork at her. 'You know something? You should listen to your grandmother and eat more. She knows what's best.'

Gina ignored his remark, turning back to her grandmother. 'Where's Nonno? I thought he'd be down for breakfast.'

'He will be in a minute,' replied Rosa. 'He had a phone call that couldn't wait.'

'In that case, I think I'll go and find him. If you'll excuse me—' She rose to her feet.

'Why don't you sit down, Gina,' interrupted Anthony. 'We have to talk. It's important.'

Gina's mouth pursed rebelliously at his tone. 'Talk? What about?' She flicked a worried glance at her grandmother. 'Is it Maria? Have you heard something?'

Rosa shook her head, her smile strained. 'No, my dear, but there are a few things worrying us.'

'OK. But let's wait for Nonno before we discuss anything,' suggested Gina. She sat down again.

A few seconds later, Luigi came in, frowning. He gave a smile as his gaze met hers. '*Buongiorno*, Gina.'

Gina acknowledged the greeting and smiled back, thinking how much she loved her grandfather in spite of his gruff ways. He sat down at the head of the table and unfolded his napkin, then placed it on his knee. As usual he was dressed immaculately in dark trousers and a white shirt. He looked so distinguished with his dark features and grey hair. Gina waited patiently for him to speak but when he didn't she prompted, 'Nonno? What is it you want to discuss?'

To her surprise, he said, 'Anthony will tell you, while I eat.'

It wasn't like her grandfather to let him take the lead. Anthony's deep voice was arrogant and immediately put her on edge.

'We've had a family conference and made a few decisions. We've decided that—'

'Just a minute,' interrupted Gina. 'You've had a family conference without me?'

Her grandfather's voice boomed out warningly, 'Gina . . .' His smile dropped from his face. 'Anthony is Maria's husband now and is part of this family, whether you like it or not. And when you start taking some responsibility for yourself, you can also make decisions around here.'

Gina's blood started to heat. 'What? For God's sake, I'm thirty years old. I can take care of myself. I don't need you to make decisions for me just because I made one big mistake in the past.' She whirled around to face Anthony. 'And why have you employed Rick Caruso?'

'It was your grandfather's decision,' Anthony informed her. 'Didn't Rick tell you?'

Gina snorted, putting her hands on her hips. 'Huh. Don't lie. I know you were behind it, even if it is Nonno paying him.'

What really annoyed her was the way Anthony always treated her as if she was a teenager who didn't know her own mind. He had an arrogant attitude towards women bordering on the old-fashioned. Maria might have been willing to accept it, but that didn't mean to say she had to.

'OK, so I suggested it,' he admitted. He gave a shrug. 'So what?'

She turned to her grandfather. 'Nonno . . . please.'

Luigi's gaze softened as he looked at her. 'Anthony is right. We don't know why Maria was shot and, until we do, I'm not taking any chances.' He waved his hand in the air. 'Rick Caruso is a man to be trusted and we could do with his help just now.'

'I'm sure anyone would help if you paid them enough,' she said hotly. As soon as she realized what she had said, Gina regretted it. She didn't mean to hurt her grandfather by her refusal but couldn't he understand she wanted to manage her own life?

Luigi's face turned thunderous as he thumped the table. The cutlery rattled and a glass toppled over, spilling fresh orange juice all over the pure white linen tablecloth. 'That's enough, Gina. I won't have that kind of talk here. Caruso comes from a fine Sicilian family. His parents have been in New Zealand as long as our family – over fifty years.' His thick eyebrows knitted together angrily.

Gina took a deep breath, not wanting to upset her grandfather any further but feeling she had to make a stand.

'It doesn't mean because Maria has been shot that someone wants to shoot me as well.'

No one spoke. An odd silence filled the conservatory. Her gaze travelled from one face to another. She added slowly, 'Well, does it?'

'You'll do what you're told, Gina,' her grandfather said. 'And I don't want any arguments. Not with Maria lying in hospital at death's door.'

She exhaled. 'Please, Nonno, I can look after myself.'

Anthony reached over and put his hand on her arm. 'Gina, you make a fuss about nothing. Listen to your *nonno*. He knows what he is doing.'

'I am listening. I don't want Rick Caruso following me around. So please . . . get him to back off.'

'He's to be trusted and he'll be discreet,' Anthony replied, as if he was speaking to a child. 'We're only doing what we think is best. Don't make things difficult.'

'Since when have you decided what's best for me? I don't care whether he's discreet or not, I'm not having it and that's final.' Her mouth tightened rebelliously.

A cough behind her had her whirling around. Rick was standing right behind her and it was obvious he had heard everything she had said. He smiled but the smile didn't reach his eyes.

'Mr Rosselini, may I have a word with your granddaughter in

private?' he asked politely. A tiny nerve beat in his temple.

'*Sí*, of course,' he said, his eyes full of speculation.

Before she realized it, Caruso had grabbed her arm, and firmly marched her into the hallway.

'Let's get one thing straight, shall we?' He towered above her, his hands curving around her shoulders. 'You . . .' he paused, 'have a family who is very worried. Your sister is lying in hospital and all you can do is stir everyone up about what you want and don't want.'

She exhaled again. 'I do not. You're wrong.'

His hands dropped from her shoulders. 'OK, prove it,' he said, his eyes narrowing.

She shoved her hair back from her face. 'God damn you, Caruso. All right. But just don't interfere in my life, do you understand?'

Caruso didn't answer. He smiled instead, a slow easy smile that quietly turned Gina's stomach inside out.

Whether she realized it or not, Caruso had just won the first round.

The electronic security system in both apartments needed updating, Rick decided. It would take some time. But what the Rosselinis did have security wise seemed to be in working order. He'd also briefed the guards he'd recently hired to patrol the property, making sure they knew to report anything unusual or suspicious to him.

A high stone wall surrounded most of the Rosselini estate. At the bottom of the garden there was a sheer drop of fifty feet to the road below. In his estimation, it was unlikely an intruder would enter from that side unless they had mountaineering gear. He had fleetingly thought about implementing electronic detection equipment but that would be a waste of time, since any bird or animal could set it off. Besides, Mr Rosselini didn't want to lock up his property as if he was in a prison. Something to do with the Second World War when he'd been a child, he'd told Rick. He'd been locked up once before and would rather be dead than have it happen again. Rick could fully understand that.

Gina interrupted his thoughts. 'I'm going to the hospital. I want to be there when Maria wakes up.'

'You only called them half an hour ago. The hospital said they would contact you if there was any change,' he reminded her. 'She's still unconscious.'

'I know, but I want to go.'

'It's safer if you stay here.'

'I don't care about myself.'

Rick was tempted to argue but quickly decided if she had her mind set, the best thing he could do was go along with it for now. Hell, he'd do the same if it was his sister lying in hospital.

'OK, if that's what you want. We'll go right now.'

'We'll take my car,' Gina said, a faint smile touching her lips. 'It's faster.'

He wasn't going to object. He'd rather take her car any day since it would be easier. Rick tried to resist the temptation to put his foot down in the Ferrari Boxer. It certainly wasn't every day he got to drive a car worth that much money. He enjoyed the sleek feel of the wheel beneath his hands and could almost swear the engine purred under his touch.

When they reached the outskirts of town he slowed down considerably. Road works held up the traffic. When he glanced in his rear view mirror a line of cars were queued up behind him. He frowned.

'Do you know who's driving the Nissan Skyline two cars behind us?' he asked. 'It's been following us for a while.' He tried to make out the driver sitting in the front seat but it was impossible due to the vehicles in between.

Gina looked back over her shoulder. 'No. I've no idea who it belongs too. Are you sure it's following us?'

He shrugged. 'It's probably nothing. All the same, we can't be too careful.' After a couple of minutes, he noticed the car turn off at the roundabout and head down another road. Perhaps he had been overcautious.

When they reached the hospital, it was busy. Obviously visiting hours had created a flurry of activity. People were heading to the lifts carrying bunches of carnations and roses. There was a queue.

'It will be quicker if we go up the stairs. That is, if you feel up to a walk?' suggested Rick.

Gina nodded, moving quickly, her heels clicking on the polished tiled floor. After climbing a flight of stairs, and walking along a long corridor, she was so absorbed in her own thoughts, she bumped into a heavily laden linen trolley as she turned around the corner.

Rick put his hand on her arm. 'Hey, slow down, will you? If you carry on at this rate, you'll end up in here as well.'

'Sorry,' Gina muttered at the orderly, who cast her an annoyed glance. To Rick's surprise, Gina bent down and helped the orderly bundle up the white linen that had fallen onto the floor.

When they reached the entrance to the intensive care unit, Gina spoke into the intercom device attached to the wall and gave her name. The door was unlocked and she went in. Maria's room was opposite the reception desk. Gina looked at the plastic drip above the bed, the monitor beeping every so often reminding them that Maria was dependent on a machine. Plastic tubes hung everywhere. A nurse came in and took Maria's blood pressure, entering it on the chart hanging at the bottom of the bed. She smiled sympathetically and then left.

Her grandmother sat on a chair beside the bed.

'How is she?' asked Gina softly. She reached out to touch her sister's hair, noticing the curls were lifeless. A huge bruise had formed along the side of her sister's forehead where she must have struck the marble pedestal as she fell.

Her grandmother dabbed her linen handkerchief at her eyes. 'They're doing all they can. The doctor says she'll come around eventually; we just have to wait. She's still stable, so that's something. They say she'll make it.'

'Thank God,' said Gina with relief. Tears welled up in her eyes. The doctor had explained earlier on when she had phoned for a progress report that it had been a miracle that Maria had survived. If the bullet had gone in a few more centimetres to her left, it would have hit her heart. On intravenous morphine, the drug would make her sleep for some time.

There didn't seem to be anything else to say, so Gina sat quietly, content just to be near her sister and her grandmother. She'd stay for as long as she was needed.

After a couple of hours had passed, her grandmother said quietly, 'Gina, go home now. There's nothing else you can do here.'

Gina hesitated. 'Are you sure, Nonna? I don't want to leave you here on your own.'

'Luigi will be here shortly to pick me up. So you see I won't be alone.' Her grandmother's mouth quavered slightly.

Gina stood up. 'All right, Nonna.' She found Rick waiting in the corridor, deep in conversation with a pretty young nurse. It certainly didn't look like any professional conversation from the girl's stance, Gina thought. She was leaning against the wall and laughing. Gina made her way over to him. The nurse saw her approaching, curtailed the conversation, gave him a kiss on the cheek, and walked away. She flashed Gina a smile as she passed.

'Got other things on your mind, Caruso?' Gina said tartly. 'Or is chatting to the nurses all in a day's work?'

His eyes narrowed. 'It's not what you think.'

'Hmm . . . I'm sure it isn't.' He'd literally been making out with a nurse in the corridor. So she'd been right about him after all. She was very tempted to say more but held back while they were in the hospital within earshot of the medical staff. Once they were outside she'd tell him a few things about his overbearing manner, she decided. She might have to put up with him accompanying her wherever she went but that didn't mean she had to like it.

They walked out the main entrance of the hospital building, and along the narrow concrete path towards the car-park.

'I can't stand it,' she said, through gritted teeth. 'I'm not used to someone following me around like this.'

His fingers dug into her arm as they stopped at the edge of the pavement, ready to cross the road. 'And I'm not used to looking after spoilt young women.'

'Why you—' she started to say, but she never had time to reply because a grey Nissan Skyline came careering around the corner at a fast speed.

Rick grabbed her arm. 'Get back,' he shouted, pushing her into the bushes. 'It's coming straight for us.'

A sharp twig scraped along her arm making her cry out. Rick landed on top of her; both of them sprawled against the flowering camellia bush. The grey car sped off into the distance, tyres squealing.

'For God's sake, what on earth happened?' she uttered, dazed, as she tried to untangle herself.

'Someone just tried to run us over, that's what happened. Damn it, the car moved so fast, I didn't even catch the licence number.'

Gina's breath caught in her throat as her hand rose to her chest. 'You mean someone tried to kill me just now?'

'I don't know whether they wanted to kill you, but they certainly wanted to frighten you.'

Gina's arm was stinging badly. Blood ran down her arm. Rick reached into his shirt pocket for his handkerchief. 'Here, use this.' When Gina made no effort to take it, he clamped it onto her skin anyway.

'Why on earth would someone want to hurt me? There must be a mistake, perhaps they didn't see us?' she said.

Rick looked at her thoughtfully. Her face was pale. Without asking, he came closer and slipped his arm around her shoulders. It provoked a quick response.

'You don't need to hold me that close,' she protested.

He grimaced. 'Come on. I'll take you into the hospital to get checked out.'

'No . . . no . . . please, I don't want to go back in there.' Her throat tightened, but she blinked back the tears, refusing to let him see how upset she really was.

'It's probably the best thing,' he argued.

'I just want to go home. I'm fine. Honestly, I am.'

After a few seconds, he gave in. 'All right.'

In spite of her reluctance to let him help her, she leaned against him. His arm slipped around her waist as she made her way across the road. The warmth of his body was oddly comforting as she tried to deal with the throbbing pain in her arm.

When she glanced upwards, she saw his jaw angled determinedly. Being so near gave her a chance to study him more closely. There was strength in that face, she realized with a jolt, and there was determination too. Suddenly she knew that whatever she felt about Rick Caruso personally and he about her, he would protect her to the best of his ability. The thought was frightening but somehow reassuring.

When they reached the car he unlocked the vehicle. Once inside, he whipped out his mobile phone and punched in the number of the police station. 'It was definitely no accident,' he reiterated, as he gave a description of the vehicle and as many details as he could remember.

When he terminated the call, he clipped the phone back onto his belt.

After they pulled up outside the house, Gina realized she was shaking so badly, she could hardly stand. Rick insisted on carrying her down the steps to her apartment.

'I don't need anyone to help me,' she protested. 'I'll be OK in a few minutes.'

He ignored her completely. Fuming, she had no choice but to bear it. He managed to unlock her front door and carried her straight into the bedroom where he laid her down gently on the bed.

'Don't move, I'll be right back,' he ordered. He reappeared shortly with a bag full of frozen vegetables wrapped in a towel and a flannel. 'This should relieve the swelling.' He applied the ice cold pack to her arm, and then used the flannel to wash the dried blood off her arm. She grimaced as he moved her arm forward to get a better view.

She winced. 'Ouch. Don't press so hard, it hurts.'

He paused, his hand lifting slightly. 'Sorry, I'm trying to be as careful as I can.' He glanced at her briefly. 'At least you don't need stitches.' He flashed a brief reassuring smile, then lifted up the bottle of antiseptic tipping a generous amount on to the cloth and applying it to her skin.

'Ouch. It stings.'

Gina was becoming increasingly aware of him, the way his deft fingers touched her skin, skimming ever so gently over the bruised area. As he worked, she noticed other things as well, like his confidence and gentle manner. Rick Caruso was full of surprises, she thought. She glanced at his handiwork and at the piece of gauze now taped firmly into place over her arm.

'So is first aid part of the deal of looking after me?' Her brow arched questioningly as she attempted to inject some humour into the situation.

He smiled. 'Only when the job calls for it. Mind you, this isn't the first time I've patched someone up although admittedly no one quite as delicate.'

She looked at him carefully. 'Thanks,' she murmured, leaning back against the pillow he'd considerately arranged behind her to support her back.

He stood up. 'I need to speak to the security guards and my old boss.'

'Old boss?' she queried, not understanding.

'Detective Dave Brougham.'

'Oh.' She'd met the detective briefly when she'd given him a statement at the hospital. She had a feeling he'd be interviewing her formally soon. At least, he'd indicated that.

Rick hesitated. 'Are you OK if I leave you for a while?'

Gina nodded. 'I'll be fine.' That wasn't exactly true. Gina recognized self-pity and didn't like it one bit. Her eyelashes lowered so he wouldn't suspect how bad she really was feeling.

He stood at the end of the bed, still unsure. 'OK. I'll probably be about half an hour. It's best you don't open the door, no matter who it is.'

She gave another brief nod and closed her eyes, feigning tiredness. But that was only to hide the tears forming slowly behind her eyelids. For God's sake leave me, she wanted to shout at him, as he looked down at her.

The door shut behind him with a resounding click. Silence descended. She reached over for her novel lying on the bedside table. Reading a few pages might help her take her mind off what had happened. She studied the cover of the book; a picture of a man and woman embracing on the front. It was a romantic story. Somehow it made her feel even worse.

Tears flooded down her cheeks. With a sob, Gina tossed the book to the far side of the room, knocking over a glass ornament on the chest of drawers.

Rick Caruso had been kind to her today. He'd probably saved her life when that car had come crashing down the road. But in all honesty, she still didn't want him to stay with her. She didn't want to rely on any man ever again. More importantly, she mustn't forget Rick Caruso had a reputation where women were concerned and, at the moment, she felt far too vulnerable. A sob stuck in her throat.

Someone had hurt Maria. He was out there watching her now. The car incident today had proved that. If Rick hadn't been there, she would have been under those car wheels.

So who was it?

And why?

CHAPTER THREE

The watcher relived the scene a million times over, enjoying every moment of it. The way Maria had fallen . . . the screams . . . the panic that ensued afterwards. And the wail of the sirens and flashing blue lights. He gave a malicious smile. Everything had gone according to plan.

Shooting a solitary figure in white was easy prey. If he'd wanted to kill Gina as well, he could have. But he knew that by shooting only one of the twins instead, it would give him more power over the Rosselini family.

Afterwards, he'd exited the hotel quickly before the cops sealed the place off. He'd already changed into grey overalls, put on a wig, then made his way down to the staff car-park. His first intention had been to ask the driver of a baker's van for a lift, but when he saw a small car with the keys dangling in the ignition, he knew that taking it would be easier. He'd driven it to the port and dumped it. Then, grabbing his black bag he made his way back to the small house he had rented in a poorer part of town. It was somewhere he could blend in easily and where no questions were asked.

The watcher got up from the chair and made his way to the dirty window to peer out. The garden was full of weeds, the result of several years of neglect. Most tenants were transient and, with little money, no one bothered very much.

He shouldn't have to live like this, he thought resentfully. All he had in his pocket was fifty dollars and a Nissan Skyline parked in the driveway. At least he had paid his rent in advance so he didn't have to worry about that for now. Sure he could sign on for government assistance, but that would mean the authorities would know his whereabouts. He didn't want that.

Feeling restless, he started to pace the room. What now? Should he go back to the hospital? He'd been there earlier waiting for the right moment to approach Gina. He needed to talk to her. But every time he got close, that private investigator, Rick Caruso, was right by her side. It was obvious to him the Rosselinis must have hired him to guard her twenty-four hours a day. That made him laugh. Did they really think they could protect her? He could kill any of them, any time he wanted. In his frustration, he'd tried to run Caruso down. It hadn't worked. Damn it.

A knock at the door startled him. Not expecting anyone, he peered out the window to see who it was. A man in a red uniform stood there looking curious. It was the postman. Deciding to answer it, he swung the door open and forced a smile. 'Can I help you?' he said politely.

The postman lifted up some letters. 'Mr Grey?'

He almost shook his head but stopped just in time. 'Yes. What is it you want?'

'These letters were found dumped at the end of the street, just by the river. Looks like some kids took them, probably up to mischief. The old lady from next door found them when she was walking her dog. Thought I'd better deliver them to you personally.' He hesitated. 'It might be a good idea to get a lock for your post box.'

'Thanks. I'll see to it as soon as I can.'

The postman handed the letters over with a smile. 'There you are.' He paused slightly. 'I'm Andy by the way. I've just started this postal run.'

'Pleased to meet you, Andy. Thanks for your help. Now, if you'll excuse me.'

'Sure. See you around then,' said Andy cheerfully, backing away.

He gave a wave, then hopped back on his bike and started to pedal.

The watcher shut the door, and locked it. In the kitchen, he slit open the first letter. It was just a circular letting the occupant know about a garage sale held at the local school. The second was a newsletter from the bowls' club. The third looked interesting. It was a letter, from a woman, obviously a friend of Mr Grey's. Enclosed was a hundred dollar bill. The previous occupant, Mr Grey, now resided in an old folk's home. Someone obviously hadn't told the woman. But then, the letter was from out of town, so perhaps no one knew her address to inform her.

A hundred dollars wasn't a lot, but it was enough to buy his meal for the day and a few groceries.

He grabbed his jacket and car keys and drove into town. He found a small café and ordered a pie and chips and a beer. As he ate, he thought about what he had to do. The Rosselini's had betrayed him. He'd brooded over it, night after night.

He drained the last of his beer. Before his glass hit the table, the waitress came up. 'Another drink?' she asked.

He glared at her, irritated that she had disturbed his thoughts. He nodded. 'Yeah, why not? Another beer.'

She must have felt his gaze on her still because she looked up at him as she stood behind the bar. Eventually, the waitress delivered the beer. 'Anything else?'

'Nope.' Ten minutes later, he finished his drink and paid his bill. Now, he'd head for the Catholic church. Sometimes Gina attended evening mass. It might be a chance to talk with her. Even if she didn't turn up, he could sit for a while and contemplate. Perhaps God would help. He gave a low laugh. Fat chance. God helped those who helped themselves.

The following morning, Rick stood on the deck of Gina's apartment surveying the view of the beach. He lifted the binoculars and zoomed in on the surfers. He recognized several whose philosophy in life was work to live. They even took time off work, or pulled a sickie, if surfing conditions looked good. Surfing had been in Rick's blood since he was a teenager and he spent as much time as he could at the beach.

Moving to Christchurch while in the police force had curtailed surfing more than he liked but he had still managed to make it to Sumner, a well-known surfing beach on the outskirts of the city, whenever he had time off. Someone had once asked him why he'd chosen surfing. He reckoned it was more to do with the sea and the way it relieved stress, than the actual sport. He'd seen the worst of humanity both as a street cop and later as a detective and member of the elite tactical response unit. Somehow, the sun, sand and surf gave him psychological release as well as the physical benefits of keeping fit. He reckoned it was better than a good workout at the gym. On a deeper level, there had been the odd moment when he'd been surfing at sunset and the sky had been streaked red and fiery against the vivid blueness of the water reminding him there was still moments of beauty in the world after a tough day at work. Now that he was back in Nelson, he tried to surf most evenings if his work allowed. Normally he would have been out there with the surfers, but work had to come first and the bills had to be paid. Besides he had his eye on a new surf board.

It had been a bonus getting this contract to look after Gina Rosselini but it was initially only for a couple of weeks. He'd been surprised the Rosselinis had hired him rather than a well-known private investigator but he knew that was due to Anthony's influence. Both of them went way back to when they'd attended high school together. They'd also been on the same high school football team. It had been a coincidence them both choosing law-related areas as a profession after graduating from school, but it had strengthened the friendship between them. That didn't mean he was blind to his friend's faults. Anthony got a bit arrogant at times but, being a lawyer, that attitude got him results.

Rick adjusted the lens of the binoculars as he swung to the left towards a sharp drop of the cliff. On the main road below, a few teenagers were leaning against their car, smoking cigarettes, their loud hip hop music drifting up to him. Another car had pulled into the lay-by beside them. The occupants didn't get out but were admiring the view across the bay. For a few minutes, he watched both cars steadily. Satisfied that they didn't pose any threat, he swung the binoculars around again in a semi-arc.

He heard footsteps behind him, recognizing them as Gina's.

'I'm going into town,' she announced.

'What for?' he murmured. He swung around again, holding the binoculars steady and for a fleeting second zoomed in on long, shapely legs walking past him. She was wearing the shortest skirt he'd ever seen. His gut tightened.

She wrenched the binoculars out of his hands. 'Shopping.'

'Shopping?' he repeated, taken aback. 'At a time like this?'

'I need to buy a few things,' she explained. 'And I have an important appointment.'

'Where?'

'I'll tell you when we get there,' she said vaguely. She lifted her arms, gathered her hair in a pony-tail and snapped on a gold clasp. The effect made her look younger, he thought.

He frowned. 'I don't think it's a good idea to go into town right now. There are too many people and it would be difficult to protect you properly. We don't know who's out there, especially after what happened to you yesterday.'

Gina lifted her chin defiantly. 'Are you telling me I can't go out?' Her voice was smooth and silky like melted chocolate.

'That's right.'

'I see,' she said slowly.

He gave a relieved smile. 'Glad you're seeing some sense.'

'In that case, how about I make us some coffee?' She handed him back the binoculars, though he had a feeling she wasn't pleased.

He shot her an uncertain look. 'Coffee sounds great. Black and strong. One sugar. Thanks.'

'I should have guessed.'

He stared at her blankly. 'Excuse me?'

'That you don't take milk.'

Sometimes women didn't make a lot of sense to him. But every male said that sometime or another. He gave a grin. 'I can drink coffee with milk or without,' he informed her. 'The legacy of being a cop, I guess. As long as it is hot and sweet, I don't mind.'

She flashed a brief strained smile. 'I'll see what I can do. But don't expect donuts.'

'Donuts?' Now she really had him confused.

'Like you read in crime novels. Cops always eat donuts, don't they?'

He felt like laughing. 'I'm no longer a cop. I'm a private investigator. And I'm Italian, so it's *zeppoli*. Donuts made Italian style.' He had a feeling she was going to swipe him one from the seething look she was now sending him. He'd better back track promptly. 'Er . . . coffee's fine. Any way it comes.'

When she headed inside he breathed a sigh of relief. Placing the binoculars on the table in front of him, he picked up a magazine on current affairs turning to the article on a recent report of disengaged staff in the police force.

Most police officers who leave on psychological or physical grounds would like the opportunity to return.

Yeah, he could relate to that, he thought, sighing. He missed the force more than he had realized. But, at least, he was lucky to work in a job similar to police work. Caruso Security Consultants had been established with the money he had received from disengaging from the police force over three years ago, when he'd been thirty years old. Although he had been well known in the area during his younger years as a cop, his reputation as a private investigator had taken time to build up and he'd been pleased with the company's progress.

After a few minutes, he called out, 'Gina, what's happened to the coffee?' There was no answer, so he called out again. Still no response. He threw the magazine down on the table and walked inside. No coffee percolated in the kitchen. Nor was there any sign of Gina. He frowned. Where the hell had she gone? Quickly, he checked all the other rooms but she was nowhere around.

'Damn it. . . .' She must have slipped out the balcony doors in the bedroom and headed upstairs to see her grandparents. Irritated at her lack of consideration, he took the steps two at a time until he reached the top level. About to enter the entrance of the top apartment, he heard the Ferrari starting up in the garage. Then it dawned on him. He bolted through the garage door, catching her just as she was about to reverse.

'Hey, what do you think you are doing?' he gasped, wrenching the car door open.

Startled by him suddenly appearing from nowhere, Gina's foot accidentally hit the accelerator. The car lurched forward scraping the car door against the wall of the garage.

'I'm going shopping. And I don't need your permission.'

'I've told you, it's too dangerous.' He swung the door, examining the paintwork. Only a small scrape but it really irked him to see such a beautiful car dented. He cursed under his breath.

Gina revved the Ferrari harder, her slim legs moving up and down. 'If you don't get in, I'll go without you,' she threatened.

He knew she meant every word. So he made a quick decision. There was no way he could keep her prisoner and Mr Rosselini did give instructions she was to lead as normal a life as possible. He'd go along with her decision for now even if he didn't agree with it. Still, she wasn't going to get it all her own way. His voice came out firm. 'All right, but you do exactly as I say. Have you got that?'

Gina smiled as she slipped her Armani sunglasses over her eyes. 'Of course,' she replied sweetly.

Rick's eyebrows knitted together suspiciously at her tone. 'Has anyone ever told you that you're far too used to getting your own way?'

'Uh-huh. Plenty of times.'

'Yeah, I thought so somehow.' He lifted his finger and wagged it.

'I mean it, Gina. One step out of line and we're straight back home. Got it?'

She nodded, though there was a curve to her lips that told him she wasn't taking him seriously.

By the time she had driven the car out of the garage and onto the tarmac area, it was Rick who said, 'Move over, I'm driving.' To his surprise she agreed and shifted over to the passenger seat.

After parking in town, Rick was around to her side in a flash and took her arm firmly the minute she climbed out of her seat.

'I'm not going to run away you know,' she said, trying to shrug him off. 'Quit holding me so tightly.'

He grinned. 'I've never heard a woman complain about it yet. Besides, after that car tried to run you down I'm taking no chances.'

Rick's cell phone went. He gave his name and listened for a moment. 'Great. That's a first. I'll be there shortly.'

'What is it?' she asked.

'My old boss. Dave Brougham. He's been busy on our behalf,' he replied enigmatically. 'I need to call into the station for a minute.'

The minute turned into five. Gina sat in the Ferrari while a young constable hovered nearby. Rick had taken the car keys with him. When he returned to the car, he was carrying a hard plastic box fastened with a padlock. He put it on the floor underneath his legs and started the car. He didn't tell Gina what the box contained though he could see her looking at it curiously.

Eventually, she said, 'So what's in the box?'

'Tell you later,' he said abruptly.

Rick followed Gina around for three hours, in and out shops in the town, until he felt like strangling her. What was she buying all this stuff for anyway?

He soon found out. She gave him directions that took them to the other side of town and to where she demanded he pull up outside the women's refuge.

'It's best you don't come in,' she warned, 'or they'll probably call the police.'

No one knew better than Rick how the women's refuge would react if he fronted up to the place. He figured she'd be pretty safe since no one knew they were stopping there anyway. Even so, he wouldn't let her get out the car until he double checked the street first.

'Are you sure this is necessary?' she asked impatiently.

'Yeah, it is.' He opened the car door for her, then lifted out the plastic bags of shopping. 'I'll be standing right out here waiting for you. If you're not out in ten minutes, I'll come in and get you. I don't give a damn what the refuge staff think.' He glanced at his watch noting the time.

She raised her eyebrows in disgust. 'I'll be out when I'm good and ready. Not before. So quit hassling me.'

Rick's mouth tightened, but he didn't reply. He surveyed the neighbourhood as he stood on the pavement. Not a person in sight. He picked up the newspaper he had bought earlier and studied it. After reading for a while, he glanced at his watch again. Gina had been away for almost ten minutes. Her time was now up. He walked over to the low, white painted house, situated behind a high wooden fence. Then he put one foot on the cross bar of the gate and peered over. No sign of her. The front door was closed, the blinds drawn tight on the windows.

Where the hell was she?

He glanced at his watch again. Fifteen minutes had already passed. He wasn't going to wait a moment longer. He had just put his hand on the latch of the gate when he finally heard the front door of the house open. Gina's voice drifted down to him. Again, he took a quick look. Gina was bending down, talking to a little boy. Rick watched for a few seconds until Gina noticed him peering over.

She bounded down the steps and opened the gate. 'Quit spying on me,' she said, irritation in her voice. She slammed the gate closed behind her.

'You promised to be ten minutes,' he retorted.

'I didn't promise anything. Being late is not a crime, Caruso.'

They stood glaring at each other until Rick finally said tightly, 'Arguing isn't going to get us anywhere. Come on, let's go.' He moved forward to open the car door for her. Curiosity got the better of him. 'What exactly did you do in there?'

'What do you think? I gave them the stuff I bought, and I had a chat to some of the women. Normally I stay for a cup of tea, but I knew you were waiting so I didn't.' She sighed wistfully. 'I saw this little boy. He was gorgeous. All dark curls and big eyes. I'd love a kid like that.'

Rick slipped into his seat and sat there, tapping his fingers against the steering wheel. He couldn't make up his mind about her. One minute he was convinced she was a spoilt brat, then she did something which completely dispelled that.

'I didn't think you liked kids,' he stated, as he pulled out onto the main road.

'What made you think that? I love children. Why shouldn't I?'

Rick hesitated. 'It's just an impression I got. You seem like a party girl. No responsibilities.'

'And you can't enjoy life with children?'

He shrugged. 'I didn't say that.'

'Well, what are you saying?'

Rick shrugged again. 'I'm not sure really. Maybe I'm a little surprised at your enthusiasm, that's all.' Silence fell. 'Why the women's refuge?' That didn't make sense either, especially when she could have easily have donated money to a charity rather than actually buying the goods. She'd even gone a step further by delivering them.

Her voice had an unexpected edge to it. 'I like to buy stuff for them when I can. They're always needing things. I'm on the committee for fund raising. Last year I arranged an art auction. The money we raised refurbished the kitchen.'

Rick raised a questioning eyebrow. 'There are plenty of charities you could support; why that one?'

She took a slow, deep breath before answering. 'I spent some time

50

there for a while when things got tough with my ex-husband.'

'In the refuge?' His forehead creased in puzzlement. 'Why didn't you go back to your family?'

'Because I couldn't. At least, not straight away.' She hesitated. 'Things were a bit complicated at the time.' Before he could say any more, she added, 'I really don't want to talk about it right now.'

There was more here than she had let on, he realized. While he was tempted to ask her more questions, she had made it obvious she didn't want to go there. He had to respect that. The last thing he wanted was to ruin the business-client relationship between them. It was already strained. He didn't want an all out war.

'OK,' he replied slowly. 'Let's talk about something else.'

She smiled unexpectedly and that gave him a jolt. Dimples appeared in her cheeks making her seem younger. Rick gave her another quick glance. Oh man . . . that babe's smile was a killer. His hands tightened on the steering wheel. Had she any idea what she did to a man? He knew he wasn't totally immune to her charms, he merely chose to ignore the familiar feelings of attraction. Besides, she's off limits, he reminded himself sharply. So forget it, Caruso.

Firstly, she was his client, and secondly, she was the granddaughter of Luigi Rosselini, a wealthy fishing industrialist. The Rosselinis owned the largest fish processing plant at the port and fishing was big business in New Zealand. Everyone knew that. Even the Italians had some sort of hierarchy in this town. The Rosselinis had money. Plenty of it. The Caruso family with their horticultural background didn't. That was simple. And not very hard to understand, he told himself firmly.

He wiped the sweat which had sprung onto his temples, leaned forward and switched on the air conditioning and the CD player. Cool air blasted out refreshing his hot skin. What made him feel even better was Brilleaux, belting out a rhythm and blues number. He tapped his fingers on the steering wheel to a song called 'PhD in Stupidity'.

'Good band,' she remarked.

So she liked the same type of music as he did, he thought. One point in her favour. 'Yeah, Brilleaux are one of the best blues bands in New Zealand,' he replied. 'Saw them in concert at the music festival last year. Absolute dynamite.'

'You like the blues?' she asked.

He nodded. 'Sure I do. What red blooded male doesn't?'

He tried to relax, pushing back his shoulders into the leather seat. Then stole a glance at her. Gina's skirt had ridden up her thighs, exposing soft silky skin. How the hell was he going to remain indifferent? Gina Rosselini was hot stuff. And, man . . . those legs.

He tried to concentrate on the words of the song, but that made it worse.

She's hot . . . she aint got a lot up top. She's cool . . . she's nice. . . .

Get a grip, Caruso, he told himself. Keep your mind on the job, he thought, glancing in his rear-view mirror. He slowed down and indicated right.

'Please, can we stop for something to eat first? I missed breakfast,' said Gina.

'Serves you right for trying to do a runner on me,' he said lightly.

'Have a heart,' she pleaded.

Rick relented. He thought about where they could get some food without having to head back into town where she'd be more vulnerable. 'OK. Here's what we'll do. We'll call in to my parents' place for lunch.'

She glanced at him. 'Are you sure they won't mind?'

'It will be fine,' he replied firmly. 'They're used to me coming and going at all times. That's the nature of my job.'

'You live at home?'

'Not exactly. I've a studio flat and office on their property, but I often eat at home. It's easier. Especially since I work long hours.' He paused slightly. 'When I'm not working I head to my beach house, out of town. It has great surfing.'

Gina picked up the newspaper lying at her feet. She gasped, 'Look at that. Haven't they anything better to write about?' The story of her sister being shot was splashed all over the front page in hideous headlines. 'For goodness sake, that must have been that photographer who pushed his way through and stood over me.' Queasiness rose in her stomach as she took in the details. Maria was lying on the ground with herself leaning over her, a shocked look on her face.

He reached over and grabbed the newspaper. 'It's better not to read stuff like that.'

'Yes, I know . . .' her voice tailed off. 'But I just wanted to see what they had written.'

He tried to change the subject. 'So what other things do you do in your spare time, Gina Rosselini? Since I'm going to be following you around for a while, it would help me to know what I'm in for. Three hours' shopping is probably stretching me a little.'

'That's just tough,' she answered in the same tone. 'I'm going to make you work very hard for your money.'

He gave her a crooked smile. 'Hard work never killed me. Seriously though, I need an idea of your movements during the week.'

She considered his question for a moment. 'I don't have any regular timetable,' she admitted. 'But I try to keep busy. Occasionally I help my grandfather with the business. Mostly to do with arranging functions for any visiting clients from overseas. That type of thing. But for the last three months, I've mainly been organizing the wedding.'

'I heard you were planning on taking a trip overseas.'

She shrugged. 'That's true. I was going to Italy to visit relatives, but when Maria and Anthony announced their engagement, Maria wanted me to stay to help, so I postponed my trip.'

'And now?'

'Oh, I still want to leave here. Travel the world. But now I need to wait until Maria is better – and they've found the person responsible for shooting her.'

'That could take a while.'

She didn't answer, her green eyes worried. 'I hope they catch him and he gets everything he deserves.' She sighed as she stared out the car window at the slowly moving traffic. 'So where exactly do you live in this town?'

'Well, it certainly isn't on snob hill,' he said bluntly. 'Damn it.' He smacked the steering wheel, furious at himself for talking that way. He sounded insulting. And, as his client, she deserved better. 'I'm sorry, I really didn't mean that.' His mouth twisted wryly. 'Sometimes, it gets to me. . . .' His shoulders lifted then fell, wondering if he should take time to explain how he felt, then deciding it probably wasn't worth it. Would a rich girl like Gina Rosselini really understand anyway?

'Got a thing against money?' she asked.

'Yeah, the lack of it,' he replied with a grin.

She laughed. 'Don't they say money is the root of all evil? Well, you might not believe this but if I could choose my life without it, I would.' She took a deep breath. 'But I can't . . . so I make the best of it and give away as much money as I can. That's why Anthony doesn't like me. He hates parting with money and he certainly doesn't like the way I spend it.'

His voice lowered. 'Come on, I don't think he's that bad. Sure, I've always known him to be careful money-wise, but he's always the first to stand a round of drinks when he's out with his mates. Besides, he's a lawyer, so what can you expect?'

'He's our family's lawyer. A while back I asked him for some of my inheritance to pay for extensions to the women's refuge. He refused, advising my grandfather I was wasting my money. He said eventually the building would be pulled down.' She sighed. 'He might have been right, but it wouldn't be for years. All the same I got the money in the end once I explained to my grandparents what exactly it was for.'

Rick listened to her words carefully. This was a new side to Anthony than the one he was familiar with. Could there be truth in what she said?

Within minutes they pulled up outside Rick's parents' place. The wooden colonial house, painted cream with burgundy window sills, had been built over a hundred years ago. An expanse of lawn, freshly mowed, rolled down to the road. Opposite the house, rows upon rows of greenhouses lined the street, all built by the Italian community.

'What's happening to the land next door?' Gina inquired interestedly. A yellow digger moved back and forward shifting dirt from one area to another. Rubble and broken glass were heaped in a corner waiting to be taken away to the dump. Gina read the large sign nailed to the fence advertising a well-known property developer.

'It's a subdivision. Some of the tomato growers have sold out. Others have gone into rural parts taking their greenhouses with them.'

'Are your parents going to follow?'

'Not likely. Papá wouldn't sell his land and greenhouses for all the money in the world. He's worked too hard for it.' However, he didn't tell Gina if his father did sell, that would be the end to his parents' financial worries. For the last few years, supermarkets had been squeezing the local tomato growers and profits had gone right down. To make matters worse, cheaper tomatoes were being imported from Australia.

Rick surveyed his father's greenhouses standing like crystal rocks against the skyline. 'In six months' time, there will be thirty new houses going up next door,' he told her. He pointed to the ravaged stretch of land. 'All this will be lawns and brick. It's a big land development area, desirable because of its proximity to the town centre.' He gave a sigh. 'Things are certainly changing around here. Within five years, we'll be lucky to see one greenhouse standing.'

'You don't sound happy about it,' remarked Gina.

'I guess you can't stop progress. Our way of life is so different now from when I was a kid. My parents' generation all worked on the land or on the sea. It was a close community. Everyone helped each other.

But now, their children are working in professional occupations. We Italians are no longer using our hands but our heads.'

'Like yourself,' she pointed out.

He smiled. 'Yeah, I guess you could say that. You can't blame them for wanting their children to do better than they did. But it's at a high cost. Families move away. The Italian ties are breaking down. Our old way of life is dying.'

Gina had never really thought about it in that light. Perhaps something was being lost along the way. Gina followed him down the stone path to the back of the property, deep in thought.

'My father should be around here somewhere,' said Rick. 'We'll say hello to him, then head over to the house for something to eat.'

Gina saw an elderly man in his seventies, hunched over some potting mixture in a big wooden tub. His tapered fingers were delicately planting seedlings like an artist painting a masterpiece. 'There he is,' said Rick.

The man looked up as they approached. 'Ah, Rick, I was wondering when you were going to turn up. I need you to—' He broke off suddenly, noticing Gina. Mr Caruso straightened his back, squinted, then shoved his glasses further up his nose adding. 'Ah, I should have known . . . and who is this pretty young thing?'

Before Rick could introduce her, Gina stepped forward and said, '*Mi chiamo Gina Rosselini*.'

Rick's father wiped his hands on his work overalls, his nails black from soil. He held out his hand. 'Ah, pleased to meet you, Gina. Welcome.'

Gina took his hand firmly and smiled with warmth. 'I've heard about you from my grandfather. He says you grow the best *pomodoro* . . . tomatoes . . . in the region.'

Mr Caruso's face broke into another broad smile. 'I know your grandfather well. I also knew your parents.' He shook his head. 'They were good people. I'm so sorry about what happened to them.'

Gina's eyes flickered but her voice was steady. 'It was a long time ago.' She paused slightly, holding his gaze. 'At least, they died together.' The memory of the crash that took her parents' lives was never far from her conscious mind.

'You must have been about six years old at the time,' Mr Caruso remarked. 'So young.'

'Actually, it was the day after my seventh birthday,' she said, correcting him. She quickly changed the subject. 'You know, I've always wanted to have a look in your greenhouses. When I was a child, we used to pass here on the way to church. My father called them temples of glass. He used to tell me how hard you all worked.' Her gaze travelled along the glasshouses surrounding them.

Mr Caruso leaned forward, speaking softly. 'But you did come here once when you were about knee high. Your father brought you in.' He smiled, his eyes reflective. 'But you probably don't remember, eh?'

Gina laughed. 'No, I'm afraid I don't.'

He gave a smile. 'I remember Rick showing you his sand pit and toys while your father and I talked business. You both played together quite well.' He chuckled as he glanced at his son. 'Then Rick tried to boss you around. But he didn't get his own way.'

'Oh, what happened?' asked Gina curiously, eager for more details. She flashed a smile at Rick enjoying his discomfort.

'Papá . . .' groaned Rick. 'I'm sure Gina doesn't want to hear this.'

'Oh, but I do,' she replied wickedly.

Mr Caruso continued, ignoring the scowl on Rick's face. 'Well, you swiped him one with your spade. He tackled you, pushed you onto the sand and wouldn't let you up until you said sorry. Unfortunately, you wouldn't give in, so we had to intervene. But all was settled with a lollipop each. Then you were the best of friends again.'

Rick coughed awkwardly. 'I think we'd better be on our way. We don't have a lot of time. And I promised Gina some lunch.'

'Take Gina on a tour of the glasshouses,' suggested Mr Caruso.

'I don't think she—'

'I'd like to,' she said.

'Excuse me, if I don't go with you,' Mr Caruso called after them apologetically. 'I have a lot of orders waiting. I really must get on with them.'

Gina nodded. 'It was lovely to meet you and to hear about Rick as a child. He hasn't changed much.'

'Yeah, neither have you,' he muttered under his breath.

She followed Rick's broad frame through the glasshouse door. 'I hadn't realized we'd met before,' she said.

'Neither had I,' he replied drily.

He guided her down the aisle towards the other end, explaining briefly the procedure from growing the tomatoes from seed until they were ready to harvest. He plucked a luscious red tomato and handed it to her. 'Here, have a taste. It matches the shade of your lipstick,' he said with humour.

Gina noticed the skin, glossy and ripe. 'That's the most romantic thing anyone has said to me in a long time,' she mused, tilting her chin up to him.

'Actually, it wasn't meant to be romantic,' he replied softly 'It's just a fact.'

'You're pretty down to earth, aren't you, Rick Caruso?'

His blue eyes steeled, but there was a glimmer of something else. 'Put it down to the job I do. Facts are what I deal with. Murder, extortion, theft.' He took a deep breath. 'Even adultery. All the vices of the human race.'

'Vices, huh? And I suppose you don't have any?'

Rick grinned. 'I didn't say that. Being a private investigator and ex-cop doesn't mean to say I'm not human.'

'Sometimes I wonder,' she said, under her breath.

Gina took a bite of the tomato, the juice running down the side of her lips. Rick lifted his finger and skimmed her mouth, wiping the juice away. 'You need a handkerchief. Sorry I can't oblige this time.'

For a moment, both of them stood staring at each other, neither of them willing to move. The heat in the greenhouse was intense, the glass panes steaming up as the sprinklers were switched on one by one. Rick swallowed, aware of something intangible.

Gina moved forward bumping against him slightly as she tried to avoid the water from the sprinkler. Her head lifted while her lips parted with apology. Rick's arms automatically reached out to steady her. What happened next was totally unexpected. His body touched hers, his mouth only inches away from her face. He zoomed in on her lips fascinated to see a trace of tomato around the edges and very tempted to taste both. He knew he ought to step back and was about to when in one artful movement, the tip of her pink tongue appeared and stroked along her lips. Water spray hissed quietly around them. His pulse raced. He leaned forward only to be interrupted by a cough from behind. It had them both jerking apart like guilty teenagers.

'Do you know where the owner is? I'd like to buy some tomatoes.' A woman's voice spoke, sharp and reprimanding.

Rick looked up, furious at himself for being caught out like that. 'My father is around the back of the potting shed. I'm sure he'll be able to help you.'

'Hmm, obviously they cultivate more than tomatoes round here,' the woman muttered to her companion as they walked away twittering to themselves.

Outside, Rick gulped in the fresh air, more from relief than from the heat. He'd damned well nearly kissed her. What the hell had got into him? He was on an assignment not a damned date.

'It is certainly good to be out of there,' he said to break the silence. The comment hung in the air and again he cursed inwardly at his lack of control.

Gina also breathed in deeply as her hand rose to her chest. She fingered the fine gold chain around her neck casually, a slight tremor in her voice as she answered him. 'I don't know how your father can bear working in that heat. The humidity under the glass was unbelievable.'

Rick walked beside her, trying to dissipate a different kind of heat, one that was generated by the sultry essence of her skin. Another glance at her made him break out in a hot sweat. He swallowed hard, his throat dry. 'My father's had a lifetime to get used to it. I'm glad I didn't follow him into horticulture. Tomatoes aren't my forte,' he replied. 'But I'm not knocking it: it's a good living and a healthy one. It's just not for me, that's all.'

Gina stopped dead. 'And what exactly is your style, Rick Caruso? Looking after rich girls in case they get into mischief?'

He gave her a long, level look, trying to keep his temper in control. He didn't know why he felt so annoyed. But one thing he did know, she hadn't been as immune to the incident in the greenhouse as he had first thought. Dangerous, he thought. Very dangerous. All the same, he knew when he answered, his words would irk her. 'Maybe you'll find out someday, Gina Rosselini.'

Gina took in the kitchen with one look. Gleaming copper pans hung on the walls and tall bottles of green, red and cream-coloured pasta sat side by side on the tiled bench. The walls, colour-washed in blue-green, resembled shades of the ocean. Stacked high in a wicker basket on the scrubbed wooden floor were fresh vegetables, juicy red peppers, strings of garlic and bunches of onions, all adding piquant colour. And all cultivated and harvested by Mr Caruso.

Gina couldn't help but compare her own kitchen against this one. She'd tried to make her apartment as cosy as possible. However, this was a real family home, she decided.

'Take a seat,' said Rick. He set down two long glasses. From the fridge, he took out a jug. 'Fresh lemonade. My mother makes it first thing.' He placed it in the middle of the table. 'There you go.'

'Thanks. I'm parched,' she remarked.

'Ice?'

'Yes, please.'

'Still hungry?'

'Ravenous,' she replied honestly.

'I'll see if I can rustle up some food.'

'Thanks. Do you cook?'

He flashed her a grin. 'Not if there's a woman around.'

If she had something in her hand she would have thrown it at him. Instead she made a face.

Rick moved efficiently around the kitchen taking out some sliced ham, mozzarella cheese and pickle. He found a loaf of baked bread in the pantry. 'It's nothing fancy, but it's fresh and it's wholesome.'

He placed the plates and cutlery on the table.

'Can I help?' she asked.

'Nope . . . you just stay put. I know where everything is. And I'll be quicker.'

It was then she noticed a photo sitting on a shelf nearby. Rick had his arms around a young dark-haired woman who looked to be in her middle twenties. The woman looked familiar somehow. Was it his girlfriend, she wondered? The thought didn't please her and she didn't know why.

Rick noticed her interest. He picked up the photo and handed it to her. 'Here, take a look. That's my sister, Elena. She's a nurse.' He grinned. 'Actually, you met her the other day.'

'I did?'

'Yeah. She was the nurse I was busy talking to in the hospital corridor.'

Stunned, she could only stare at him. 'Oh. . . .' That nurse. The one she had practically accused him of flirting with. 'I . . . er . . . hadn't realized.' Her face flushed. She took a sip of lemonade, then placed the glass back on the table. 'I guess I thought—'

He interrupted her. 'Yeah, I know exactly what you thought. Just shows, doesn't it? You can't jump to conclusions. Because nine times out of ten it will be wrong. Being a cop taught me that.'

He had a point. 'OK. I made a mistake, I admit it.' Gina took in the photo again. 'She's pretty. Is she married?'

'She was. Her husband died a couple of years ago. A work accident. He was a construction worker.'

Gina's heart went out to the woman. 'I'm really sorry.' Now she felt even worse.

Rick placed the photograph back on the bench. 'Things were a bit rough for her especially since she's got two young sons. Luckily, my parents rallied around.'

'Hmm . . . I guess that figures being Italian. There's nothing like family, is there?' She took another bite of bread, and swallowed. Her thoughts were never far away from her own sister. 'So where's your mother? I thought she might have been here.'

'She's out.' He glanced at the clock on the wall. 'But she'll be back any minute. She has a cleaning job at a local motel. My father's not too keen on her doing it, but she's got a mind of her own.'

'You agree with him?'

Rick finished his mouthful as he leaned back. 'Yeah, I do. I'd say she's got enough to do around here as it is.'

'You don't approve of a woman working outside the home?' Gina asked testily.

'I didn't say that – but I certainly wouldn't approve if my wife had children. I'm not into putting kids into child care. If you have kids, you look after them.'

'The Italian macho male,' she said mockingly.

'Maybe,' he answered seriously, 'but when you think about it, it's just down-to-earth common sense.'

Just then, his cell phone rang. He answered it. 'Caruso.' The conversation was brief. 'Twenty minutes,' he said, flipping his phone closed. He looked at Gina. 'We have to call back to the station and see Dave Brougham. He wants to talk to you.'

'OK.' Gina's stomach lurched. More questions.

The door opened and Rick's mother walked in. When she saw the two of them sitting there, her eyes shone bright with interest. 'Rick, you're home now. We weren't expecting you.'

'Just a quick visit,' he explained. 'We were passing, so we stopped in for a quick bite to eat.' Rick got up immediately, put his arm around his mother and gave her a quick hug. As they drew apart, he introduced Gina.

'It's nice to meet you,' said Mrs Caruso, with a warm smile.

Gina took in the woman in front of her. She was attractive with fine features, in her early sixties with grey peppered hair. Her figure was full giving her a homely look.

'I hope Rick put plenty of food on the table,' she added.

'Thank you. He did. I couldn't eat another morsel if I tried.'

Rick lifted the dishes into the sink. 'It's time we were on our way. Sorry, but I'll have to skip the washing-up this time. We've got an appointment to keep.'

His mother turned to Gina, her hands on rounded hips. 'Hmm, excuses. Now isn't that just like a man? Leave the dishes for the woman to do.'

Gina rose to her feet. 'Surely our appointment can wait. Perhaps I can help you, Mrs Caruso. It won't take long to wash these.'

'Gina, we need to get going,' reminded Rick.

Rick's mother smiled. 'Thank you for the offer, but it really is OK.' She turned to face Rick 'You'll have to bring Gina back again sometime. Perhaps for a meal.'

'Maybe.' His tone was dismissive inferring he wouldn't be bringing her back any time soon.

Gina ignored his rudeness. 'I'd love to come back, Mrs Caruso, whether Rick brings me or not.'

Surprise crossed Rick's face, but he didn't say anything. He opened the door, and then turned to his mother. '*Ciao.*'

They had only gone a few yards down the concrete path when Gina squinted her eyes in the bright glare of the sun and said, 'Oh, I've left my sunglasses on the kitchen table. I'll just run back and get them.' She hurried back up the worn path until she reached the kitchen door.

When she went inside, she found Rick's mother humming softly to herself, her hands already in the sink. 'I just forgot these,' said Gina, and reached out for her sunglasses lying on the table. She slipped them on.

Mrs Caruso turned and dried her hands on a towel. She smiled at Gina, her brown eyes sympathetic. 'I'm sorry about your sister; it's an awful tragedy. Please, if there is anything I can do, anything at all, you will let me know?'

Gina's throat tightened unexpectedly. Rick was lucky to have a mother like this, she thought, and she hoped he damned well realized it.

'Thank you. You're very kind, Mrs Caruso.'

Mrs Caruso put her hand on Gina's arm. 'I know Rick is looking after you. And he will look after you, you know. He's dependable. A good man.' She smiled again. 'And don't forget you're welcome here anytime.'

'*Grazie*,' Gina replied shakily, feeling a sudden urge to cry on this woman's shoulder. Although she had only met Rick's mother a few minutes ago, she couldn't help but wish that if her mother had been alive today, she would have been like this woman standing in front of her. It wasn't that she didn't love her grandparents and wasn't grateful to them for looking after Maria and herself all these years but there was something about having a mother and father which nothing could ever replace. Would her life have been different if they had lived? It was a question she had often asked herself.

By the time, she got to the car, Gina had almost returned to normal.

Rick noticed her quietness. 'Is there something wrong?'

Gina swallowed again, not sure how to answer. 'No, should there be?' she lied. She paused slightly. 'I like your mother and father,' she said simply.

He grinned. 'Yeah, we have our ups and downs sometimes, but we're a pretty close family really.'

'I'm surprised you've never married.' When she realized what she had said, she could have kicked herself for speaking so impulsively. What business was it of hers if he hadn't got himself hitched?

He threw his head back and chuckled. 'Marriage?' He shook his head. 'I'm not ready to settle down. Besides, I'm not sure I even want to get married. I've seen too much of what can go wrong.' He paused reflectively. 'When I was a cop, marriage split ups were common. The stress, long hours on duty. I've seen some guys really cut up when their marriage fell apart. There's no way I want to go through that.'

'You can hardly apply that situation to your parent's marriage.'

'No, that's true, but they're an exception. But if and when I do marry I want to make sure it's the right person.'

It was Gina's turn to laugh out loud, the bitterness coming through in her voice. 'We all take a chance whether you like it or not. There are no guarantees in this life.' And, because her curiosity got the better of her, 'Tell me, have you got a girlfriend? Or is it true what they say, you have a few women scattered around town?'

'You should never listen to gossip,' he said, his mouth lifting at the corners.

'I wasn't listening to gossip,' she said indignantly. 'It was our housekeeper, Maggie. She mentioned that her daughter, Jennifer, went out on a date with you and came home drunk.'

'Hmm. That sounds like gossip to me.' He shrugged again. 'Yeah, I remember her daughter very well. Nice girl.' And because he couldn't resist it, he added teasingly, 'With a nice butt to match.' But what he didn't tell Gina was Maggie's daughter hadn't been his date. She had been drunk at a party and he took her home because he could see she was inviting trouble wanting to drive home herself. He had merely been acting like any responsible male would. Being a cop for years had left some habits deeply ingrained. But he didn't see why he should explain himself to Gina.

Rick fell silent as he concentrated on the road ahead. In twenty minutes, Rick drew up outside the police station. It was a four-storey, grey-stone, depressing looking building in the centre of town. As Rick escorted her up the concrete steps, Gina felt the whole of the town was looking at her. Rick held the swing doors open and she stepped inside first. The waiting area was smaller than she expected and, as there was someone already at the counter being served, she took a seat on the nearest chair to wait.

'I won't be a moment,' said Rick, moving forward. He attracted the attention of a female police officer, busy typing at a computer behind the reception desk. A broad smile lit up her face.

'G'dday Rick, back so soon?' she said.

Rick leaned forward on the counter, his voice low. 'Dave is expecting us. He wants to interview Gina Rosselini.'

The officer on duty glanced over at Gina curiously. 'Yeah, and I bet she's a handful.'

'Can't comment. She's a client.'

'Really? That's not like you.' She looked over at Gina again. 'She's attractive too. And stinking rich. Looks like you got yourself a cushy number.'

He saw the glint in her eye. He replied with a grin, 'It's strictly professional.'

'Yeah, and pigs might fly. . . .' She paused slightly. 'When you've had enough of playing private investigator I reckon you should come back. We miss you heaps.'

'How come you never told me?' he said, his smile widening.

Her mouth twitched. 'I did. At your leaving party.'

Rick groaned. There were some things he preferred to forget.

She leaned forward. 'Things just aren't the same around here without you.' Still chuckling, she picked up a phone within arm's reach and, after a few seconds of conversation, swung back to Rick. 'Dave will be with you as soon as he can. Do you want a coffee while you're waiting?'

'No thanks. If I remember rightly, the coffee is pretty disgusting around here.'

She laughed. 'We've improved a lot since you were on the beat. We've now got a state of the art coffee machine. Real coffee too. None of that cheap supermarket stuff.'

'Impressive. But I'll save it until next time.'

Rick took a seat next to Gina and said quietly, 'Brougham shouldn't be too long.'

'Do you know her?'

'Who?'

'The cop on reception. The one you were just talking to.'

'Sure. We patrolled together a few times. Why?'

She shrugged. 'No particular reason.' But the truth was she was curious. She couldn't help noticing the easy manner in which he talked to her.

While Rick read a magazine, Gina surveyed the other occupants in the room. A drunk, sitting in the far corner, had fallen asleep, his head lolling as he snored. On the other side, a young girl with a sullen look on her face, who looked no more than sixteen, was getting a ticking off from a youth aid police officer.

Gina's gaze shifted to the woman who had just walked in, escorted by a female cop. The woman was a hooker, there was no mistaking the fact. She wore a short, tight, red skirt, and a low-cut black top to match. Her make-up was plastered on thickly. The woman tried to shake herself free, but the police officer firmly marched her into an interview room.

'You've no right to hold me. I haven't done anything wrong.' Gina heard the woman say in a shrill voice.

It was a sad reminder of those unfortunate in the world and Gina was only too aware of it. But one thing she knew, the hooker hadn't been arrested because of prostitution. That occupation was legal in New Zealand.

'I hate police stations,' Gina murmured uneasily.

'You've been in one before?'

'I suppose you could say that.'

A door opened and another officer appeared dressed in plain clothes. It was Senior Detective Dave Brougham. He greeted Rick first, then said, 'This way, Ms Rosselini.' When they reached the interview room, the door swung shut behind her with a click. Gina jumped. She stood there, unsure what to do. 'Please take a seat.' His officious manner immediately put her on edge.

Gina sat at one side of the formica table, keeping her eyes focused on the man in front of her. Detective Dave Brougham was well built and in his early forties. He had red hair and fair skin. She'd met him for the first time on the day Maria had been shot when he'd taken her statement at the hospital. He'd been polite and sympathetic but she had a feeling that wouldn't last.

He smiled briefly. 'Right, then, Ms Rosselini . . . thanks for coming in. There's a few things I'd like to go over with you.'

Gina shifted uneasily, clutching her handbag tighter. 'Well, what would you like to know? I've already told you everything I can think of.'

'How about we start at the beginning? Tell us what exactly happened on the day of the wedding.' He switched on the small tape recorder at the side of him.

Gina repeated her story, telling them the events of the morning. 'Maria and I got dressed at home and then the limousine called for us just before lunchtime. We were running a little late due to the busy traffic, but everything was going to plan.' She paused slightly. 'Maria was nervous. I guess she had every right to be. We talked in the limousine on the way to the hotel. Everything seemed fine until . . .' She faltered a little. 'You know the rest.' She felt like crying again but fought for control. It wouldn't help Maria if she burst into tears every time she was interviewed.

'Would you like to take a break?' asked the detective, unexpectedly.

She looked at him in surprise. 'No . . . no . . . I'm fine. Really I am. I just want to get this over with.' Gina rummaged in her bag for a piece of paper. 'This is a complete list of all the guests' names you asked me for. The hotel handled the catering, but I also hired some extra people like the musicians.'

Brougham surveyed the list, and then laid it down in front of him on the table. 'Are you sure that's all that happened. There's nothing else you can recall? I want you to think really carefully.'

'No . . . no . . . there's nothing else.'

'What about the guests who didn't come to the wedding?'

Gina's brow's knitted together. 'You mean cancellations?'

'That's right.'

Gina frowned, concentrating hard. 'If I remember rightly, a couple of guests phoned at the last minute. One of them was Anthony's secretary, Denise Thompson, who was sick and couldn't make it, and also an elderly cousin of my grandfather's who'd had a fall and broken her arm.'

The Detective scribbled on the pad in front of him. Then he looked up. 'Do you have any idea why anyone would want to shoot your sister?'

Purposely, she kept her voice level. 'You've already asked me this and really I have no idea. Maria was quite popular. She had lots of friends.' Her voice tailed off again as she stared into space. Her chin lifted. 'There is one thing . . . I'm not sure but . . .' She shrugged, 'well, it may be nothing.'

Brougham's eyes narrowed. 'We're willing to look at any detail no matter how insignificant you think it is.'

Gina bit her lip as she held his gaze. 'I just remembered. The week before the wedding, Maria had a couple of distressing phone calls.' She paused again, trying to remember exactly what the caller had said. 'Maria was a bit upset over it, but she didn't want to make a fuss especially when we were so busy with the wedding arrangements.'

'Did she recognize the caller?'

Gina thought for a moment. 'No. I don't think so, but she did say it was a woman's voice.'

'And she didn't tell you what the caller said?'

'No, she didn't. Maria dismissed it as a misunderstanding and didn't want to talk about it.'

'You didn't think that a bit odd?'

'Actually, I did, because we always tell each other everything. But I respected her wishes.'

The detective wrote something down on the pad in front of him. 'We'll make enquiries and see if we can trace the call.' He paused briefly. 'We found the room the shooter was in. He rented the room under the name Mr Grey, then disappeared.'

'I've never heard of him.'

'A red rose was found on the windowsill in the room? Does that mean anything to you?'

Gina shook her head. 'No. It doesn't.' She hesitated. 'But red roses are my favourite flower.'

'Who gave you red roses last?'

'Maria did. On my birthday. A few weeks ago.'

'What about Anthony? Do you get on OK?'

'What do you mean?' she answered warily.

'We know there were harsh words said between you the night before the wedding. I understand you had an argument.'

Gina's mouth parted in surprise. 'Did he tell you that?'

'I'm not at liberty to disclose that, I'm sorry.'

Gina took a deep breath. 'Yes, that's true. We had an argument. He was being his usual awkward self so I might as well be honest about it. He was upset because I'd taken more staff on for the wedding. He said we were way over budget.'

'So you don't get on?' Brougham prompted.

Gina hesitated. 'I suppose that's one way of putting it. We rub each other up the wrong way.' She took a deep breath before adding, 'I had my doubts over his sincerity in marrying Maria.'

'In what way?'

'It's difficult to explain,' she said lamely.

'Then please try.'

'OK. Maria will inherit money after her marriage. It was a condition in my parents' will.'

'I'd hardly say Anthony's short of a dollar or two himself especially since he is one of the top lawyers in the city,' Brougham said drily. 'Somehow accusing Anthony Monopoli of being a fortune-hunter doesn't make sense.'

'I don't mean he's a fortune-hunter exactly. He's merely ambitious. Marrying my sister, Maria, granddaughter of the owner of Rosselini Fishing Industries, would lift his status in the business community even more. The inheritance would be the icing on the cake.'

'I see,' replied Brougham thoughtfully. 'You and Anthony used to date, didn't you?'

'No, we didn't,' she answered sharply. 'I met him for dinner on a couple of occasions to discuss business.'

'What sort of business?'

'A couple of projects I had in mind. That's all.' For some reason, her gaze moved to Rick who was absorbing her every word. Why did she feel the need to justify her actions to him of all people?

'Anthony is just a friend. And now he's also a relative by marriage,' she emphasized, suddenly feeling as if the conversation was leading up to something of which she was totally innocent.

'So it isn't true you had an affair with him?' Brougham accused.

Gina felt her face suffuse with colour as her hands balled in her lap. 'No, it damned well isn't. And you've no right to make accusations like that.' She looked from one man to another furiously. 'I thought we were discussing who would want to hurt Maria, not nasty gossip.'

Detective Brougham replied calmly, 'We have to look at every angle. I'm sure you can understand that.'

Oh, she could understand it, she thought, furiously. But she didn't like it. While she was tempted to argue their method of reasoning, it would only prolong the interview. Right now, she wanted out of the place fast.

'Is that all, Detective?'

He stared at her as if he couldn't make up his mind about something. 'Not quite. I still have a few more questions.'

Somehow, Gina had a feeling the worst was yet to come. Her hands clenched in her lap.

'What about your husband? Jason Gallagher.'

'I thought you'd get around to him eventually.' She breathed in deeply, trying to keep her voice steady. 'Jason wasn't at the wedding, if that's what you mean. He didn't have an invite.' Her eyes were cool, distant. 'And we're divorced, by the way.'

'Have you seen him lately?' asked Brougham.

Gina hesitated slightly, though she kept her gaze level. 'I don't want to see him.' Oh God, this was getting worse, she thought. 'Look, I don't see what this has to do with what happened to Maria.'

Brougham said quickly, 'Don't lie, Ms Rosselini. Why don't you tell us why you met your ex-husband two hours before the wedding?'

CHAPTER FOUR

Gina gasped. She gripped the arms of the chair. 'How did you know that?'

Brougham gave a low laugh. 'I can't disclose that either, I'm afraid, but let's just say the police have their ways.'

She saw Rick's accusing look. She hadn't lied outright: she'd merely avoided the question.

'It's not like you think,' she said frantically. Why was she trying to explain herself again to him anyway?

Brougham leaned forward. He said calmly, 'We're trying to help. So why don't you just tell us what happened?'

Gina took another deep breath. 'I knew it would come back to haunt me. Jason was released from rehab a couple of weeks ago. He rang me on the morning of the wedding and said that he needed some money badly. I . . . I gave in to him. I arranged to meet him at the beach and wrote him out a cheque.'

'I see. And how much was it for?' asked Brougham.

'Fifty thousand dollars.'

Brougham whistled. 'That's a lot of dosh. Why didn't you call us?'

'I didn't have time. If the police turned up that would have upset the wedding. I had to think of Maria. So I had no choice but to give him the money.'

'Have you heard from him since?' continued Brougham.

'No, I haven't.' He looked like he didn't believe her. 'I'm telling the truth.'

'We could have him arrested on grounds of extortion,' he offered. 'We should nip this in the bud since he might try that again.'

Gina remained silent. She knew that was entirely possible, but the next time she wouldn't be under so much pressure and she wouldn't give in to his demands. 'I don't want to take this any further. I'll be ready for him next time.'

'Did he say why he wanted the cash?'

'Jason promised me he was going make a new life for himself. He just needed a helping hand.'

'And you believed him?' asked Brougham.

'I . . . I'm not sure,' she replied honestly. 'I guess I wanted to. He seemed to mean what he said.' She hesitated. 'Jason wanted me to go with him. He told me how he was going to make up for what had happened between us. But I refused.'

Brougham arched a brow. 'Do you know where he is staying?'

'No, I don't. He didn't say. And quite frankly, I didn't want to know.'

'You should have told us,' Brougham admonished. 'This could be important.' He made a few more notes on his pad. 'He's not Italian, is he?'

'No, he's not.' She hesitated. 'My grandparents held that against him. They were against me marrying him. It caused a lot of difficulties.'

Brougham looked thoughtful. 'How is your sister by the way?'

'She's stable . . . the doctors are pleased with her progress. It's a relief to know she's going to make it.'

'We'll continue the surveillance outside her hospital room just in case there is another attempt,' he informed her.

'You don't think they'll try again, do you?'

Brougham spoke carefully. 'We don't know, but we have to cover all our options. We've also posted a patrol car outside your house and one down on the main road below your property.' His gaze flicked to Rick, then back to Gina. 'We'll work in conjunction with Rick and whatever private security arrangements he's made.'

'Thank you,' she murmured.

Rick spoke quickly. 'The Rosselini family's security arrangements aren't that tight. A few things need updating. I'm looking into that now. I've hired more security men to guard the property and I'm putting in an additional alarm system. But all this is going to take time.'

Detective Brougham nodded. 'Sounds like you're doing all you can.' His gaze met Gina's. 'There's a limit to what the police can do protection-wise, but I'm sure Rick will do everything he can to make sure you're kept safe. You've got one of the best people in the business. I've known him for years. We did our training together at the Police College in Wellington.'

So Rick had a professional reputation. Somehow it didn't surprise her. 'That's reassuring to know.'

Brougham stood up. 'OK. That's all for now, Ms Rosselini. Thanks for coming in. If you could please step outside, I'd like to speak to Rick privately.' Brougham held the door open for her. 'We'll be in touch.'

Once Gina had left the room, Brougham switched off the tape recorder and turned to face Rick.

'What's your take on Ms Rosselini?'

'For the record, I'd say she loves her sister and her grandparents. I think she's telling the truth.'

'She lied about meeting her husband.'

'She avoided the question,' corrected Rick. 'There's a difference.'

'You sound like you're defending her.'

'She's my client; I'm paid to.'

'Actually, I'm surprised you took on the Rosselini job. I didn't think you'd be into protecting the rich and famous.'

Initially, Rick hadn't thought so either, but he had always been open to new challenges.

'You know how it is. Got to take the work when it comes along. Times are lean. In case you hadn't noticed, we've got a downturn in the economy. Plus I'm a one man band. I have to be versatile.'

Brougham's eyebrows rose. 'Yeah, well, if I don't get more help around here, I might join you. Need a partner?'

'That bad, huh?'

Brougham sighed. 'Same old story. We're short staffed. Work too many long hours. This Rosselini case is stretching us. And my wife's on my back about taking a holiday. She reckons I live here more than I do at home. I'm starting to think that myself.'

Rick could believe it: Brougham was totally dedicated to the job. He was highly respected by his colleagues. 'Take my advice, you're better off staying in the force. At least you get paid overtime.'

'You tell my wife that,' said the detective, wryly. 'Incidentally, getting back to the case, we've had the ballistic report back. The bullet that hit Maria was .223 calibre. One of the weapons stolen from that sports shop raid a couple of weeks ago was a Remington in that calibre. It could be the weapon.'

'Yeah, I remember hearing about it.'

'If the attacker was responsible for that robbery, he could be planning other raids now that he's armed,' Brougham pondered. 'Or he could be planning to finish off Maria Rosselini.'

'Do you think it's Gina's ex-husband?'

'I really don't know. But we'll try and find out where he is for a start. Bring him in for questioning.'

'With fifty thousand dollars, chances are high he's skipped the country,' remarked Rick.

'Possibly. We'll check that out with passport control.' Brougham reached over for another file sitting on his desk. He opened it. 'There's something else. I did a bit of digging. Remember that scandal about four years ago, to do with Rosselini Fishing Industries?'

Rick searched his memory. 'I think I was away at the time, working in Greymouth, on that Triad drug smuggling case. But I remember my cousin, Mark, mentioning it. He's a fisherman. Wasn't it to do with fishing quotas? Some court case hit the news?'

'Yeah, that's right. One of Rosselini's vessels was forfeited to the

Crown. A guy called Dani Russo was the owner and skipper of the boat and contracted it to Rosselini. Russo was convicted of quota fraud. Well over the catch limit. He said Rosselini put pressure on him to overfish. Rosselini denied all knowledge of what he had done. Russo took the rap.'

'So what's this got to do with Maria?'

'She was involved in giving evidence against him. Millions of dollars were at stake at the time.'

'So why didn't you bring it up with Gina?'

'I needed to look through the file first.'

That made sense to Rick. He made a mental note to ask Gina about Maria's involvement.

'Any luck tracing that Skyline which tried to run us down?'

Brougham shook his head. 'Nothing yet, but we're working on it.'

Afterwards, Rick thought about what Gina had said. Her husband had demanded money and she had given it to him. So why would he shoot Maria afterwards? Unless there was something else they didn't know about. And what about Dani Russo who had committed quota fraud? Could that also have some connection?

Brougham might be in charge of the case but that didn't stop Rick from fitting the pieces together as well. As a private investigator, he'd worked closely with the police on many occasions. He'd never forgotten what it was like to be a cop. If anyone asked him what it was he missed about the force, he'd say it was the team work and the comradeship. He'd often tried to define what made a good cop and had never come up with a specific answer. Cops were human beings too and made mistakes along the way in spite of their good intentions. He might not be a cop now but the way he felt about the law and protecting the public hadn't changed. The only difference was who paid him.

Rick returned to the waiting room. He saw Gina sitting there. She was pale, too pale under the tan. 'You OK?'

'No . . . no . . . I'm not.' She turned on him, her eyes flashing. 'I thought you were supposed to be on my side. How could you let Brougham question me like that?'

He frowned. 'What are you talking about?'

'All those questions he was asking about Anthony . . . and Jason. How do you think he made me feel?'

Rick recognized she was strung up tight. He could hear it in her voice. 'Probably damned uncomfortable,' he replied, 'but you have to remember he's trying to find out who shot Maria. He's a police officer.'

'He kept making insinuations about me and Anthony.' Despair washed over her. 'Damn him.'

'He was just doing his job. He's one of the best officers in the force. And he gets results. I ought to know, I worked with him for long enough.'

'Well, you would stick up for him, wouldn't you? Being an ex-cop shows exactly where your loyalties lie.'

Warning lights glinted dangerously in his blue eyes. 'That's enough, Gina. You know nothing about being an ex-cop.' He gripped her arm firmly as they walked along the path.

Gina knew then she had hit a nerve. An odd bleakness had come into his eyes but was gone so quickly she nearly wondered if she had imagined it. She bit back the retort on her lips.

After a few moments, she added, 'I'm sorry. I didn't mean that. I don't know why I let him get to me. I guess it's also because of the questions about Jason.' She took another deep breath. 'Here I am trying to forget I was ever married to him, and just when I think I have my life on track again, he turns up demanding money. I had no choice but to pay him because I was thinking of Maria. I know I should have told Brougham.' Her voice lowered regretfully. 'What else was I to do at the time? After Maria had been shot, I didn't want my grandfather to find out I'd met Jason again. I didn't want to make things any worse because he was so upset already over our marriage. Am I so wrong to want to protect my family?'

He grimaced. 'No, you're not. But the information might have been important. Brougham would have kept it in confidence.' He took her arm, leading her forward and said in a low voice, 'Come on, let's take a walk down by the river.'

They crossed the busy road and headed down the stone steps which led under the road bridge and along the sloping bank. Weeping willow trees lined the edge of the river, sweeping low, the branches trailing lightly into the clear green tinged water. The river was calm and smooth, not a ripple out of place. They followed the narrow concrete path a little way, then stopped to sit down on a battered wooden bench covered in graffiti.

Gina took a few deep breaths to steady herself.

'Feeling better?' he asked, after a while.

She turned to answer, but before she had a chance, he gave her a smile which made her heart do a quick somersault. The shock of it was so physical, she raised her hand to her breast. To hide her confusion, she stammered, 'I . . . I'm not sure.' Then fell silent. When she found her voice again, she added, 'Maybe I did overreact back there. Police stations don't agree with me. I guess I can thank my ex-husband for that.'

Rick's eyes focused on her, turning a deeper shade of blue, and for one split second, Gina felt she had to try and explain some things to him.

'My ex-husband was a gambler and he had a drink problem. He got involved in the drug scene to pay off his debts. The cops were always chasing him. Give him his due, he really did try to put things right for a while but it didn't work out that way.' The excuse sounded lame and she knew it. She didn't know why she was even trying to defend Jason because deep down inside she knew he deserved everything he got. And what was more, the misery he put her through nearly destroyed her.

Rick said gently. 'It might help to talk.'

'Talk? That's kind of hard to do right now.' She hesitated. 'Still, if you think it might help us find who tried to hurt Maria, I'll tell you everything.' She paused slightly as she collected her thoughts.

'Like I said, Jason was into drugs. He became a dealer. When the police came to arrest him at our home, he wasn't there. They searched the flat. Found some cocaine. So the cops took me instead. It wasn't a pleasant experience being locked up and it's certainly not one I want to repeat.' Her heart began to beat faster as the memories came rushing back. She could still hear the sound of the slamming cell door echoing in her mind. 'I'm surprised Detective Brougham didn't bring it all out during his questioning: I'm sure it's all on file.'

Rick frowned again. 'Did you know Jason was dealing drugs?'

'Of course I didn't,' she said indignantly. 'I had no idea he had drugs stashed away. Luckily, I had a good lawyer, someone recommended by Anthony, and I was cleared.'

'And what about Jason?'

'He got off the drug charges. We separated. Then he eventually went into rehab. Our divorce came through six months ago.'

'Do you still love him?' he asked tentatively.

Gina clenched her hands together in her lap. Love him, she thought? She hated him. Detested him for what he had done to her. And the shame he had brought on her family.

'No, I don't love him. He hurt me badly at the time. I made a big mistake in marrying him, and paid for it. Jason is out of my life forever. Now, I just want to forget about that whole sordid episode. But Maria being shot has brought it all up again. What if it was Jason who shot Maria? That keeps going around in my mind.' She shook her head. 'I didn't want to accuse him back there. Why, I don't know. When I met him the other day, he seemed to have changed. He asked me to go back to him. But I refused.'

Rick exhaled. 'We don't know yet if it was him. But if it was, you're not to blame for his actions, so don't even think that way.'

'Aren't I?' she asked, her heart sinking. 'I'm not so sure.'

The watcher entered the church early before evening mass. He hovered at the back waiting for his eyes to adjust to the darkness, then when they did, he slowly he made his way to a wooden pew on the left. He slid onto the seat next to the aisle. Several people were praying in the front row. An elderly lady, her back slightly curved, fumbled with her rosary beads. He heard her drop them on the floor. She muttered something. When she half turned around to retrieve them, he saw her face. It was Rosa Rosselini. If she was here, then Gina might be as well. But as he looked around, he couldn't see her.

The chapel door creaked as it opened. He half turned to see who had entered, but kept his face down. It was her. Gina. A man followed her in. Rick Caruso, he realized. He should have guessed he'd be with her. He noticed she wore a white lacy dress emphasizing her olive skin and dark hair.

She whispered some words to Caruso and, while the private investigator sat down at a pew on the right, she continued walking towards the altar. She passed him by. She was so close to him, he could have reached out to touch her. The watcher curled his fingers into the palm of his hand to prevent him from doing so.

She picked up a candle and lit it and placed it on the iron holder at the alter. Then after crossing herself, she turned around and walked back down the aisle again. The watcher lowered his gaze.

The priest and other clergy entered. The smell of incense permeated the air.

The church was filling up, he realized. Should he stay, or go? He wasn't sure, but the opportunity to observe Gina for a bit longer was just too tempting.

The next day, Gina called in to see Maria at the hospital. She paused in the doorway at intensive care and said to Rick. 'I'd like to stay for a while.'

'Sure. I'll wait out here in the corridor until you're ready.'

Gina entered the room, approaching her sister quietly. Maria was asleep. Her sister looked so pale, the dark shadows under her eyes even more pronounced. All of a sudden an uneasy feeling came over Gina as she moved closer to her.

'Maria, can you hear me?' said Gina softly. 'I'm right here beside you. You have to get better . . . we have so much to do together.' For a moment, the impossible ran through her mind. What if Maria died? She froze. But she couldn't die, she told herself sternly. The doctor had already told them she was making good progress. She had come around very briefly earlier on, but the doctor had given her another sedative because she was in such a lot of pain.

She kissed her sister lightly on the cheek and said a short silent prayer.

It was evening when Gina arrived back at her apartment. The first thing she did was call in to see her grandmother to tell her about her visit to see Maria.

Her grandmother patted her hand. 'She's in the best place. The doctors said we have to be patient.'

'I know, but it's so hard.'

'I have something for you.' Her grandmother opened up her handbag and handed her a small white box. 'Look inside.'

Gina did. A silver amulet shaped like a horn lay against the silky material. 'Oh . . .'

Her grandmother smiled. 'It's a *cornicello* . . . to wear around your neck. It's an old Italian custom to ward off the evil eye.'

'Nonna . . .' protested Gina.

'Promise me you will wear it, *sì*?'

She kissed her grandmother's cheek. 'I promise.' She slipped it around her neck. '*Grazie*. It's beautiful.'

'I'm going down to the beach for a swim,' Gina told Rick.

'Why don't you use the swimming pool? It will be safer.'

'Because I prefer the sea,' she said simply.

'OK. Give me ten minutes. I just need to see your housekeeper. She wants me to check the security alarm.'

Gina nodded. But she couldn't help feeling resentful. Everything she wanted to do had to go through him first. It was driving her crazy. After grabbing a towel and changing into her swimsuit, she sat down to wait. Ten minutes passed. Then another five. She stood up impatiently. Obviously Rick was going to be longer than he thought. Surely it wouldn't do any harm to go on ahead? He could follow later. There were security guards patrolling the beach as well as near their house, and a police car was parked on the main road only a few yards away. She'd be within shouting distance if she needed any help.

Slipping on her sandals, she made her way out of the grounds stopping to speak to a security guard at the main entrance gates. 'Please, will you tell Rick I've gone down to the beach?'

'Perhaps you'd best wait, miss,' he advised.

'I'm sure he won't be long. I'll be fine,' and she continued on her way giving him a bright smile, hoping it would convince him. As she glanced back, she saw the security guard looking worried and speaking into the hand-held radio.

Next to their property, on the other side of the high wall, winding steps led down to the beach. She hurried down them taking care not to slip. A warm breeze skimmed her face. Once she reached the golden sand, she kicked off her sandals, dumped her towel, and waded in.

It felt so good. The water cooled her skin and calmed her turbulent thoughts. The interview at the police station earlier on had really upset her and then afterwards seeing Maria lying so helpless in the hospital. Life was particularly hard at the moment, she thought ruefully. But she had been through tough times before, she reminded herself. And Maria would recover. She had to keep positive.

For a while she swam, then lay flat on her back floating as she gazed up at the sky, absorbing the crystal blueness. This was better than any work out at the gym, she decided, as the tension eased out of her. While she used to attend the gym regularly during the winter, in the summer she exercised in the pool or the sea, taking advantage of the warm weather.

Suddenly, someone grabbed her from behind.

83

'Aghhh!' She screamed as she lost her balance and slipped under the water. Her arms flailed outwards.

'Please . . .' she begged, half choking as she surfaced. She tried to twist around but she was pinned tightly. Whoever it was, she was no match for his strength. Oh God. Rick had warned her to wait. She steeled herself waiting for the blow to come.

Then she heard his deep voice. 'I've been out of my mind looking for you. Why didn't you wait for me?'

She turned to face him. 'Because you took so long. You . . . you . . . you frightened me out of my wits.'

Rick grimaced. 'I was just trying to make a point.'

'Well, you did. Are you satisfied?' To her dismay, tears sprang into her eyes. 'I don't need you to look after me. I don't need anyone. Just leave me alone.'

'Hey, take it easy,' he said soothingly, as he grabbed her wrists. 'You have to understand, there's some crazy guy on the loose. You can't just go off on your own whenever you feel like it.'

By now, she was past caring. 'Can't I? I'd like to see you stop me?' She shrugged herself loose from his grip, trying to choke back a sob at the same time.

He must have heard it, because he reached out for her again, this time drawing her closer by the tops of her arms. 'I'm sorry. I really am.'

For a few moments, she let herself be drawn into his embrace. Having him so near brought back memories of the past and she remembered a time when Jason had held her like that, apologizing and declaring he loved her. He had almost destroyed her. She would never allow *that* to happen again.

'Are you OK?' asked Rick, his face full of concern.

His voice brought her to her senses. This man was the complete opposite of Jason and this certainly wasn't a romantic interlude. It was a business arrangement, she reminded herself. He was her bodyguard, damn him. He had no right to do what he did just now but he had done it for her.

'I don't know,' she replied, still trembling. She pulled back from him even further. Her gaze slid to his chest, noticing his body was a deep mahogany, tanned from hours spent in the sun. Rivulets of water ran down his muscled chest, making his skin gleam in the sunlight. Her gaze shifted slowly across the planes of his body, where she saw the white scar, jagged and ugly, right below his breast bone. She stared longer than she meant to.

'It's a knife wound,' he explained, his mouth twisting slightly.

Guiltily she flushed. 'I . . . I didn't mean to—'

'Yeah, sure you did. I can see the questions in your eyes,' he said quietly with a directness which disconcerted her. 'So, aren't you going to ask how I got it?'

Gina flinched at the hard note in his voice. 'Would you tell me if I did?'

'I might.'

She waited. Their eyes met, held. 'Go on. . . .'

'I was a cop in Greymouth at the time. It was late at night and I was running after an offender. His accomplice was hiding in the shadows and I didn't see the blade coming.' His eyes flickered. 'I guess you can imagine what happened next.'

She stared at him. 'It must have been terrible.' Her curiosity got the better of her. 'How long were you in the police force?'

He pursed his lips. 'About ten years . . . mainly front line duties. Burglaries, domestics, cruising the streets. That kind of thing.'

Her gaze fell to his chest. 'And you left because of that?'

'Partly,' he answered carefully. 'There were other reasons. But I won't go into them; they're long buried.'

Up to now, Gina realized, he hadn't talked much about his police career, or his private life, and she wondered what else had happened there.

Finally, he said, 'Come on, let's get out of here. We can talk back at your apartment.'

'I need a few more minutes,' she told him, still feeling raw. He might be protecting her but she wasn't going to let him take over completely, not after the fright he had just given her. He could wait for her until she was ready. She lifted her chin, ready to challenge him.

To her surprise he relented. 'OK. Go right ahead. I'll wait on the beach. Just shout if you need me.'

Being on her own gave her time to think. Rick's confession had been unexpected. He'd been honest with her and that couldn't have been easy for him. No wonder he had left the force after something like that had happened.

A few minutes later, she made her way out of the water. When she reached Rick, he was sitting on *her* towel watching her. He was now wearing a tracksuit top with his swim shorts. Conscious of his gaze, the dark glasses he wore made it impossible to read his expression.

'Enjoy your swim?' he asked.

She was going to say she had until he had come along, but the unfairness of that thought prevented her.

She nodded. 'Swimming always clears my thoughts.' She stood there, dripping wet. He handed her the towel. 'Thanks,' she murmured. After shaking the sand off the towel, she dried herself, then slipped on her sandals.

Rick stood up. 'Ready?'

She nodded again.

As they walked side by side, he said, 'I know you've been asked this before, but is there anyone at all you can think of who has a grudge against Maria?'

She paused thoughtfully, turning to face him. 'I've been thinking. Some years ago there was a court case involving Maria to do with Rosselini Fisheries. Maria had to give evidence against an employee, Dani Russo. It caused ill feeling with some of his crew.'

'You mean, someone might have held a grudge?'

'It's possible, I suppose.' She thought again for a moment. 'Apart from Dani Russo, I suppose Jason is the obvious suspect.'

Rick removed his sunglasses. 'We're looking for a motive. But sometimes people don't need a reason to hurt others. There's a lot of crazy people out there.'

'Jason got angry when I refused to go back to him,' she pointed out.

'Angry enough to shoot Maria?'

Gina hesitated. 'I don't know. Surely he would have shot me, not Maria.'

Rick shrugged. 'He could have shot her to get at you. He'd know how close you were. Or maybe he hit her by mistake. Realistically, there could be a thousand reasons and scenarios. We need some leads and at the moment there aren't any. Not until the police come up with something, anyway. Or until they find Jason and question him.'

Gina bit her lip. She dug the tip of her sandal into the sand making a pattern. 'Maybe the attacker was after Anthony and hit Maria by mistake?'

Rick's eyes narrowed. 'What makes you think that?'

She shrugged. 'Just an idea I had.'

His finger brushed against her shoulders briefly. His touch was so light, she almost thought she imagined it. She hadn't.

'Just because you don't like Anthony, that doesn't mean to say he's a suspect. You need to have a stronger reason.'

Gina shook her head, not convinced.

He took hold of her arm, his expression serious. 'Gina, what is it? Is there something you're not telling me about Anthony? If there is, I'd like to know what it is?'

Gina hesitated. Anthony and Rick had been good friends for a long time. They had even gone through high school together. 'You're right; I was just speculating. Anthony has been known to be very fond of women. Maybe some woman took offence after he dumped her and wanted revenge.'

Rick frowned again. 'You mean a disgruntled girlfriend?' He thought for a moment. 'You really don't like Anthony, do you?'

She cocked her head to the side. 'I guess that's obvious. We have never got on. And that makes things difficult because he was made a trustee of my financial affairs. My grandfather made an arrangement with him to safeguard both Maria's and my inheritance. It's not something I agreed to. I had no choice.'

'He's a trustee?'

She nodded. 'Our parents left us five million dollars each. Half was paid to us when we reached twenty-one, the other half when we marry.'

Rick whistled. 'That's quite an inheritance.'

'My parents loved us,' she said defensively.

'What about Maria? How do you feel about her marrying Anthony.'

'Things won't be the same without her, but I'm not selfish enough to prevent her having the happiness she wants. I do know she loves him and wants to marry him. I would never stand in her way. We might be twins, but we respect each other's opinions and choices.'

Rick flashed her an odd look. 'At least you're honest about it.'

'Why shouldn't I be? I've got nothing to hide.'

He caught on quickly. 'Meaning Anthony has?'

A disapproving note crept into her voice and she felt she ought to give him some justification for her reasoning. 'Anthony is known for his philandering ways and I can't see him changing because he's married. Maria deserves someone who won't hurt her.' She shrugged. 'I guess I can foresee problems when the novelty of marriage wears off for him.'

'Perhaps, Maria knows already. Have you considered that?'

'What? No way. If she did, she would have told me.'

'Are you sure? Maybe she just accepts him for what he is. Some women do, especially if they're in love.'

Gina looked at him in disbelief. 'You don't understand. Maria has these visions of sweet love . . . living happily ever after. But life's not like that. I've tried to warn her. . . .' She shook her head in frustration.

'Don't you think that what happened to you is maybe prejudicing your feelings a little? She has every right to her dreams, Gina.'

That gave her a jolt. Maybe he was right, she considered suddenly. All the same her voice became defensive again. 'I just want her to have the happiness I didn't have when I got married.'

'I know,' he offered gently. 'But what about you? Where are your dreams now?'

Her shoulders stiffened. If only he would stop prying. She kept her voice steady, though inwardly she felt herself tremble again.

'What do you mean?' she said, playing for time.

'Would you fall in love again?'

His blue eyes were so piercing, Gina felt they were stripping her of her senses, one by one. She tried to dismiss it all lightly with a shrug of her shoulders, but somehow couldn't prevent the bitter note creeping into her voice. 'I once believed in love but look where that got me.' She held his gaze. 'You ask a lot of questions.'

His mouth twisted. 'Put it down to the job I do.'

She took a deep breath. 'You would have heard a lot of gossip about Jason and me.'

He pursed his mouth. 'Some. But I never took any notice. Small towns are like that.'

'Do you want to know what really happened to me?'

Rick nodded.

'OK.' She took another deep breath to steady herself. 'My husband came home in a rage one night. He had lost a heap of money at the gaming tables. And he was drunk. I challenged him about it and told him that unless he quit drinking, I was leaving.' She paused slightly. 'He lost his temper and hit me. The next day I lost the child I was carrying.'

Rick's jaw dropped.

It explained a lot of things about her, thought Rick afterwards, and the things he'd heard about her too. Her relationship with a man like that would have left its mark in more ways than he could ever imagine. She'd told him her grandfather had cut her off financially once he'd learned she'd married without telling him, especially to a man her grandparents disapproved of. Gina knew that a condition of her inheritance was that her family had to approve of the marriage, but she hadn't told Jason that. When he found out, he was furious. That's when things started to slide downhill. Pride had made her hold out in the marriage for as long as she could.

Her grandmother, knowing she was in dire straits, had secretly arranged some money to be deposited in her bank account on a regular basis to help Gina when she was in need. It wasn't enough; Gina's husband had spent it on high living.

Rick didn't know that Gina had lost her child though. That came as a surprise. But he suspected the Rosselinis were pleased she divorced Jason to avoid any long term scandal. It was obvious Gina didn't like Anthony being in charge of her financial affairs, but Rick knew her grandfather, Luigi, had a shrewd business mind and he'd made these legal arrangements to protect her from any other men who were after Gina's money. Anthony was trustworthy where her finances was concerned, even Rick knew that, no matter what other weaknesses Anthony had in his personal life. Rick suspected there was a clash of personalities between Anthony and Gina due to a number of reasons and that was going to make it difficult for her unless she could come to an understanding with him. He only hoped time would ease her hurts.

Rick sat at the kitchen table drinking a cup of coffee and mulling over the facts. Brougham had rung him earlier to say that he'd gone through the case notes. Maria had been the whistle blower in the quota fraud case. She'd turned Russo in to the police. Her evidence in court stated that Rosselini Fisheries never knew what was going on; Dani had acted on his own. The court case had caused a huge rift between the employees at Rosselini Fisheries, depending on whose side they took in the affair. Dani Russo was sentenced to five years' imprisonment and Rosselini Fishing Industries were eventually cleared of any wrongdoing.

Rick told Gina about Brougham's phone call. 'Did Maria talk much about the court case?'

'Often,' she admitted. 'She felt pretty bad about it. She hadn't wanted to give evidence at first, but once things were set in motion, she couldn't back down. It was a pretty tough time for Maria, but I admired her for seeing it through.'

'What about the crew on the boat? They must have known what Russo was up to.'

Gina shrugged. 'I guess some of them must have. Everyone was interviewed by the police. I know some of the staff in the factory resented Maria. She had new ideas. I guess they'd been working there for years and didn't like her coming in to tell them what to do.'

'Tell me about Maria.'

'What do you mean?'

'What is she like?'

Gina gave a sigh. How could she describe her sister? 'Maria is thoughtful and kind. She's passionate about what she believes in. When she left school, she went to university to study marine biology. She's also a great believer in protecting our environment and our fisheries. At university, she organized a demonstration against Japanese whaling. She was unpopular for a while in the factory because of her beliefs. But it sounded like she won most of them over with her arguments.' Gina hesitated. 'She loved working at Rosselini Fisheries, but Anthony wanted her to give up the job when she got married and start a family straight away. I think it was the only thing she held out on because she loved her job.'

A thoughtful look crossed Rick's face. 'Do you share the same interests?'

'No, our interests are very different. I studied drama and theatre at university.'

'That explains a lot.'

'What do you mean?' she asked, interested.

His mouth twitched. 'Your temperament.'

She smiled ruefully. 'It has its down side.'

'Yeah, I've noticed.'

'I've been trying hard to curb my temper.'

'Yeah, I've noticed that too.'

'How do you do it?' she asked.

'Do what?'

'Keep so calm.'

He shrugged. 'Years of being a cop, I guess. During an emergency it comes in handy. The last thing people in trouble want is someone who can't control a situation.'

'You're lucky.'

'Luck's got nothing do to with it: it takes practice.'

'Maria is always telling me to calm down. To think before I act.'

'Does it work?'

She laughed. 'No, I still get into trouble. I am always the impulsive one.'

Detective Brougham had been pressurizing Gina to speak with Maria all day.

'How is she?' he asked.

'Getting better, but it's going to take time.'

'Can she talk?'

'A little, but she's not that coherent.' Her sister's words were slurred due to the drugs. Gina could see it was an effort for her to talk.

'Can we ask her some questions? It could help with the investigation.'

'She's not well enough.'

Brougham exhaled impatiently. 'Any idea when?'

'I'm not a doctor, Detective Brougham. She needs a few more days.'

He nodded. 'Call me.'

Gina nodded, feeling irritated. Couldn't he see how ill her sister was?

Gina was standing beside her sister's bedside when Maria's eyes fluttered open as if she sensed her presence. Her lips moved slightly. Gina leaned closer. 'What is it?'

'He . . . he . . . might try again,' murmured Maria.

Gina didn't tell her sister the same thought had occurred to her. 'You're safe. The police are outside your room twenty-four hours a day.' Gina told her briefly about Rick but she had no idea if Maria heard her. 'I'll go along with it for now, but I don't like it.'

A flicker of a smile.

Gina's heart rose. At least, it was a start.

'Maria, do you know who shot you?' The words slipped out before she could stop them.

No answer. A few seconds passed. Maria's lips moved slightly. Gina couldn't make out what she was trying to say. A solitary tear ran down her sister's cheek. It was obvious she was becoming distressed.

'It's OK,' soothed Gina. 'Don't try to talk if it's too much.'

After Gina left, Maria's eyes fluttered. She could see images. Many faces of those she used to work with at Rosselini Fisheries, all swirling around her. Dani Russo's furious face emerged from the shadows, more prominent than the rest. Fear struck her. She could remember every little detail of that day. The day she'd told him what she'd done.

He had been in the factory office, talking to some of his crew. He'd been in good spirits, having just returned the day before from being at sea for four weeks. Things had gone well. Their catch had been the best for months. She had called him over to the side, so the other staff couldn't hear. 'Got a minute, Dani? It's urgent.'

'In here.' He beckoned her into a small side room. 'What is it?'

She sat down, her heart beating out of control. 'A Ministry of Fisheries officer came to see me. He said there had been a lot of dead fish found floating around your trawl area. He accused us of dumping fish of poor quality and size, and catching more to make up for it. I had to tell him the truth – that you'd falsified the quotas from the last catch. If I hadn't, he was going to lay charges.'

Russo gasped. 'You what? Are you crazy?'

'I warned you the over-fishing had to stop. If everyone fished like you do, ignoring the quotas, only taking the best, we'd have no fish left in the sea.' She took a deep breath to steady her nerves. 'The officer said if we came clean, he'd see what he could do. Perhaps we'd get a fine. It would be heavy, but it would mean we could start again. Keep to the quotas. Keep everything legal.'

'You idiot. You think you can trust *them*? He only said that to scare you. He had no proof, only suspicion. You fell into a trap.'

'He had proof,' she emphasized. 'He said one of your crewmen would give evidence. He had a camera and he'd taken photos.'

Dani scowled. 'Did he say who?'

'No, but—'

Dani cut her off, his mouth tight with anger. 'He was lying, putting the pressure on. Not one of my crew would have betrayed me. You might have a fancy diploma from university, but you've not had the experience I've had. Sometimes we have to take more fish than we're allowed to cover the lean times. It's a very competitive industry and we have a reputation of selling high quality fish. How the hell do you think we stay in business?'

But the truth was, in her naïvety, she had no idea. All she had been trying to do was keep to her ideals. She wanted to do her best for the company and to protect the environment at the same time. Someone had to make a stand. Why not her? So she'd braved the fall out. After all, she was a major shareholder in the company. And her grandfather had put her in charge of the quota department after she qualified from university. She hadn't told Gina how much she had suffered at the hands of the other staff after the investigations had started. And especially when the police were called in to lay charges. The Ministry of Fisheries officer told her that if she gave evidence against Russo, they wouldn't touch the company.

Sometimes she'd even felt her grandfather had disapproved of her actions, though he'd never actually come out and said so. He'd stuck by her. But it had been at the expense of losing Russo, one of their most experienced skippers. Afterwards she wondered if her grandfather had actually been innocent of it all. Things had got nasty in court and Russo accused her grandfather of being an accomplice. Of course, her grandfather had denied it.

She'd never forget the day Dani was sentenced to eighteen months in prison. It had shocked her. After the trial, Dani's wife had accosted her as she was leaving the courthouse. 'Was it worth it?' she'd said, sobbing. Then, clutching her two children by the hands, she was ushered into a waiting car.

Maria jolted. Something pricked her arm. A nurse whispered in a hushed voice, 'Rest now. . . .' The warmth of morphine hit her veins. Dani Russo's image receded, stepping back into shadow. She could no longer hear him shouting obscenities at her. She floated.

The last thing she heard was Gina's voice in the background, her soothing tones reassuring her. She should have told her sister earlier on how worried she'd been about Dani Russo. It had to be him: he'd come back for revenge.

Gina wasn't sure what to think when she walked out of intensive care. Her senses told her Maria was trying to tell her something important.

'Is everything OK?' asked Rick.

Gina told him what had happened.

'You think Maria knows who's responsible?'

'I don't know. She was upset. She was trying to tell me something. Perhaps tomorrow, when she wakes, we'll know more.'

At her apartment, Gina picked up her mail which her grandfather had left on a shelf outside her front door. The first letter was in a bright gold envelope: an invitation to a cocktail party in two weeks' time to celebrate a friend's engagement. The second one shocked her.

'What's the matter?' Rick asked.

Gina couldn't tell him. The words froze in her throat. Rick snatched the letter and read the contents.

'*It's your turn next.*' No signature. At the bottom of the letter, a small red rose had been stapled.

Carefully, holding the envelope by its outer edges, he held it up to the light to get a closer look. His eyes narrowed. 'It's been posted locally. I'll let Brougham know about this. He'll want it sent down to the station so they can test for fingerprints.' After a quick phone call, within minutes someone appeared at the door and he handed them the letter he'd slipped into a plastic bag.

Gina shivered, feeling sick inside. Did someone hate her that much? She went outside on to the deck, knowing that anyone on the hillside or down on the beach could be watching her through binoculars. Her chin lifted defiantly.

Well, they weren't going to scare her.

That evening Rick received a call to say his father had had an accident and was in hospital. A ladder had slipped while he was clearing the gutter on the roof of the house. He had fallen onto the concrete injuring his leg.

'Damn it, why didn't Dad ask me to help him?' Rick said worriedly, as he spoke at length to his mother on the phone.

'He knew you were busy with the Rosselini case. He didn't want to bother you,' explained his mother.

Rick sighed with frustration. 'I'll head over to the hospital as soon as I can.' He hung up.

'I'll come with you,' offered Gina, overhearing the conversation.

'That's not necessary,' he replied sharply. 'I can arrange for a colleague to take over while I am away.'

'That's true,' she reasoned, 'but I could visit Maria while you're busy with your father.' Her face took on that stubborn look Rick recognized immediately. 'And it's not as if you are leaving me alone,' she argued, 'there is a police officer on duty outside Maria's room, so I'll be quite safe.'

After a moment's hesitation he agreed. He could see the sense in what she suggested. 'All right then. I don't want you moving from Maria's room until I get back.' He wagged a finger at her and she smiled again, giving her promise so willingly Rick almost had trouble believing her.

When they arrived at the hospital, Rick delivered her into the care of a uniformed constable while he set off in search of his father in the surgical ward. It was an ironic situation. Both of them had close family in hospital. He only hoped he could trust Gina to keep her word and stay with the police officer. Rick took the lift to ward nine and enquired from a nurse which room his father was in.

She pointed. 'Room five.'

Rick's father was propped up in bed. He looked up when his son entered and his face broke into a smile. 'Rick, at last . . . what took you so long?'

'*Mi scusi*. I got delayed with work.'

'Ah, I know. It's the Rosselini girl, eh?'

Rick gave a wry smile. 'Yeah, that's right.' He drew up a chair and faced his father. 'How are you feeling?'

'A bit sore. Aghh, it shouldn't have happened,' Mr Caruso said, shaking his head in disgust. 'The ladder slipped and I fell.' He shrugged his thin shoulders. 'It was bad luck. Look at my leg in plaster. Luckily, it was only one leg I broke. It could have been worse.'

Rick thought so too, but refrained from saying so. In his estimation, his father ought to have been taking it easy at his age after a lifetime of hard work in the tomato-growing business. Unfortunately, Rick's father's work habits were deeply ingrained and it hadn't been so easy to convince him.

He swapped glances with his mother sitting opposite. He could tell she was thinking the same thing from the disapproving look on her face.

'Maybe we should sell up,' she said. 'That real estate man called in again. He says we'd get a good price for the property.'

Rick agreed. 'It would be easier for all of us if you would consider selling. You could have a nice little cottage in the country. Why don't you think about it?'

Mr Caruso looked thunderstruck. 'No, no, no. I have worked too hard. All these years doing back-breaking work to get the place established.' He jabbed his finger in the air. 'Others might want to sell up. But we are here to stay.' His father set his mouth determinedly, not willing to discuss the issue further. 'Another thing, if anything happens to me, the business is yours, so don't forget it, eh?'

Rick knew his father had hopes he would take over the business eventually, but he certainly couldn't envisage it. That wasn't to say he couldn't put a manager in if he had to. If anything did happen to his father, his first thought at one time would have been to sell the property, but lately he hadn't been so sure. Could he really destroy what his mother and father had taken a lifetime to build up? There was more than just money at stake; it was a lifetime of passion and hard work and sacrifice.

Rick patted his father's arm. 'OK, stop worrying. We'll get someone in to help you until you're back on your feet again. I can do the odd thing around the place to keep things ticking over.'

His father looked relieved and sank back into the pillows exhausted. Shortly afterwards, the nurse came in to check on him.

'Your blood pressure is a little high. I think you should rest now, Mr Caruso,' she advised.

'*Grazie*,' he said gratefully.

Rick's mother got to her feet reluctantly. 'I'll go back to the house, Enrico.' Concern was etched on her face. She leaned over and kissed him on his weathered cheek. 'You sleep now. Don't worry about things.'

'I'll try,' he mumbled tiredly, as his hand clutched the sheet. 'Don't forget the sprinklers need turning on tonight. The tomatoes need water. And check number one greenhouse, there's been some bugs lately. I don't want them spreading.'

'I'll see to it,' promised Rick. Once outside the room, he whispered to his mother, 'Don't worry about him, he'll be fine. He'll have those nurses wrapped around his finger in no time.'

Within minutes, Rick had picked up Gina from her sister's room. 'I hope I wasn't too long,' he said apologetically.

'Not at all. I'm only too glad to spend time with Maria.'

'Any change?'

'She came round briefly, but didn't say anything.'

Side by side they walked down the corridor and down the stairs until they reached the car-park.

'I'll drop you off at home first, then I need to call in to my father's place. There's some urgent matters to see to.'

'Why don't we call in there first. It would save time.'

She was right, he thought. 'You don't mind?'

Gina shook her head. 'Of course not.'

Within half an hour, Gina was sitting in the kitchen having a cup of tea with Mrs Caruso discussing an Italian recipe while Rick offered to check on the greenhouses.

'Well, if you're sure you can spare the time,' his mother said, looking relieved. 'Maybe I should ring Mark, your cousin. He's back home at the moment. He doesn't go back to sea for six weeks.'

'That might be a good idea; I can't be in two places at once. And I have to finish this case I've taken on,' Rick replied, glancing at Gina.

'I'll come with you,' offered Gina, standing up.

'No, that's OK. But thanks anyway.'

After an hour, Gina, feeling restless, had finished her cup of tea and told Mrs Caruso she'd find Rick. She could do with some fresh air anyway. She had just entered one of the greenhouses when she heard Rick's voice. 'Do you make a habit of making life difficult?'

She jolted. 'Why would I want to do that?'

'Because you never do as you're asked. You said you'd stay in the house.'

'I just needed some fresh air,' she explained.

'OK, So how about giving me a hand?'

'Depends on what it is?' she said warily.

He gave her a reassuring smile. 'Nothing strenuous. Just turn on some taps.'

'OK. Even I can manage that.'

Once inside number two greenhouse, he asked her to walk towards the far end.

'The taps are near the floor. I'll be nearby,' he told her. 'Just holler out if you have any trouble.'

Helping out in the greenhouse wasn't something she had exactly planned on doing. But she had been adamant about accompanying him, so she'd have to go along with it. Gina turned on the first tap.

'That was easy,' she murmured.

Water whispered, then whooshed as five sprinklers came on automatically. Gina fought her way through the foliage until she came to the next one. It was like being in the tropics, it was so hot. She could feel herself starting to perspire and her mouth had gone dry. When she reached the next tap, she tried to turn it on but it wouldn't budge. Dropping to her knees, she twisted and strained, leaning with all her weight, still to no avail.

Without even hearing him approach, Rick leaned forward across her shoulder, his muscled arm touching hers. Gina startled, twisted around, and looked right into his eyes. She saw the warmth but it was tempered with wariness. A trickle of sweat ran down his temple but he brushed it away with his arm. The extra few seconds he took to turn on the tap, enabled her to observe him more closely. His nearness was disconcerting, she couldn't deny that. But there was fascination as well and it held her long enough to notice the density of his muscles and the way they moved as his grip tightened on the tap. She kept completely still, watching and waiting. His arm flexed, shoulders lifted. The sheer power of his maleness sent her into spirals of panic as she realized how attracted she was to him. And, what was more, it seemed to her, he was quite unaware of it. But she was quickly to change her mind when he gently helped her to her feet. The soft regular whooshing of the sprinklers pulsated with a hidden energy matching the rate of her heartbeat.

His finger slipped underneath her chin, tipping her head upwards.

'Maybe it wasn't such a good idea coming in here, after all,' he said softly, looking down at her.

She couldn't help the smile tugging at her lips. 'Afraid, Caruso?'

'No,' he mused. 'What gave you that idea?'

'No particular reason.'

'We've another three greenhouses to check. We'd better go.' His hands dropped to his sides.

Go where, Gina thought? For a wicked moment, she had an image of Rick lying tangled amongst silk sheets, his sleek body naked with hers. Shocked at her thoughts, she stared at him harder than she meant to. Finally, she managed to get the words out, 'So have we finished in here?'

His voice deepened. 'Actually, I don't think we've even begun.'

Gina, feeling like a kid out of school and not like the sophisticated woman she always made out to be, couldn't make up her mind if he was talking about them or the taps they were supposed to be turning on. She took a deep breath to steady herself. What was it about this man that left her feeling so uncertain about herself?

'What's next?' she asked.

'That depends,' he answered enigmatically. Then he gave her a smile. 'How about dinner out tonight?'

Asking Gina out to dinner had been on impulse, but Rick really didn't think it would do any harm especially if they took extra security guards with them for added protection. He flicked his wrist to look at his watch. There was time to visit Brougham beforehand. Earlier on, he'd received a call from the detective. A psychiatric report from the rehab clinic had arrived on Gina's ex-husband, Jason Gallagher, and he wanted to discuss it.

Rick took a seat opposite Brougham. 'I'm surprised the clinic released the report,' stated Rick.

'They refused at first, so we reminded them about the Freedom of Information Act. And that it could be a matter of public safety.' Brougham opened the file and took out a document.

'Take a look at this. Gallagher's got mood problems. Big ones. His psychiatrist informed us he was obsessed with Gina. He would do anything to get her back.'

'Even commit murder?'

'That's what we want to know. There's another thing. Jason Gallagher is a crack shot with a rifle. If he'd wanted to kill Maria, he could have.'

'So where did he learn to shoot?'

'A stint in the army. Dishonourable discharge.'

'Do we know where he is?'

'Nope. The forwarding address he left at the rehab clinic doesn't exist.'

Rick frowned. 'He's lying low. He'll know you're looking for him.'

'That's what I thought. Also, we checked Gina's bank account. The money she gave him is still in there. According to the bank, Gallagher went in to cash the cheque, but he was told the cheque had been cancelled.'

Rick frowned. 'That's strange. Gina never mentioned anything about cancelling the cheque after she'd written it out.'

'She didn't, the bank manager did. He contacted Anthony Monopoli when Jason presented the cheque to the teller. The bank had been forewarned by Monopoli that any large amounts written out by Gina had to be OK'd by him. Turns out Anthony refused payment when he heard who the payee was.'

'Sounds like a good enough motive for Gallagher to shoot one of the Rosselini's. You've questioned Anthony about this?'

'He's confirmed it. But interestingly enough, Anthony didn't say anything to Gina at the time. He was busy getting ready for the wedding and was going to tell her about it later. He completely forgot about it when Maria was shot.'

That sounded believable, thought Rick. 'What about Dani Russo? Any further information about him?'

'He was released from prison a couple of weeks ago. Didn't serve his full time. Good behaviour.'

'They could be in cahoots,' offered Rick.

'That's a possibility too.'

'We've got a lot of possibilities here and no definites,' stated Rick.

Brougham gave a grin. 'That's what makes crime interesting, Rick.' He paused. 'By the way, we got the forensic report back on that anonymous letter to Gina. No trace of fingerprints. Ordinary writing paper with the words typed out. The brown envelope is sold in a thousand stores around the country. Postmarked locally.'

'If it is Gallagher, it seems strange he hasn't contacted Gina again,' said Rick with a frown, 'especially if he didn't get his money.'

'Unless he's waiting for the right moment,' Brougham suggested.

That was Rick's thought exactly. And he had a feeling it would be sometime soon.

Gina stood there seething. 'I'm going to complain to the bank. Anthony had no legal right to refuse the cheque.'

'Legal or not, they did,' said Rick. 'Anthony had previously advised the bank to contact him before any large amounts were cashed.'

'I had no idea.' Gina moved forward to use the phone, determined to give Anthony a piece of her mind, but Rick got there before her. 'Don't.'

Her gaze locked onto his. 'Why not?'

'Because you're all wound up. Having a discussion with Anthony in that frame of mind will make things worse.'

Gina was tempted to ignore him, though something held her back. 'You're my bodyguard, not my counsellor.'

'Sometimes I end up doing both.' He gave a brief smile. 'If the occasion demands it.'

Gina sighed. 'I bet you do. So what do you suggest?'

'Forget it for now. Or, at least, leave it for a few days. Nothing can be gained from a heated discussion with Anthony. When you've calmed down, arrange a meeting with your grandfather. Tell him things aren't working with Anthony being your financial adviser and lawyer. Request that you have someone else.'

She considered his words. Maybe he was right. 'OK.' She hesitated. 'Except that when I tell my grandfather about the cheque, he's not exactly going to be sympathetic.'

'Perhaps. But you can only try. . . .'

Later on, Gina saw her opportunity once her grandfather had retired to the study to go over some business reports. She knocked on the door. 'Nonno, please, can I talk to you?'

He beckoned her inside and pointed to a chair. 'Sit.'

She explained what had happened and why. 'I know what it looks like, but I wrote the cheque because I thought I was doing the right thing.'

'Why did you not come to me?'

She smiled regretfully. 'I wish I had, but I didn't want to upset anyone.'

Her grandfather gave a deep sigh. 'You want someone different to handle your financial affairs?'

Gina nodded. 'Now that Anthony is family, I think it would be better to have someone more objective. It would lessen the conflict between us.'

Luigi nodded. '*Sí*. That makes sense.'

'Where did you get that?' said Gina. The sight of the big black automatic holstered under Rick Caruso's left arm stunned Gina. 'You're not allowed to carry a handgun in New Zealand. You of all people should know that. If you're caught you'll be in big trouble.'

Rick slipped into his jacket and settled it so the gun and the holster harness vanished. 'I used to be a member of the police tactical unit, like the Armed Offenders but more so. I think this threat to you and your family justifies it. Don't look so worried, it's legal. I'm officially one of only three civilians in the country permitted to carry a handgun. The police commissioner himself had to OK it. I only got it thanks to my record and Dave Brougham's recommendation.'

'So that's what was in the black plastic box you picked up at the station.' She hesitated. 'What sort of gun is it?'

Rick slipped the automatic out of the holster and held it for her to look at.

'Ugly thing,' Gina blurted, pulling a face.

'It's a Glock 17, standard police issue,' Rick replied, pushing the pistol back into the holster. 'A very comforting thing to have around. Not as effective as a rifle but better than throwing bricks,' he added with a grin.

'I hope you don't have to use it,' Gina said.

'So do I, but I will if I have to,' Rick promised. 'Now, let's go out to dinner.'

In the bedroom while getting changed, Gina thought about the gun. Somehow it emphasized the danger she and her family were in.

She slipped on a creamy silk dress she'd bought recently. It had thin double straps and a fitted bodice and reached her calves. She reached into her jewellery case for her greenstone necklace and matching teardrop ear-rings and put them on. It wasn't a date, she told herself. Yet she couldn't ignore the flutter in her stomach at the idea of them both sitting at a table in a restaurant. He was probably trying to keep her amused, and enjoy himself at the same time, she justified.

Rick gave a whistle when she walked into the living room. 'Nice.'

Her face flushed. 'Thanks.'

'I hadn't reckoned you'd be a greenstone girl,' he said teasingly. 'I thought diamonds would be more your style.'

She fingered the smooth stones hanging around her neck. 'I do have diamonds,' she admitted. 'But I wanted to wear this necklace and ear-rings tonight. They belonged to my mother. My father gave them to her as a wedding gift.'

'Then that makes the greenstone very special,' he replied quietly, 'especially if it's given with love.'

His words made her wonder if she would ever find love like her mother and father had done. Her throat tightened.

'Just a moment,' she said, 'I've forgotten something.' She went to her bedroom to give herself time to compose herself. She reached out for her perfume and dabbed some on her wrists and behind her ears.

'I'm almost ready,' she shouted through to him. Then taking a deep breath to steady herself, she returned to the living room.

She watched Rick double check his Glock and tuck it into his shoulder holster, under his jacket.

'Is that supposed to make me feel better?'

'Just a precaution,' he explained. 'We'll use my car. Less obvious than the Ferrari.'

Rick drove out the wrought-iron gates, waving to the security guard. The gates clanged shut behind them. A security van containing two guards was parked at the kerb. It followed them down the street. Rick had only driven a few yards when the Toyota veered to the side. A sharp bang almost deafened him.

'Don't tell me we've got a flat?' he groaned. He pulled the station wagon over towards the pavement and climbed out. He bent down on his haunches to examine the tyre. The two security guards climbed out of the van and came over. 'What's the problem?' one asked.

'A puncture, damn it,' said Rick with dismay.

Gina opened the passenger door and climbed out. 'Shall we get my car or a taxi? It might be quicker.'

Rick turned around. 'No, I'll change it. You'd best sit in the van for now.'

The back window of the Toyota suddenly exploded, spraying glass everywhere.

'What the hell. . . ?' said Rick. He grabbed Gina by the arm. 'Get down,' he shouted, 'Someone's shooting at us,' and pushed her towards the pavement.

He whipped out his Glock. Huddled beside the car, he peered around the back end but couldn't see anyone. The two guards were behind them, pinned against the side of their van. One signalled to him. Rick interpreted the gestures as saying the shooter was across the other side of the road.

Another shot rang out, missing Rick by millimetres and slamming into the back end of the car. 'Jesus. . . .' His arm reached out for Gina. 'Keep down.'

She nodded. 'I intend to.'

Within minutes, a police car, the red and blue strobe light flashing furiously, sped down the road towards them. The breaks squealed as the car slowed to a stop and two uniformed officers carrying Glocks climbed out quickly and crouched behind their car.

'What's going on?' one called.

Rick filled him in on the details. 'Someone is taking pot shots at us, but I can't make out where it's coming from. It could be somewhere behind those line of trees.' He pointed. 'Or even that two-storey house over there.'

A large, white-painted colonial-style house stood directly opposite on the other side of the road. A window on the top floor was open slightly and the heavy maroon curtains drawn, but there was no sign of any inhabitants.

'I'll radio headquarters. We need back up,' the officer replied urgently. He spoke into his radio. After a few seconds, he said to Rick, 'Armed Offenders Squad is on its way.'

The police officer kept low, behind the open car door. He turned to his colleague. 'Isn't there an old lady living in that house? Maybe we'd better check she's OK.'

His colleague replied, 'I'll go.' Crouching low, he made his way further down the road, out of the firing line and crossed over to the line of trees.

Gina peered over the bonnet into the semi-darkness to see what was happening. Rick hauled her down. 'Do you want to get yourself killed?' he growled. 'Don't even move a muscle until I tell you.'

'I was only looking,' she protested.

His arm tightened protectively around her and she could feel his warmth melting into her body. Sensations shot through her which had nothing to do with the danger they were in.

The Armed Offenders Squad didn't take long to arrive. Within twenty minutes, a vehicle sped down the road towards them and screeched to a halt. Police officers, dressed in black bullet-proof jackets and helmets, each carrying a Bushmaster rifle with a Glock on his thigh, climbed out.

After a quick discussion, several members of the squad fanned their way across the road. The officer in charge came up to Rick. 'Best you both stay here until we check things out.'

Half an hour later, AO Squad members returned. After a quick discussion amongst themselves, the officer in charge spoke to Rick. 'Looks like the shooter is long gone.'

'And the elderly neighbour across the road?' Rick enquired.

'She's safe. She was out visiting family when it all happened.' He spoke into the radio briefly, then turned to Rick again. 'It would be safer if we get you both inside the house.'

Rick agreed. He held out his hand and helped Gina to her feet. 'You OK?'

'I think so,' she replied shakily.

Rick and three police officers escorted Gina up the driveway, keeping as close to the bushes as possible. The only sound was that of the gate shutting behind them.

Gina tried to stop thinking that she or Rick could have been killed, but the events of the past hour were taking their toll. Tears poured down her cheeks. Looking down at her silk dress, she was dismayed to see it covered in dirt, completely ruined. She tried to brush off some leaves but all she succeeded in doing was spreading a black sticky substance across the front. Oil, she thought, which she'd picked up from the road while huddled in the gutter. She didn't even know why she was worried about her dress when she had almost been murdered on the street. But, at least, it was something to focus on.

She had been so looking forward to going out tonight especially since Rick had managed to convince her she wouldn't be neglecting Maria if she took a couple of hours out for herself.

Rick unlocked the door to her flat. She went straight into the bedroom to change into jeans and a shirt and washed her hands. In the hallway, she could hear Rick talking to one of the police officers standing at the door but couldn't make out what they were saying.

'What's happening?' she asked, afterwards.

'The police have sent out a couple of patrol cars to scout around. Brougham has been informed, but there's not much more we can do tonight.'

The phone rang, startling Gina. She turned around to answer it but Rick was there before her. 'Don't. Let me.'

'You think it might be him?' But even as she said the words, she knew that was exactly what Rick was thinking.

Only she knew from the look on Rick's face it wasn't. He spoke quickly. 'Yeah . . . I understand. She's right here.'

She stepped forward. 'Who is it? Detective Brougham?'

'No.' He hesitated. 'The hospital. . . .'

She took the phone from him quickly, feeling a sense of unease. 'Hello.'

A man's voice spoke. He was tense, the tone urgent. 'This is Dr Stevenson at Nelson Hospital. I think you should come straight away.'

Gina's heart started to pound uncontrollably. 'Why? Is there something wrong?'

There was silence for a few seconds. Gina's chest started to tighten. 'Dr Stevenson?'

'I think you should come as soon as you can,' he repeated. 'Maria's had a massive heart attack.'

'Is . . . is she going to be OK?'

'I'm sorry,' he replied.

'What . . . what do you mean you're sorry?' A chill shot through her. 'Are you telling me she's . . . she's . . . dead?'

Another pause. A longer one this time. 'Yes . . . I'm afraid we did everything we could.'

Gina put her hand to her mouth. Dizziness assailed her. She felt a light pressure on her arm from Rick. She forced herself to speak into the phone but had trouble forming her words. 'I see. I'll be there as soon as I can.'

When she hung up, she turned to face Rick. She didn't need to tell him; he'd heard the conversation.

'I'll drive you to the hospital,' he offered, his expression grim.

'I can't believe she's gone.' A sob stuck in her throat. Blindly, she tried to move past him, but he caught her wrist gently. 'Gina. . . .'

'Yes?' she whispered.

'Is there anything I can do?'

She shook her head. 'No. Nothing.' She swallowed hard, her gaze searching his face. 'Why did she have to die?'

'I wish I could tell you,' he said gently.

She let him gather her close. The warmth from his body was comforting. She rested her head against his chest for a few moments, trying to make sense of it all, but couldn't.

'I don't want to see her dead. I want to remember her alive.'

'Your grandparents will need you,' he replied encouragingly.

She swallowed again. 'I know. I need to go to them.' She wiped away the tears that were now running down her cheeks.

It had been pure luck the watcher had heard Rick Caruso ask Gina out for dinner. He'd been checking out the Caruso property when they had called in for lunch. They hadn't noticed him as he'd pretended to be a surveyor, measuring out the boundary next door to do with the property development. None of the workers had taken any notice of him since there were plenty of workmen about.

He'd edged his way closer, eventually climbing over the fence and hiding around the corner of the greenhouse. He could hear every word they'd said. When the private investigator had taken her in his arms, he had reached for his automatic in his pocket, his fingers curling around the gun's butt.

Later that evening, he had hidden in the trees opposite Gina's apartment, waiting for them to drive out. Just as he had anticipated, the black gates had opened. He'd blown their tyre with one quick shot. Then, after they climbed out the car, he'd fired at the back window. The third bullet was meant for Caruso, but the man moved faster than he'd thought.

Next time, he wouldn't miss.

At the hospital Gina saw her grandfather waiting for her in the corridor. He stood in the doorway of Maria's room, a grim look on his face.

'Nonno,' she uttered. He gathered her in his arms in a bear-like hug.

'You're safe ... thank God,' her grandfather said. His glance moved to Rick, a slight nod in silent acknowledgement. 'We did the right thing in hiring you. If you hadn't been with Gina tonight ...' His voice tailed off.

'I'm fine, Nonno,' she reassured him.

Luigi gave a deep sigh. 'Come, we must be with your sister,' he said in a low voice. 'It is only right.'

'Were you here, Nonno? With Maria? When ... when ...' She couldn't bear to say, 'when she died.'

'Sí. We had just arrived.'

It brought some comfort, at least.

At first Gina was hesitant to enter the room, but it was expected of her. She took a deep breath, knowing what she was about to do would be one of the hardest things she had ever had to do.

Her gaze was drawn straight to the bed. To the prone figure of her sister. She stepped closer, her grandfather right behind her.

111

She looks like an angel. Hadn't she said those same words to her sister on her wedding day?

Pain shot through her, so intense, she thought she would cry out. Her hand clutched the edge of the bed to steady herself. 'Oh Maria. . . .' Gina's voice broke. She bent closer and brushed her lips against her sister's cheek, then smoothed back the tendrils of her hair. Her sister's skin was still warm.

Her grandmother's weeping sifted through to her consciousness. She was sitting in a chair in the corner of the room. With a determined effort, Gina moved towards her, slipping her hand into her grandmother's.

'*Nonna* . . .' choked Gina.

'I can't believe it,' Rosa sobbed. 'First your mother. Now this. What is God playing at?'

'I don't know,' answered Gina. She heard footsteps enter the room behind her. She turned. It was Anthony.

'I came as quickly as I could.' His gaze slid to the bed, then to Gina. 'I don't understand . . . she was getting better, wasn't she?' he said hoarsely.

No one answered. He stepped forward, standing next to Gina. Shortly afterwards the doctor joined them, explaining what had happened. 'We did our best,' he said. 'I really am very sorry.' His tone was completely sincere and Gina didn't doubt him for one moment.

Gina mustered her strength and put her hand on the doctor's arm. 'I know you did and we're all very grateful. Really we are.'

The doctor nodded, then with another sympathetic glance added, 'I'll make sure you're not disturbed. Please . . . take as long as you like.'

Two hours later, Gina still stood beside her sister's bed though her grandmother had long since left. She took a sip of the coffee Rick had fetched her, and winced. Bitter. So bitter it left a sour taste in her mouth. But, at least, it had shocked her out of the state of numbness.

Her gaze slid to Anthony, watching him. She could see his anger radiating in him. It frightened her. She had never seen him like this. He looked up, the light in his eyes fierce. 'I loved your sister. No matter what you thought.'

She couldn't help herself. 'Really? Even when you were visiting your secretary?'

Anthony's mouth tightened. 'It wasn't like that. My secretary was ill; I was concerned for her.'

'What about all the other women?' she accused.

'I swear to you, I never touched another woman after Maria and I became engaged. It was only malicious gossip you heard. None of it was true.'

This town was filled with gossip. She hated it. Despair filled her. 'I want to believe you but. . . .' She searched his face for any sign of falseness, but, to her surprise, she found none. Gina didn't have the heart to fight with him anymore. Only one thing united them now: Maria. Perhaps he had loved her sister more than she realized. And she had been blind, her judgement flawed because of her own experiences.

'I'm sorry,' she said quietly. 'I do believe you. Please forgive me.'

Dawn broke at five o'clock in the morning. When the sun rose, golden rays tumbled in through the hospital window as if creating an aura around her sister. The sunshine failed to warm Gina. She felt so cold and empty. Desolate. She had known times in the past when she had been low in spirit, but nothing she had experienced before had ever compared to this.

She hadn't even realized Anthony had left until Rick came into the room. His hand squeezed her shoulder. 'Come on, let me take you home. You need some sleep,' he said gently.

For once, Gina hadn't the energy to argue. She was glad someone was there to take over. With a sigh, she followed him out the room, feeling like her heart had broken into a million pieces.

CHAPTER FIVE

Gina stood on the freshly mown lawn at the cemetery, dressed in a black lacy top and long skirt which rebelled against the hot February sun. She moved forward and threw the perfectly formed white rose into the open grave. She'd chosen white roses for purity.

She couldn't have picked a better spot for her sister to rest, she thought, as she gazed at the ocean from the hillside. The sea reflected silver blue against the sky of the heavens. To the left and right and behind her, the sweet smelling pine forest, shades of dark green, stretched endlessly, over the mountains, framing the city and busy harbour.

Her vision clouded as the priest's final words rang out. He made the sign of the cross.

'Ashes to ashes . . . dust to dust. . . .' His violet robe, cuffed with embroidered gold, swayed as the wind breezed straight off the sea. The smell of freshly dug earth drifted past her along with her grandmother's cloying perfume. She was suddenly conscious of someone in a light grey suit standing next to her and she knew it was Rick without even looking.

'I'm right here if you need me,' he said softly.

She nodded gratefully and dabbed at her eyes with her handkerchief. In front of her, the polished mahogany coffin was being lowered into the grave with ropes by four men in black suits.

Gina felt herself slipping back in time to her parents' funeral.

Only she had been a child then. And Maria had shared her grief, slipping her hand into hers for reassurance as they stood side by side at the grave. Gina distinctly remembered the red roses. Masses of them. She had never seen so many roses. When no one had been looking, she had slipped a tiny bud into her pocket and taken it home to press in a small book of poetry her mother had once given her. She still had the rose and the book.

Her grandmother's husky voice brought her back from the past. 'Rest in peace.' A handful of fragrant rose petals were thrown into the grave.

Yes. Rest in peace, my beloved sister. But I will never be at peace until your murderer is brought to justice.

Gina's gaze swept the area. Many friends and staff from Rosselini Fisheries and some distant relatives had attended, as well as business associates of their family. Gina also noticed Senior Detective Brougham standing at the edge of the large crowd observing the mourners. Taller than most men, he stood out distinctly because of the way he held himself; a man used to giving orders. While she thought it respectful of him to attend, he had a reason as he had explained earlier on. It was commonly known that sometimes a killer would attend the funeral of their victim.

Her gaze skimmed from face to face. *Who is the murderer? Who hated them enough to do this?*

Near the cemetery gate, a lone figure of a woman stood half hidden by pink rhododendron bushes. She's staring at me, Gina realized. Unease gripped her.

'There's someone over there, standing in the trees,' Gina murmured to Rick.

'Don't worry, I saw her,' Rick said quietly. He leaned forward, his voice low. 'It's probably just a spectator. I've already sent someone over to check her out.'

So that was the reason he had stepped closer, so close she could feel his breath on her neck. He was worried about her safety.

She glanced again at the pine forest beyond the pink flowers. Did he really think there was someone in there waiting to shoot her?

The violinist began to play a haunting tune she recognized as *Meditation for Thais*. Notes drifted, rose, until finally a crescendo stormed the air, then gradually descended, the last note lingering so beautifully, it made Gina want to capture the notes in the palm of her hand and hold on to them forever.

Maria's life had been too fleeting. She should have grown old beside her. They could have talked of their youth, their losses and their joys, the children they might have given birth to, the men they had known.

Now she would talk to a grave and no one would answer her back. She wanted Maria to know she had loved her dearly. That she had treasured their friendship as sisters. And valued their closeness. They shared a blood bond that even death could not destroy.

All these thoughts swirled around her mind until she felt like she wanted to scream with the unfairness of it all.

And the priest's words droned on.

The watcher's gaze fastened on Gina like a hunter looking for prey. The blood in his veins still sang from the havoc he had caused. He took in her slim figure and her tear-streaked face as she stood at the grave. Now she would know what it was like to suffer. To lose someone you loved. To lose everything you valued.

Punish all of them. Punish Gina.

He knew perfectly well it was risky to attend the funeral, but was more than willing to do so. The voice in his head had urged him on.

He kept his head down, the fedora half covering his face. He stole the odd glance at those around him. Of course, they wouldn't know who he was. With his immaculate well-cut black suit, polished Gucci shoes and expensive gold watch, he blended in with all the other well-dressed mourners. He'd placed himself in the middle of the crowd, well away from the detectives.

He had time on his side. Plenty of it. He couldn't afford to make any mistakes. He thought about his next move.

The interment was nearly over. Gina lost count of the number of people who offered their condolences. Now she would have to face many more people at the Club Italia where refreshments were being served. Many families had baked and cooked, their own way of sharing grief.

Her gaze settled on Anthony, talking quietly to her grandparents. He was bearing up quite well, but then he was used to playing a part. Just like an actor. She'd seen him in action at the courthouse when Maria had persuaded her to go along. She didn't want to feel negative about him, especially at a time like this, but she couldn't help it.

Her grandparents spoke to her briefly, giving her a big warm hug before they moved away to the waiting limousine.

Minutes later, Gina found she was the only one left standing beside the grave. Dear God, she couldn't move, didn't even want to. For to do so would mean she'd have to turn her back on Maria, lying so alone in the ground.

'Take all the time you want,' Rick said, his voice low, as if he sensed her reluctance to leave.

'I think Maria would have wanted me to stay a while. I need to be here. . . .'

Rick nodded his understanding. He then moved away from her, but not too far that he couldn't reach her in a few steps, if he had to. The security men were already making their way back from the forest having checked the area. She heard them say to Rick, 'All clear.'

When Rick returned to her side, Gina asked, 'Did they find the woman?'

'No. Whoever it was disappeared very quickly.' He guided her by the elbow. 'Come on, how about we head down to the beach for a walk? The sea air will do you good.'

'The beach?' she said, surprised. 'But everyone will be expecting me at the Club Italia.'

'Everyone will cope fine without you for a while. People will understand better than you think.'

Nearby, the watcher sat in his car waiting for Gina and the private investigator to climb into the limousine. No doubt, they would head to the Club Italia. He planned to go as well. But first he had to pick someone up along the way, someone he'd employed to do a job for him.

He started up the car and followed the limousine, keeping well behind. When the limousine signalled left to turn off the main road, he began to get alarmed. This wasn't the way to the Club Italia. It looked like they were heading down to the beach. Frustration consumed him. He couldn't follow them. Not dressed like this. He'd stand out. The only thing he could do now was carry on to the Club Italia until Gina arrived.

Putting his foot down, he sped right past.

The girl he was to pick up was waiting on the street corner, just as he'd planned. She was about sixteen years old, the daughter of one of the gang members he'd had dealings with. She'd been keen to earn some money and he'd promised her a hundred dollars.

'You think you can do it? Just like I explained,' he asked, after she hopped in.

' 'Course I can.' She slid a glance at him. 'Is that your real name, Mr Grey?'

He tapped his nose. 'Never you mind. That's my business.'

She made a face.

The huge breakers pounding the white sandy beach reflected how Gina felt. Her heart was torn, bruised and battered. An uncontrollable sense of anger shot through her. She felt like hitting out, at anything, anyone. Taking a deep breath, she focused on the waves as they churned and frothed. Somehow the turbulence made her feel worse.

'A penny for them?' asked Rick, walking beside her.

She sighed. 'You don't want to know.'

'Try me.'

'I just can't talk right now.' She was just too choked up.

'Then don't. Let's walk.'

Walking might ease the rage, she realized. Or it might make it worse.

The sun belted down. Gina's clothes were sticking to her back and tiny beads of perspiration ran down her spine. Already she could feel the sun reddening her face. On a day like this the sun could burn in minutes. 'I should have brought some sun block,' she murmured, not realizing she had spoken aloud.

'I'll borrow some. Don't move. OK?'

Gina watched him. He made his way over to the surfers, a few metres away, who were busy waxing their surf boards. He came back with an orange bottle.

'Courtesy of the surfing club,' he informed her, as he squeezed a generous amount of lotion into her hand.

She flashed him a grateful smile. 'Thanks.'

'All part of the job, ma'am,' he mused.

His words struck her hard. For the second time that day, she crumbled. Was that all it meant to him? A job? He was only doing all this for her because he was being paid for it, she reminded herself. How could she have forgotten that?

Somehow it made everything seem even worse. Upset she turned away and started to walk, eager to put as much distance between them as she could. She needed to be alone. Damn him.

'Gina, where are you going?' He caught up with her, touched her arm. Unable to bear his touch she jerked away.

'Leave me.'

Rick tried to grab her again. 'Wait.'

'I don't want you here,' she retorted. 'I've never wanted you here. Just get out of my life.' Images of her dead sister, the casket, the priest hovering over the grave flashed through her mind.

This time he grabbed her arm firmly.

'Let me go,' she warned. She lifted her other arm and swung it round to hit him.

Rick's reflexes were quick and he caught her arm in mid air. She started to struggle, but he held on to her tighter. 'Let me go, will you?' she shouted again, an element of panic in her voice.

She struggled, lost her balance and fell onto the sand, pulling Rick down with her. Winded, she looked up to see Rick half lying over her, still holding her wrists firmly. She couldn't move.

His mouth was tight. 'Why are you angry with me?'

'Not at you.' She was angry at everything. The whole damned world. Her words slipped out before she could stop them. 'You're fired, Caruso.'

He gave a low laugh. 'You can't fire me: you didn't hire me in the first place.'

He'd done nothing but help her. And she was behaving like a spoilt bitch. Yet, still she couldn't help herself. 'I don't need you.'

'You're wrong. You're just upset. Not thinking properly.'

She knew he was right. But that didn't make it any easier. Trying to twist away, she only succeeded in hurting her arm. He held her firm.

'OK. I guess we're going to be here all day,' he threatened.

Stalemate. Her head turned to the side. She could see the surfers had put down their surf boards. They were heading their way to see what was going on. One of them pointed at her. Gina's face flushed.

'For God's sake, they're watching us. Let me up, will you?'

He shook his head, his eyes glinting. 'Not until you calm down.'

If Gina hadn't felt so miserable, she would have laughed at the situation. She swallowed hard instead, hoping she wouldn't break down. Tears welled in her eyes. 'OK . . . OK. I promise I won't take another swipe at you.'

He released her hands and stood up warily. He held out his hand to help her up but she ignored it. She brushed the grains of sand from her clothes and swung her handbag over her shoulder. She wasn't putting up with this, she thought, with frustration. First thing, when she got back home, she was going to tell her grandfather she didn't need a bodyguard any more. The murderer could take another pot shot at her for all that she cared. Maybe that would be a good thing. It would draw him out.

'I'm going back to the car,' she said.

He didn't answer and, to her surprise, he didn't follow her, though she could feel his gaze. It seared her. Don't look back at him, she told herself. She knew if she did she would crumble.

Rick walked over to the surfers and held out the plastic bottle to one of them. 'Thanks.'

'No worries,' replied a surfer with sun-bleached hair.

Another surfer stepped up and clapped him on the back. 'Hey, mate, that was quick work. How did you get her flat on her back so quickly?' He offered Rick a can of beer from their chilly bin.

Rick declined the beer, grinning. 'It's the Italian charm. I'll give you some lessons sometime.'

He walked away leaving them chuckling to themselves.

In the limousine, he slid onto the seat next to her, saying nothing.

'I'm sorry,' said Gina, turning to face him. 'I hadn't meant to lash out at you. I've never hit anyone in my life.'

'Forget it,' he said quietly.

But Gina couldn't.

The watcher pulled up the grey Nissan outside the Club Italia. He adjusted his wig and fedora in the car mirror. Satisfied no one would recognize him, he climbed out. He passed a patrol car with two officers sitting inside, busy talking. He gave them a quick glance and continued walking.

Instead of going in the front door of the Club Italia, they walked straight past and turned down an alleyway until they found the back entrance. A couple of full wine crates stood outside the kitchen door as did several empty blue plastic trays and cardboard boxes. He lifted up a crate of wine and entered the kitchen, the girl following him. No one took much notice of them since the waitressing staff were too busy serving food. A security guard stood in the corner chatting up a waitress. The watcher's heart started to pound as the man glanced at him as he approached. Fortunately, the waitress offered the security guard some oysters and the man was distracted.

'Wine delivery,' he announced. 'Where do you want this?'

Someone shouted. 'Not in here. See Bill in the bar. He'll tell you.'

He nodded and carried on his way, passing by the security guard who was now busy stuffing his face. 'Keep close to me,' he instructed the girl. In the bar, he delivered the crate to a man standing behind the bar serving drinks. 'Bill?'

A heavy-set man turned to face him. 'Yeah, that's me.'

'Someone asked me to bring this through for you.'

Bill glanced at the crate of wine and pointed. 'Just put it over there, will you?' He put the crate down, swapped glances with the girl, then both of them slipped out amongst the guests. There had to be at least a couple of hundred people milling around, he thought, talking and eating. It would be easy to blend in.

He saw Gina's grandmother sitting in the corner, her handbag at her feet. He whispered to the girl. 'That's her, over there. Give me five minutes to get to the car. Remember what I said. And don't forget to smile.'

The girl walked over. 'Excuse me, Mrs Rosselini, your granddaughter wants to talk to you privately.'

'Gina? Where is she?'

The girl whispered, 'In the ladies room. It's something important.'

Rosa lifted her handbag on to her knee, frowning. 'Luigi, I'll be right back.' She stood up.

The girl followed her. Rosa had just opened the door of the ladies room when the girl pushed her hard. She fell through the doorway, dropping her handbag. The girl grabbed it as another woman went to Rosa's aid. She heard Rosa cry out, 'Wait. . . .'

The girl sprinted down the hallway and through the front door.

He was waiting in the vehicle, the engine running, just as he had told her. She ran down the steps and half fell into the car as he took off. The tyres squealed as he took the corner and sent them racing away. A quick glance in the mirror told him the police car that was parked outside wasn't following him. But, as he turned the corner, he saw someone run out of the building to alert them. He put his foot down hard on the accelerator.

She held up the handbag. 'Easy.'

He gave a smile. 'You did well. Now, look for the keys.'

The girl rummaged in the handbag and pulled them out. 'Here they are.'

He had to get to the Rosselini apartment quickly before the alarm was raised. Ten minutes later he pulled up to the kerb, just a few metres away from the wrought-iron gates of the Rosselini apartments. The girl lifted up a large bouquet of flowers he'd placed on the back seat earlier on. Together they walked towards the security guard. The guard stepped forward when he saw them. 'Can I help you?'

'We're friends of Gina's. We couldn't make it to the Club Italia, so we just wanted to drop these off for her on the way home. My name is Grey. This is my sister, Julia.'

The guard looked uncertain. 'I'm sorry, no one's allowed in.'

'We're good friends of the Rosselinis.'

The girl smiled brightly, adding, 'We've got Gina's favourite flowers. Red roses. She'll be so pleased to get them. We'll leave them at her door.'

The security guard relented. 'OK, but make it quick.'

'We will,' they said in unison.

One minute later they stood at the door of Gina's apartment. He took the bunch of keys out of his pocket. It had been a gamble the old lady might have a key to her granddaughter's apartment and he'd been right. The original plan had been to steal Gina's bag somehow and get her keys, but with her not turning up at the Club Italia, he'd had to think again.

The third key fitted and they stepped inside. 'Don't touch anything,' he warned the girl. He checked to see she was wearing gloves just in case she did.

He went into the kitchen and took out a knife from the drawer.

'What are you going to do?' she asked, wide eyed.

'You ask too many questions.'

She scowled at him.

In Gina's bedroom he looked around. On the wall hung a black and white photograph of Gina and her sister with their grandparents. 'Perfect,' he murmured. He lifted it off the wall and set to work.

The girl whispered urgently. 'Hurry up. We've been here too long.'

She was right. By now, the police might have alerted the security guard at the gate. He laid the red roses on the table.

Both of them hurried up the steps, crossed the parking area, and walked casually past the security guard standing at the gate.

'All done,' he said to the guard, giving him a friendly wave.

The security guard unlocked the gates and watched the man and the girl walk through them, side by side. Then he went back to his coffee and newspaper.

When Gina heard what had happened to her grandmother she felt sick with worry. As for getting Rick fired, the last thing she wanted was a showdown with her grandparents especially with her grandmother suffering from shock. Maybe she'd wait a little longer before she brought up the subject of Rick Caruso.

She'd helped her grandmother to bed and made her a cup of tea. Her grandfather had wanted Rosa seen at the hospital, but her grandmother had refused. 'I don't need the hospital. I'm fine.'

Instead, the doctor came to visit her grandmother at the apartment. 'She's got a few bruises and is shaken up, but nothing a few days' rest and some painkillers won't fix,' he told them.

After he left, Gina said, 'Are you sure there's nothing else I can get you, *Nonna?*'

Her grandmother's voice sounded sleepy. 'No ... no ... nothing.'

Gina watched her grandmother's eyes close. Satisfied her grandmother was fast asleep, Gina got up quietly and left the room. Rick was waiting for her. 'All OK?'

'She's resting.' She sighed. 'It's like a vendetta. I've heard stories about vendettas from my grandfather, but I never thought for one moment that would ever happen to us.'

'Your grandmother said her house keys were in her handbag. I'll arrange for the locks of her apartment to be changed,' said Rick. 'It's best to be safe.'

'*Nonna* has a key to my apartment as well,' muttered Gina. 'It was on her key ring.'

'In that case, I'll check out your apartment straight away.'

'I'll come with you. Please,' she pleaded.

He nodded. 'OK. But wait outside. I'll go in first.'

Gina watched Rick slip the key into the lock of her front door.

A few minutes later, he came back grim faced. 'Just as I suspected.'

'What's wrong?' Fear shot through her.

'Don't touch anything.'

She stared at him but he gave nothing away. 'Why can't I go in?'

He hesitated. 'Because someone's been in your bedroom.'

'What?' She pushed past him. She saw the red roses lying on the table.

'Gina,' he shouted. 'Don't!'

Too late. She took in her bedroom at one glance. The large photograph of herself and her family lay on the bed, the glass smashed. Her eyes widened. 'My God. . . .'

Her face and Maria's had been removed from the photograph.

Rick saw the priest to the door. Gina's grandmother had arranged for him to bless Gina's bedroom after the forensic team had finished. Gina had gone along with it.

Three days passed. Rick was worried. Gina had shut herself in her bedroom, only coming out to briefly eat and drink, though Rick noticed that what she had eaten had been very little. She had refused to take any calls from friends. When he had tried to approach her, she had said, 'Just leave me alone.'

'He's trying to scare you,' said Rick.

She exhaled. 'You think I don't know that?' She slammed the bedroom door behind her.

When Gina opened her bedroom door on the fourth morning, Rick was waiting for her, determined to coax her out of the grief-stricken and terrified state she had sunk into.

'Come on, we'll go for a drive by the sea. You'd like that,' he said gently.

'I don't feel up to it.'

Before she had a chance to return to the bedroom, he stepped in front of her, barring her way. 'Then let's talk.'

Her chin lifted. 'I don't feel like talking either.'

He saw the distant look in her eyes. Recognized it. He'd been there once himself. But he'd survived. Somehow he had to get through to Gina that she had to as well.

He took both of her hands in his and pulled her over to the couch. 'Then listen.' He saw her mouth purse rebelliously. 'Please,' he added.

She nodded, though her face was wary.

He chose his words carefully. 'Shutting yourself up in your room isn't going to make it any easier. You can't bring Maria back.'

'I didn't ask for your opinion.'

'Yeah, well, I'm giving it anyway. For what it's worth.'

He saw the angry glint in her eye but that didn't deter him. He had nothing to lose, but she did.

He continued, 'Death is never easy. We never know when it's our turn . . . it's something we have to accept. No matter how unfair or unpleasant. Or even heartbreaking.'

She pulled her hand away sharply. 'Is this a lecture? Because I don't need it.'

He could see she was fighting for control. He could see it in the way her mouth trembled. He pushed on. 'You have to face people. Pick up your life again.'

'I can't,' she explained, swallowing hard. 'I don't know what to say to them. For the past three days, I've been questioning everything about my own life. Every decision I've ever made. And what's even worse, I can't even envisage a future. There just doesn't seem to be anything to look forward to.' Her voice cracked. 'I'll never be the same person again.'

'No one ever is. But losing someone close can make you a better person – if you let it.'

She gave a bitter laugh. 'In what way?'

'You'll be more willing to take chances. Live life to the full. Not so afraid, and more appreciative of those you care about. We have to take some good from the bad.'

He could see she was considering his words. 'The trouble with you, Caruso, is that sometimes you sound so damned convincing.' She shook her head. 'But right now, underneath the fear, I feel such a terrible sadness.' She put her hand over her heart. 'Everything is so overwhelming. So painful. I'd give anything to stop feeling this way.'

'That will pass,' he said knowingly.

She gave a deep, heartfelt sigh. 'You talk like you've had experience of death.'

'I have. A cop deals with it often.'

'But it's more than that, isn't it?' she persisted, searching his face. 'I can tell.'

But he didn't let on as she hoped he would. He just gave her another of his enigmatic smiles and more words of comfort before he left the room so she could rest quietly and be alone with her thoughts.

*

The next morning, Gina stepped out of the shower and dried herself, then surveyed her face in the mirror. Dark shadows circled her eyes. Her skin had a pale pallor. Not surprising. She'd spent a lot of time crying over the last few days. The whole of the previous night she had sobbed into her pillow. And when the first rays of dawn had filtered through the window, she found she had no tears left. Only a deep sense of loss remained.

More importantly, she realized, if she didn't do something to stop the fear drowning her, she couldn't catch the killer. Maria needed justice. They all did. She wouldn't rest until the killer had paid for what he had done.

Rick had been right: she had to face people.

Forcing herself to take several slow breaths, until her breathing became more regular, the tension in her stomach eased. But her thoughts continued to race ahead.

There has to be a way to draw the killer out. I can do it. I know I can.

She reached for her make-up to repair the damage to her face, but the effort was almost her undoing again. She reached out for a glass and filled it quickly with water. She'd once read somewhere that you couldn't drink and cry at the same time. It was worth a try. Anything to help her snap out of this tearful and volatile state she had fallen into.

After draining the glass, she felt more composed. She started to apply her lipstick though her hand shook too much. Not satisfied with the uneven line she had made, she wiped the lipstick off with a tissue, then, concentrating, began all over again.

If only her stomach wasn't so clenched tight in a knot.

I have to try to relax. Focus. Make a plan.

After a final check in the mirror, she decided she looked as good as she could under the circumstances. She found Rick in the living room. 'I've been thinking about what you said.'

'And?'

She tried to smile, hoping she could convince him. 'You're right.

So how about we eat out tonight?'

Surprise entered his eyes. 'That's like diving into the deep end without learning to swim. You might like to wait a few days before you go on a public outing. At least until you're feeling stronger.'

'I'm strong now.' But was she really? She'd do all she could to bring the murderer to justice and realistically she knew she couldn't do that hiding away in her bedroom. She firmed her voice. 'I mean it. I really do want to go out tonight.'

He considered her request for a few moments. 'I don't know. It could be risky. Look what happened last time.'

'Risky or not, it's something I have to do. Like you said, I have to start sometime.'

He gave her a quick smile that had her heart skittering all over the place. If she didn't watch out she might fall in love with him, she realized, with a jolt. And she couldn't do that. Not now. Not with Maria's killer on the loose. It would distract her. Besides, hadn't she convinced herself she didn't want a man in her life? She had to stay focused on what she had to do. Find the killer. Whoever it was. Whatever it took. Her resolve deepened.

'So what do you say?' she prompted.

'OK. I'll book a table. The Boat Shed Café. Seven o'clock.'

She nodded. 'Perfect.'

Gina phoned the hairdresser, Donna James, and made an appointment. Donna had done her hair for the wedding and she was one of the top hairdressers in the town. Two hours later, she walked out of the salon, feeling a lot better, and more confident. She'd had her hair trimmed and highlighted with gold streaks.

She took care in choosing what she would wear. She changed her clothes several times before settling on an olive-green dress with thin shoulder straps. She was tempted to remove the *cornicello* from around her neck and wear her greenstone necklace but she had promised her grandmother she would wear the amulet. She studied her image in the long mirror, satisfied she looked her best. Silver sandals and a clutch bag completed the outfit.

The last time she and Rick had both attempted to eat out, the killer had been waiting across the road, ready to shoot them. Could the killer be waiting there for her again? Tension coiled in her stomach at the thought. He could reach her any time he wanted. He'd proved that already.

She lifted her chin defiantly as she surveyed herself in the mirror. Let him. She'd be ready.

Rick assured her that everything would be fine. 'No one knows where we are heading. I've got security men checking our route out beforehand. They'll be watching us closely. Some are in plain clothes. Others are in uniform.'

'What about the café?' she asked.

'There are only two doors at the front. No other entrances. So the security guards can easily keep an eye on us.'

'Was that why you chose it?'

'No,' he replied honestly. 'I knew it was your favourite café. Your grandfather told me.' He hesitated slightly. 'He mentioned you and Maria used to go there often.'

She wondered what else her grandfather might have told him.

Once again Rick chose to use the unobtrusive Toyota instead of the Ferrari. The rear window had been repaired. The café was situated on Rocks Road, alongside the sea. Known for the best seafood in town, it was popular with locals and tourists alike. The café also had a breathtaking view of the Cut – the entrance to Nelson harbour. In the distance a white lighthouse stood along the boulder bank.

When they walked in, the staff greeted them warmly. 'We've reserved you a table by the front window,' said the head waiter, showing them to their seats.

'Good,' answered Rick. He had asked for that. Facing the sea meant no sniper could position themselves to take a shot at Gina.

The waiter handed them the menu, and brought a jug of water and two glasses then left them alone while they settled in.

'Nice place,' remarked Rick, leaning back in the chair.

'We're lucky to get a table. It's usually very busy on a Saturday.' Gina looked around the café, noticing the place was filling up. 'Do you think the murderer is watching us?'

'Possibly,' he replied, thoughtfully. 'Realistically, he could be anywhere.'

She skimmed the faces in the café. Somehow, she couldn't imagine one of them being the man they were looking for. 'If it's Jason, he could be in disguise. But I am sure I would recognize him.'

'And if it's Dani Russo?'

She shook her head. 'It's been years since I've seen him. I wouldn't know him at all. Then again, it might be neither of them. It could be someone I've never even met.' She paused slightly. 'I don't want to spend my whole life wondering, waiting for him to make a move. I can't live like that.'

'You won't.'

'How can you be so sure?'

'My gut feeling. Plus his *modus operandi*.'

'What do you think he will do?'

'I don't know. But he left you red roses. That tells us something: it's his signature.'

She frowned. 'What do you mean signature?'

'Sometimes killers leave something that has meaning for them. And for the victim.'

She frowned. 'But red roses – doesn't that mean love?'

'Possibly.'

She thought about the colour. 'It could mean blood. He's out for revenge. It *is* a vendetta.'

'It's starting to look that way.'

And that made Gina wonder. She took a sip of water. Then she heard someone call her name. Startled she looked at Rick. His gaze met hers. 'Easy now,' he murmured. She saw his hand slide under his jacket. 'Someone's coming your way.'

Slowly, she turned to see the chef, dressed in white trousers and shirt, make his way down the aisle, a bottle of wine under his arm.

He stopped in front of her and placed the bottle on the table.

'With our compliments, *s'il vous plaît*,' he said with a heavy French accent. 'In memory of your sister, eh?'

A lump stuck in her throat as her hand reached out to touch one of the finest Chardonnays, produced in the region.

'Thanks, Pierre. It's very thoughtful of you.' The chef's warm brown eyes were full of compassion. He'd always had a soft spot for Maria, she remembered.

His acknowledgment was a sympathetic smile and a nod of his head before he turned tail and headed back to his domain in the kitchen. The head waiter and the rest of the staff were speechless.

'I feel so honoured,' she whispered. 'Pierre never comes out of the kitchen.'

Eventually, the chatter around them resumed to normal.

'Maria knew Pierre's daughter. They were good friends,' explained Gina.

'Sometimes tragedy can bring out the best in people.'

'Or the worst,' – thinking of her own behaviour at the beach. Shame washed over her. She might not agree to Rick being hired as a bodyguard but that didn't excuse her bad behaviour. 'I really am sorry about what happened at the beach. It's been on my mind ever since.'

'Consider it payback for when we were kids,' he mused.

'Oh, you mean that fallout we had in the sandpit that your father told us about.'

He nodded.

She smiled. 'I guess that makes me feel a little better.'

'Besides, most people understand what grief can do,' he said.

'Do you?'

He pursed his mouth. 'Probably better than most. Being a cop has given me insight into how people react. It's proved useful at times.' His gaze held hers again. 'But how about we concentrate on what we're going to eat. I'm starved.'

'Changing the topic of conversation?'

132

He gave a low laugh. 'It wasn't intentional; I really am hungry.'

'Huh, typical. A man always thinks of his stomach first,' she said lightly.

'Not always. There are other things a man thinks about.'

'Hmm, I won't argue with you on that one.'

'Good.' His eyes glinted. 'Because I'd probably win.'

Her chin lifted. 'That sounds like a challenge.'

'Take it any way you like.'

She couldn't help but smile. 'OK. A truce. Let's order.'

'Sounds good to me.' Rick studied the menu, raising his eyebrows. 'Fancy prices for fancy dishes. Must admit, if I'm not eating Italian, I'm more of a steak and chips man. But . . .' He paused, looking impressed. 'Mussels in garlic sound tempting.'

'They're Rosselini mussels,' she informed him. 'All the seafood in this café is supplied by us.'

'In that case, mussels it is.' He added quickly, 'And I'm paying. I was the one who asked you out to dinner, remember?'

'That was the first time. This time it's different,' she argued. 'Besides, I can afford it. And I did read your contract with my grandfather. It states all expenses are paid. Consider this one of them.'

'No,' he said firmly. She detected the steely note in his voice. 'This is one time you're not getting your own way.'

'Most men would have taken advantage of my money,' she pointed out.

'You know the wrong men,' he said drily.

He had a point, she thought.

While he was reading the menu, she studied him closer. Unexpectedly, his gaze lifted and met hers in a questioning look. 'Something wrong?'

'No . . . no . . . I was just thinking,' she murmured. A shock rippled through her making her realize how attracted to him she was. She lowered her gaze quickly, trying to ignore her pulse zooming skyward again.

The waiter poured them both a glass of the fine honey-coloured Chardonnay, then took their order.

Gina lifted her glass. 'Here's to life.'

'Yeah . . . that it keeps getting better.'

'For a PI, you always seem to be so positive. How come?'

'Must be in the genes,' he responded. 'Being Italian might have something to do with it. Live and let live.'

'So what do you do in your spare time?' she asked, curious. 'Or do you spend most of your time working?'

'I'm a surfing junkie. I hang out at the beach any chance I can.'

'At long last, one of your vices.'

'Surfing isn't a vice, more like an addiction,' he mused. 'Surfing keeps me fit, psychologically and physically. You should try it sometime. I'll give you a few lessons.'

'Why, that almost sounds as if you're asking me out.'

'I guess I am,' he replied steadily, holding her gaze, 'but it will have to be after I finish my contract with your family. Then we'll be on equal ground.'

His blue eyes held a hint of something else, though of what she wasn't quite sure. She decided to push further.

She said slowly, 'You mean, when you're not an employee?'

'Exactly.'

Then, because she couldn't help herself, 'I'll be holding you to that. You won't forget, will you?'

Suddenly she recalled that only a few days ago she couldn't wait to have him fired. Now she was practically arranging a date with him.

He chuckled. 'Somehow, I don't think I'd forget a date with a beautiful woman.'

'I'm not beautiful . . . my nose is too long and my mouth is too wide.'

His expression turned serious. 'You're wrong . . . I think you're beautiful.' His voice was low with a sexy inflection making her think of silken sheets, champagne and Rick Caruso all at once.

'Compliments will get you everywhere,' she said softly. 'Come to think of it, that's the first compliment you've paid me.' Certainly, it gave her a taste of pleasure, however fleeting.

'Actually, I can think of many compliments.' His eyes held a teasing light. 'But I wouldn't want you to get the wrong idea.'

'How about if I got the right idea?'

'Then we'd need to be very careful, wouldn't we?'

Yes, very careful.

Her pulse fluttered again.

The waitress arrived with the meal. In between mouthfuls, Rick entertained her with humorous stories of his time in the police.

She angled her chin at him. 'Sounds to me you didn't get much time to do any policing, you were too busy enjoying yourself.'

'Oh, there was plenty time for that.'

'Has anyone ever told you you're a good storyteller?'

'Only my sister's kids, Ben and Sam,' he replied with a grin. 'They're both dynamite.'

'You're full of surprises, Caruso.'

'Yeah? You've told me that before.'

'Have I?' It had slipped her mind.

'You're not quite what I expected either,' he said softly. His gaze held hers.

She was curious to know what he meant. 'Care to explain?'

'Some of the things you do. Even say.'

He was getting too close, far too close, she thought suddenly. She picked up the menu and tried to focus on the words. She looked up. 'Dessert?'

'Anything you recommend?'

She said wickedly, 'Death by Chocolate.'

His mouth twitched. 'Sounds a nice way to die. I'll take the risk.'

Later on, as she lay in bed thinking about the evening, Rick's image hovered around her. She recalled the clean cut of his jaw, the deep blue of his eyes which changed colour so readily, depending on his mood. Tonight he'd been good company. Different somehow. Or maybe it had been her. How she had responded to him. Whatever it was, he wouldn't be her protector forever. She would never allow it.

But for once, she wished he'd stick around a little longer.

Rick Caruso couldn't sleep, so in the end he pulled on his jeans and wandered outside on to the deck. He leaned against the wooden rail gazing at the dark ocean in front of him. The night was warm, humid. Fresh sea air entered his lungs and helped clear his thoughts.

This assignment was becoming more difficult than he had expected. And he knew why: he was becoming emotionally involved. Damn it – it was something he hadn't expected. This had never happened to him before. Even now, as he thought of their evening together at the café, Gina's laughter was still with him. And yet, he still couldn't figure her out. There were times she came across as lonely and vulnerable and then she'd do something that completely dispelled that notion. He suspected she had put up a barrier between herself and the world. Hadn't he done the same thing after he'd been injured in the police force? For a long time he lay in that hospital bed knowing that the officer he was working with on that fateful night had died. He hadn't told Gina that his partner that night was a woman and that he'd been dating her. Yeah, he knew all about survival. All about guilt. He was the one who was still alive. As for Gina, she'd lost her parents at an early age, had a disastrous marriage, and now the loss of her only sister in tragic circumstances. Yet, she still carried on bravely. Sure, she had her moments of grief. She'd spun out a few times. He couldn't blame her. Yet, he couldn't help but be impressed with her courage and spirited nature.

Maybe being one of the rich Rosselinis wasn't all it was cracked up to be. They had their problems just like everyone else.

He sighed. In a few days his contract with the Rosselini family would come under review. All the recommendations to do with security had been carried out. It was possible Mr Rosselini might not renew his contract. What would happen to Gina if he didn't? He hoped like hell the police had made some progress with the case. It made him sick to the stomach to think somebody might harm her. He pulled himself up sharply. What the hell was he thinking?

He had a business to run. Clients to see to. Most of all, a life of his own. Still, he had hired security guards on the property around the clock which would be permanent. He only hoped it would be enough. First thing tomorrow, he'd see Mr Rosselini and finalize the long term security arrangements. With a killer on the loose, it would pay to double check everything.

CHAPTER SIX

Deep in thought, Rick was sitting outside. According to the latest update from Dave Brougham, the police were continuing to search for Jason Gallagher. Danni Russo had been taken down to the station for questioning but they'd had to release him due to lack of evidence. Rick had racked his brains trying to think of a motive and as far as he could see there wasn't one, unless someone held a grudge. That meant either Russo or Gallagher.

Leaning back in his chair, he concentrated on a power boat vibrating through the water as it raced towards the horizon. The wind gusted again, fresh and salty, while white gulls screamed above in protest. He relished some time on his own, if only for a few minutes. It was a habit he'd got into when he'd been a cop, and somehow it had never left him.

'Good morning,' said Gina, her voice light and fresh, as she walked out. A scent of lilac floated through the air as she passed.

'Morning,' he grunted, purposely missing out the word, 'good'. He rubbed his unshaven jaw. Mornings had never been the best part of the day for him – not until he'd had at least two cups of strong coffee. He'd probably overdone the alcohol the night before, and he'd broken his cardinal rule of not drinking when he was working.

He surveyed Gina as she leant on the balustrade of the deck facing the sea. She was wearing stretch white shorts, emphasizing a part of her anatomy that definitely had all the right proportions.

Her halter neck top revealed bare shoulders, her skin gleaming copper as she had obviously rubbed something over them. Her hair was still damp from her shower.

'You're not wearing your sun hat,' he remarked.

She whirled around. 'I know. I've misplaced it.' She shrugged. 'I probably left it on the beach somewhere.' She turned her face to the sun. 'Those rays are strong at this time of the year. Even though I've inherited my mother's olive skin, I can still burn.'

'There's no atmospheric pollution in this part of the world,' he said. 'The sun's more intense in the southern hemisphere.' Rick slid his own bush hat across the table to her. 'There you go.'

She plonked it on her head. 'It's a bit big, but thanks.'

'It suits you,' he remarked, thinking she'd probably look good in anything along with that killer babe smile.

The wind gusted and the hat lifted into the air and spun outwards like a frisbee. Gina rose to her feet to retrieve it and covered the distance in a few steps. But Rick moved faster and reached it first. She bumped into him and his arm shot out to steady her. She tried to snatch the hat from him, but he had already swapped it to his other hand. Before he knew it, his arms had circled her. She looked up at him. Neither of them spoke. One hand pressed in the small of her back brought her even closer. If he had hesitated before, he didn't now. His head bent forward while his other hand slid upwards to curve around her neck.

'Gina,' he murmured.

'Uh huh,' she replied softly. Then, before he knew it, his mouth was hard upon hers. The softness of her lips challenged as much as it rewarded. He could feel his blood starting to pump.

It was Gina who pulled away first. Shock floored her eyes. 'Do you make a habit of kissing your clients?'

He flinched. 'No, I don't.' His voice was calm, too calm, and if she had known him better she would have realized that underneath he was as shaken as she was. Using his well-honed control he'd developed as a police officer, his blue eyes narrowed on her face while his hands fell to his side. He wanted her to rage at him, tell him he'd overstepped the line. Even tell him he was fired again and he'd accept it this time. Instead, he got indifference. It cut deep.

'A kiss is just a kiss. And they're all the same, one way or another,' she said coolly.

His jaw tightened. 'Liar.'

She started to turn away. He grabbed her wrist. 'It won't happen again,' he told her through gritted teeth. 'I never make the same mistake twice.'

'Neither do I,' she retaliated. She pulled away hard and he had no choice but to let her go. 'Gina . . .' he called out, but she ignored him and carried on walking. He cursed under his breath.

Once inside, Gina sought refuge in her bedroom and thought about what had happened. Oh God . . . she had let herself fall into the kiss. But what she hadn't reckoned on was her willing response. And yet she knew perfectly well, no one had ever kissed her in that way, not even her ex-husband. She couldn't deny how her body had betrayed her at his touch. But it was only a chemical attraction, she told herself sharply. Two people thrown together due to circumstances in a highly tense situation. There was no love or romance. How could there be? She'd cut herself off from men after the fiasco with her marriage. Those nightmare months of living with a man who'd abused her mind and her body had taken their toll.

Hadn't she made a vow never to get involved again?

That private investigator was proving to be a problem. He had to get rid of him so he could get to Gina on her own.

Soon it would be dark. The watcher had thought of another plan the night before and knew it would work.

Within twenty minutes, he stood on the edge of the Caruso property. He slipped on his latex gloves and climbed over the half erected fence. He moved silently past the row of olive trees planted when Mr Caruso had been a new immigrant from Italy. Silver-green leaves rustled with the night breeze. He was careful not to knock over a stack of broken plant pots placed along an uneven path.

During the previous evening, after the workmen had left, he'd surveyed the property from the building site next door. Rick Caruso's office and studio flat were situated in a small separate building. He made his way towards it. He tried the door, not expecting it to be open, but there was no harm in making sure before he assembled his variety of tools. He worked on the lock as carefully as possible, a trick he'd learned from a burglar he'd once met.

Once opened, he stepped through the doorway and shone his torch, keeping it on low beam. The light found a desk. That would do, he thought, opening one of the drawers. He stuffed the envelope inside. Perfect, he smiled. But he wasn't ready to leave yet. His gaze travelled around the room, settling on the filing cabinet. Curious, he tried opening it, but it was locked. He turned ready to leave. A can rattled outside. He froze. Was it someone approaching? He couldn't hear any footsteps. He moved forward slightly. Then he heard it: an unmistakable noise of cats wailing disturbing the peace of the night. Breathing a sigh of relief, he made for the door, his sneakers moving silently on the wooden floor. He shut the door behind him and locked it. No one would have guessed he'd even been in there. Keeping to the shadows, he quickly made his way back along the fence. By the time, he reached his car, he was gasping for breath. He flicked his wrist to look at his watch. It had only taken thirty minutes.

Since the incidence of the kiss, Rick noticed Gina had acted as if nothing had happened. He wasn't fooled, but he had no choice but to act the same.

'I'd like to take a drive up the coast. Can you take me?' she asked politely.

'Not today,' said Rick, more abruptly than he meant to. 'I'll arrange for someone else to take you. I'm meeting your grandfather this afternoon to discuss the security arrangements before I leave.'

She arched a brow. 'Leave?'

'My contract is up in a few days.' He hesitated. 'Unless your grandfather decides to renew it.'

'The killer hasn't been caught,' she reminded him.

'I know.'

'So tell me,' she said slowly, 'what exactly do you recommend for me, Mr Expert on security? Put me in chains so I can't move from my flat? Rewrite my whole life plan even?'

He groaned. Could he really answer that without getting his face smacked? What he wanted to do was sweep her off her feet, carry her onto that soft silky bed in her room and slam the door behind him. Certainly thinking about it made him answer very tightly.

'The security arrangements are for all of your family. Not just for you.' He knew he sounded harsh, but he damned well couldn't help it. He was only there to protect her, to fulfil his contract, and that was all.

He saw something in her eyes. Hurt. Damn it. He'd handled her request badly. All she had wanted to do was go for a drive – she hadn't asked for the moon.

'I might be able to take you,' he amended. 'But it would have to be tomorrow.'

'Don't bother,' she threw at him, her eyes glinting. 'I'm not that desperate.'

He had to put things right. To get things back on an even keel between them like it had been the previous night. 'What happened before . . . when I kissed you. . . .' He took a deep breath. 'The fault is all mine. I had no right. No right at all.'

She shrugged. 'It doesn't matter. Let's forget it. It didn't mean anything anyway.'

No way could he forget it. Nor did he want to. And he had a feeling that Gina thought the same in spite of her words. He was conscious of a rift opening up between them but he wasn't sure what to do about it.

She moved closer. He had the urge to reach out, pull her close to him. He squashed it flat. Get a grip, Caruso, he thought disgustedly.

'There's something about the sea that draws me,' said Gina, her hair whipping around her face. 'When I was a child, my father used to take me down to the beach to play in the sand.'

'That's what every father should do,' he replied.

'At the weekends, my parents would drive Maria and me in their convertible up the coast. We'd always stop for an ice cream. I used to have chocolate, and Maria strawberry. We'd sit on the rocks and watch the sea.'

The wistfulness in her voice almost tempted him to cancel his appointment with Mr Rosselini until the evening. They'd have plenty of time if they left now. He was just about to suggest it when he heard footsteps behind him. Two dark figures in police uniform appeared around the corner, a serious look on their face.

'This is an unexpected visit,' Rick said, recognizing the men. 'Must be important.'

The tallest officer spoke first. 'It is. Brougham wants you down at the station. Right now.'

'You mean you want me to bring Ms Rosselini?' Rick clarified.

He shook his head. 'No he doesn't want to see her; he only wants to see you.'

Rick frowned. 'Why? What's all this about?'

The two police officers swapped uneasy glances. 'We can't say at the moment.'

'So what if I refuse?'

'Well, I guess we'll have no choice but to arrest you.'

Rick exhaled sharply. Something was up. 'I see. That serious?'

Both men nodded.

No point in delaying, he thought. If Brougham wanted him that badly, he'd better oblige. He turned to Gina. 'I'll alert security I'm out for a while. If you leave the property, make sure you take a security man with you. If there are any problems call me on my mobile straight away.' He grabbed his leather jacket. 'OK, let's get this over and done with.'

It was odd sitting in the back of a patrol car being escorted to headquarters. How many times had he driven in the front seat with a suspect in the back? Probably thousands, he thought ironically. The ride gave him time to think about what had happened earlier on between himself and Gina. He cursed himself furiously for stepping over a boundary which he had convinced himself earlier had been set firmly in place. If he was honest with himself, one part of him wanted to make love to her, the other was still on duty. Maybe later on there might be time for a friendly date as he'd promised, but that was as far as it should go. She was much too complicated. And yet, her unpredictability and depth added to her attraction.

He leaned back against the seat and forced his thoughts to why Brougham wanted to see him so badly. If it had been anything to do with Gina, he would have rung first to alert him.

Rick surveyed the streets through the window. The shops had just opened for the day and already the traffic was heavy especially with the road works on the main highway. A red light forced them to stop to let pedestrians cross. Rick drummed his fingers on his knees impatiently.

When they reached the police station, Brougham was in a foul mood. Surrounded by files and a desk covered in papers, he was busy talking to a colleague. Rick took a seat opposite him until he had finished.

'You look like you've been up all night.' Rick commented.

Brougham took a swig of coffee from his mug. 'Yeah, I guess you could say that. We've had two burglaries, one arson attack and a runaway teenager. Even worse, we're not getting anywhere with the Rosselini case. Forensic didn't find anything in Gina's apartment. Not even a fingerprint on the roses.'

Rick decided to cut to the chase. 'Why do you want to see me so urgently?'

Brougham drew his chair in. 'We had an anonymous phone call early this morning informing us some drugs were stashed in your office. We sent a police officer around to check it out.'

Rick stared at him in disbelief. 'Drugs? You're kidding me.'

Brougham grimaced. 'We found cocaine. Any idea how it might have got there?'

'No. I damn well haven't. I don't know anything about it.' He paused slightly. 'You realize someone must have planted it.'

Brougham face looked thoughtful. 'So who else has access to your office?'

'Just my parents. But there's no way they'd get involved in anything like that. For a start my father is still in hospital. He's got a broken leg.'

Brougham wrote something on the pad in front of him. 'Anyone else working at your place?'

'Only my cousin Mark. But there's no way he'd be involved either.' He briefly outlined what had happened to his father and why his cousin, Mark, was working for them. 'He's helping out with a few chores. I trust him completely.'

Brougham looked up. 'He wasn't at your place when we went around this morning. We'll need his address to interview him.'

Rick gave him the information. 'You realize someone is trying to frame me.'

'Any idea who?'

Rick thought for a moment. 'No. Some criminal I put away in the past maybe.'

'If I didn't know you so well, I'd arrest you,' said Brougham drily. 'Anyway, just a few more questions. Then you can go.'

'Sure. Go ahead.'

But he never had time to utter any of them as a plain clothes detective burst open the door and said, 'We just had an emergency call. Gina's disappeared. They can't find her anywhere.'

By the time Rick reached the Rosselini residence, he cursed himself for the hundredth time. He shouldn't have left her alone. Only she hadn't exactly been alone, he reminded himself, he'd arranged a security guard to take his place. And there were others patrolling the property.

'She's left a note . . .' Rosa said, fumbling with the piece of paper and handing it to Rick.

He quickly skimmed the contents.

I'm going for a drive by myself. Don't worry about me.
Love Gina.

Luigi stepped forward. 'I've told her she's to have someone with her at all times. Why doesn't she listen to me?' He turned to the security guard whom Rick had appointed while he was away. 'Why didn't you stop her, eh? It's your job to look after my granddaughter.'

The security guard shifted awkwardly. 'I tried to reason with her, sir. But she wouldn't listen.' He looked towards Rick for support. 'As soon as I realized what she intended, I came upstairs to inform Mr Rosselini.'

Rick nodded. He knew only too well what Gina was capable of when she set her mind on it. He'd already come across Gina's stubbornness before. 'It's OK, you did your best.'

The security officer looked relieved as he moved away.

'Do you know where she might have gone?' asked Rick.

Luigi shook his head, his face worried. 'No.' He shrugged in the Italian way of accepting the inevitable. 'But when I find her, I'm cutting off her allowance. She has to do as we say.'

'You can't pin her down, Luigi,' interrupted Rosa, a note of warning in her voice. 'I've told you that before. She needs to be free to do what she wants to do. If you try to cage her, you'll lose her.'

'None of us is free,' grumbled Luigi. 'We've all got responsibilities. It is time Gina learned this.'

Rosa clicked her tongue. 'Don't talk such rubbish. She left a note, didn't she? I don't blame her wanting to get away on her own. I feel like that sometimes too.'

Rick wasn't about to get into an argument about what Gina needed or didn't need, because he knew they had to find her as quickly as possible.

'Gina asked me this morning to take her for a drive up the coast,' he told Luigi. 'Have you any idea what direction she might have taken? Does she have a favourite spot she'd stop at?'

'Not that I know of,' Luigi replied, shaking his head. 'She could be anywhere.'

'I'll ask Brougham to put a ten one out to all patrol cars. We should hear something soon.'

Rick paced up and down. He'd already rung Gina on her mobile, but she wasn't answering. He racked his brains trying to think where she might have headed. While drinking his second cup of coffee, a call came through from Brougham. A red Ferrari had been seen heading north towards Cable Bay. A traffic officer sitting in a lay-by had pulled her up.

It took thirty minutes to reach her. Rick flung open the car door and strode towards her. 'What the hell do you think you are doing?'

She flung a hostile glance at him. 'The officer had no right to stop me. I wasn't breaking any law and I wasn't over the speed limit. So would you mind telling me what this is all about?'

'You should have taken a security guard with you.'

Her green eyes flashed. 'I would have *if* you had been available.'

'I didn't have a choice this morning,' he reminded her. 'Something urgent came up.'

'Look, I didn't mean to upset anyone. I just needed some time out. Before I knew it, I was behind the wheel of my car and zooming on to the highway.'

He didn't know whether to believe her. Something in her tone made him suspicious, but he'd play along with it for now. 'At least you're safe.'

'Would it worry you if I wasn't?'

He frowned remembering his reaction when he heard she had disappeared. It was just a normal response, he reassured himself. No point in reading more into it than necessary. 'Of course, it would.'

Then, because she couldn't resist it and knowing it would take some heat out of their argument, she said, 'Good. I wouldn't want to make your job too easy.'

He gave a low laugh. 'Oh, something tells me you'd never do that.'

CHAPTER SEVEN

The watcher had driven past the Rosselini residence three times. On the last occasion, he noticed the cop cars parked outside. Something was going on. He strained his eyes but it was difficult to see for the large flowering rhododendron bushes bordering the fence. He pulled over to the side and watched for a few more minutes. At that moment, the red Ferrari with Gina and her bodyguard came racing down the hill and turned into the driveway.

He slid down the seat and pulled his baseball cap over his forehead. He'd come back later, when it was quieter, he decided. Still, he was surprised to see Caruso still around, especially after he made that phone call to the police telling them about the cocaine stashed in Caruso's office.

He thought they would have kept him down at the police station for a while and that would have given him plenty of time to get Gina on her own. Only it hadn't worked out like that, damn it. She'd taken off within minutes, just as he was attempting to climb over the wall to the house. He'd bounded back to the car and, although he'd followed her for a while, he'd seen the cop car pull her over, so he'd had no choice but to continue on his way, and turn around as soon as he could. He'd lost her. His hand smacked down on the steering wheel in frustration.

As for Caruso, the cops had let him go sooner than he had reckoned. He'd known Caruso had been a police officer in the past.

They were like a brotherhood. Always watching out for each other. Disgusted, he put the car into first gear and discreetly drove past, planning his next move.

Gina couldn't afford to tell Rick the truth. By going for a drive on her own, she had been hoping to draw the killer out. Rick would never have allowed it. And, if he knew what she was up to, her freedom would be curtailed even more.

All morning she had been waiting her chance again. She saw it when he was busy supervising the workmen installing another alarm. Only he caught her as she had opened the car door, ready to climb in.

'Going somewhere?'

She whirled around. He was right behind her. How did he manage to move so quietly? 'Damn you, Caruso. Do you have eyes in the back of your head?'

'Yeah, I do where you're concerned.' His eyes glittered. 'Get out.'

Gina felt her face heat. She certainly wasn't going to argue with him in front of the security men standing nearby. With her bag hitched over her shoulder, she marched down to her apartment. He caught up with her. 'So that's what you were up to.'

'What do you mean?' she said, feigning innocence. She should have known she couldn't fool him.

'You were hoping to lure the killer out.'

'OK. So what if I was?' She shrugged. 'It was worth a try.'

His eyes narrowed. 'Forget it.'

'You can't be with me twenty-four hours a day. What about at night?' she threw at him.

'Babe, if I have to, I'll sleep right beside you.'

'You wouldn't dare.'

'Try me.'

Fuming, she paced the living room. She was considering her options when an urgent message came through. Detective Brougham wanted to see her urgently upstairs along with her grandparents and Anthony.

'What do you think it's about?' she asked Rick.

'I don't know. But if Brougham wants you all together, I'd say it's something very important.'

Gina took a seat next to her grandmother and waited for Brougham to speak.

The detective cleared his throat. 'There have been some new developments.' He looked at each of the members of the family seated in front of him. 'We've arrested Dani Russo for the murder of Maria. The rifle that shot your sister has been found in his garage after a tip off. Russo's fingerprints are all over it.'

'So it was him,' exclaimed Gina.

'A court of law will judge that,' reminded Brougham. 'But we believe so.'

'And have you found Jason?' she added.

'Jason Gallagher is dead.'

'Dead?' repeated Gina, stunned. 'But . . . but I don't understand.'

'Gallagher left a note in a motel saying he was committing suicide; that he couldn't live without you. The motel manager contacted the police first thing this morning to let us know. The note left specific instructions where they could find his body and the car. He drove off a cliff. Earlier today, we sent divers down and they've confirmed the car's there. Vehicle recovery are in the process of bringing it up.'

Gina couldn't believe it. Jason was dead. Suicide. Because of her. When their divorce had come through she couldn't have been happier realizing it officially finally freed her from the nightmare of the last three years. She'd been relieved she was no longer legally tied to him. But why had he done this now? Had stopping the cheque tipped him over the edge? She knew he had been desperate for the money.

Luigi gave a deep sigh of relief. 'So it's over then.' He walked over to Rosa sitting in a chair nearby and took her hand in his.

She gave him a brief, sad smile. 'It will never be over for me,' she added quietly. 'Not with Maria gone.'

Gina absorbed everything that had been said. Something still bothered her. 'What about the anonymous letter I received? Did Russo send it?'

'It's possible he could have. Though none of the notepaper found in his house matched.'

'What about the grey Skyline?' Rick added. 'Have you managed to trace who it belongs to?'

'It belongs to Gallagher. He must have been trying to scare you. Perhaps frustration when he didn't get his fifty thousand dollars. We can only surmise.'

'Are you sure that's all there is to it?' said Rick. 'It seems to all fit together too neatly.'

Brougham took a breath. 'We don't know all the specifics but certainly nothing points otherwise. Russo was supposed to report to a parole officer during the first six weeks he had been out of prison. He failed to turn up. It would be more likely he killed Maria, rather than Gallagher. He had the motive. It's unlikely Gallagher would have committed suicide if he was guilty.'

'So what now?' asked Gina.

'There will eventually be a post-mortem on Gallagher when we bring him up. Then a final report from the coroner. That will give closure to the official side of things.'

'Will Russo get bail?' asked Rick.

'Unlikely. We'll certainly be appealing against it.'

Afterwards, Rick accompanied Brougham to the door so he could talk with him privately.

'I'm not entirely convinced about Russo. It's too circumstantial. Something tells me it's still not over.'

'Got any facts to back that up?'

'Nothing other than a gut feeling.' And it had never proved him wrong before.

Brougham looked thoughtful. 'OK. I'll bear that in mind. But don't forget, Russo had the rifle hidden in his garage. Forensic confirmed it is the murder weapon. You'd best keep the Glock for the time being until we find Gallagher's body.'

'Thanks,' Rick replied, relieved he didn't have to hand back the weapon just yet. It could be the balance of life and death, his or Gina's.

The following morning as Gina sipped her coffee she couldn't believe the whole episode had finished and soon their lives would return to normal . . . well, as normal as they could do under the circumstances, she corrected herself. There would be a murder trial eventually, but she would be ready to face it.

Her gaze lifted, settled on Rick. What kind of man was he really when he was away from the job, she wondered? Already she had found that one minute he could be hard and rough, the next tender. Only hours ago he had threatened he'd sleep right beside her if she tried to give him the slip again. The trouble was, she had almost been tempted to call his bluff.

'How about a few days away from here?' suggested Rick.

She hadn't expected that. Surprised she looked up. 'Where have you got in mind?'

He flashed an easy smile, making her pulse suddenly skitter again.

'My beach house. It's pretty secluded, but it's my kind of place. We could drink red wine, watch the sun go down and listen to some blues. Sound good?'

She hesitated. 'Well, I . . .'

'Of course, if that type of place doesn't appeal to you . . .' He left the words hanging. 'Maybe a five star hotel is more in your line?'

'No, you've got me wrong,' she replied in the same tone. 'It sounds wonderful. The kind of place I'd love. It's just that . . .' Just what, she asked herself? Stop reading more into it than there is. It's only a friendly invitation.

'You're worried about being alone with me,' he said drily.

Hearing him voice her concerns made her face flush.

'I'll be a perfect gentleman,' he promised. 'My sister will also be staying and she'll be bringing her two kids along too, so you'll have a chaperon.'

That surprised and disappointed her all in one breath. 'Your sister?' she said slowly.

'Elena. She needs a break and she's got a few days' leave from work. It's the school holidays, so I said I'd help out with the kids so she can relax for a while.'

It sounded good, she thought. 'OK. So when do we leave?'

'As soon as you're packed. Throw some gear in a bag and we'll go. I was speaking to Elena last night and she'll be arriving this evening if all goes well.'

'You don't waste much time,' remarked Gina.

He gave a grin. 'Got anything better to do?'

'No,' she admitted.

Later, Gina wondered how she managed to pack so quickly. But then again, there wasn't really that much to take. It wasn't as if they were going to hit any night clubs. Or shop in any trendy malls.

He hadn't wanted to take her Ferrari, preferring his own Toyota station wagon as it could carry more luggage. She agreed.

On their way out of town Rick stopped briefly to see Anthony at his law office to let him know where he would be in case he needed to be contacted. Anthony opened the door, looking harassed.

'Is everything OK?' Rick asked.

'I'm not sure.' He paused briefly. 'My secretary, Denise, hasn't turned up for work again. It's a bit worrying.'

'Have you rung her?'

Anthony nodded. 'There's no answer.'

Rick suspected there was more to it than Anthony was letting on. 'Maybe she's just not answering on purpose.'

Anthony shrugged. 'Maybe . . .'

Rick recalled what Gina had told him about Anthony. 'Is there something going on between you and your secretary?'

'Like what?'

'Come on, Anthony.'

Anthony exhaled. 'Who told you?'

'Does it matter?'

'OK, we had an affair. So what? It finished long before Maria and I were engaged. The problem is Denise took our break up hard. Things have been a bit awkward between us since then. I've tried to keep things professional, but you know how it is. . . .'

So Gina had been right about the other woman. There were more questions he would have liked to have asked Anthony but now wasn't the time. 'I'll catch up with you later. I'm on my way to my beach house. Gina's coming with me.'

Anthony raised his brows. 'She is?'

'Any objections?'

Anthony shook his head. 'None at all.'

'It's a bit off the beaten track. That's why I bought the place,' said Rick.

The ocean, a Prussian blue in the evening sun, shimmered with an intensity taking Gina's breath away. Why didn't the sea look like that from her apartment? Maybe it was the magic of the place, she thought, as she took in the long wild coastline and the golden sands stretching endlessly.

A few minutes later they reached the beach house, a rustic wooden building perched only metres from the edge of a cliff. Gina suspected there'd be a sharp drop to the beach in front of it and, when she climbed out of the car to investigate, she was right. Large rolling breakers pounded below, luring anyone with a surfing soul to play amongst the foaming brine. She knew Rick heard the call as he stood there looking seaward. He had brought the surf board with him, tied to a roof rack.

Rick hauled their bags out of the rear of the Toyota and laid them on the deck near the French doors. Gina noticed the old ship's bell at the door and the half-moon pottery of a smiling face hanging on the wall to the left. The earthy charm about the place pulled at her.

'I never imagined you owned a place like this.'

'I keep it secret. Only invite close friends or family. I try to come down here as much as I can.'

She took in the flowering honeysuckle as it climbed up the front of the house and the daisies bordering the path. Pink roses bloomed in two identical terracotta pots. She bent down to smell them. 'The garden's well kept.'

'I've got a confession to make. My father attends to the place once a month.'

She gave a smile. 'I should have known.'

He picked a white daisy from a large bush nearby and popped it behind her ear. 'Suits you,' he said, tilting her chin one way, then another.

She laughed, feeling more carefree than she had in days. 'Well, thanks,' she said, and before she realized what she had done, she reached and kissed him lightly on the cheek. 'That's for taking such good care of me.'

His eyes darkened. From the way he looked at her, she thought he might have taken her in his arms, but he stepped back as if to put some distance between them. Just then his mobile phone rang. 'Sorry.' He gave a shrug. 'I have to answer it. I've still got the business to run and you never know who is trying to get hold of me.'

While he spoke at length on the phone, she walked up the steps and sat down on the deck to wait.

After a couple of minutes, Rick hung up. 'That was my sister, Elena. She can't make it here until tomorrow. Something's come up. Do you want me to take you back to town until then?'

She shook her head. 'We've spent over a month together in my apartment and one more night on our own isn't going to make a bit of difference.'

He laughed. 'Good.' He pushed open one wing of the French doors. 'Come on, I'll show you around.'

'You don't lock the door?' she asked, surprised.

Rick gave her a crooked smile. 'The day I lock it is the day I find somewhere else to live.'

When Gina entered the large living area, she gasped. The room was painted a sunflower yellow but what astounded her was the candles. They were everywhere.

'No electricity?' she asked.

'Only a generator and a big bunch of batteries and gas cooker.'

A large open fireplace had a blackened kettle sitting in the cold, empty grate. For an instant, she could imagine a roaring fire and toasting marshmallows, listening to Billie Holiday, while the wind pounded at the windows with its fists.

The room itself was simply furnished but that was part of its charm, she decided. A chunky old-fashioned-looking sofa sat against one side of the wall. Several bottles of red wine were stacked nearby in a wine rack while on a table in one corner stood a CD player. At the other end of the room, a bookcase full of paperbacks reached to the ceiling. If she owned a place like this, she'd live here all the time, she decided.

'Want to take a look at your bedroom?' he asked.

'Love to.'

The bedroom was spacious. A large brass bed, made up in white linen, faced the French windows. Apart from a large rimu dresser and a basket-weave chair the room was simply furnished. A collection of shells were displayed on the dresser. She picked one up admiring the green and blue pattern of the paua.

'There are plenty more shells on the beach,' he said, moving closer. He lifted a hand to her cheek and ran his thumb across it lightly. It was such a natural gesture that it made her smile. He stepped away to look out the window. 'Wind is getting up. We'll light the fire tonight. It heats the hot water.' With quick strides, he lifted up the log basket. 'I'll chop the wood. Make yourself at home.'

'Thanks,' she murmured. She started to unpack the box of groceries, placing what they had bought on the kitchen bench. 'Where do you want these?'

He pointed. 'Over there. In the cupboard.' She quickly thought about what she could make for dinner. A quick pasta dish with the fresh vegetables, tomatoes, and basil, would work well, so she left them on the bench ready for use. It didn't take long to chop the ingredients. The pungent aroma of basil filled her nostrils. One thing she'd always been good at was cooking and using herbs. When she was a little girl, her mother had helped her develop her own garden plot near the kitchen. Every day she had watered it faithfully. And when her first harvest of herbs was ready, she had been so proud. She gave a small sigh. It was memories like those which kept her parents alive for her.

It took a while to get the hang of the gas cooker as the flame was so temperamental but she persevered. She stirred the rich tomato sauce, humming softly.

Rick was still outside chopping wood. She couldn't see him but she could hear the thud of the axe as it hit the log. He soon appeared through the doorway with the log basket. 'It's a bit dark in here. I'll light the candles,' he said, his muscles straining with the weight of the basket as he deposited it close to the fire.

Although it was late summer, the sea breeze cooled the evening, so Gina was glad of the heat from the fire. Within minutes it roared. She leaned forward to open the kitchen window to let out the steam from cooking. Brisk night air rushed in.

Rick uncorked a bottle of red wine and poured two glasses. He handed her one. '*Salute.*'

'*Salute,*' she repeated, and took a sip. 'Dinner's nearly ready. Hope you're hungry.'

'You bet.'

He took a seat at the table and Gina could feel him watching her as she worked at the kitchen bench.

'Have you thought any more about travelling to Italy?' he asked.

Gina threw over her shoulder. 'Hmm . . . often.' Concentrating on the task in hand, she lifted the dish of pasta out of the oven and set it down in the middle of the table, ready to serve. 'I guess there's nothing to stop me now. But it would only be for a holiday, not to live there. My home's here. It's strange really, sometimes I think of myself more Kiwi than Italian.'

'You do?' He arched a brow. 'Why?'

'Because I grew up here. That's not to say I'm not proud of my Italian heritage, I am. My grandmother tried to instill in me some of the old ways. At first, I didn't want to know, but as I got older I realized it shows us who we are. Where we came from. We can never forget our roots.'

'What about on a personal basis? You didn't take any notice of your nonna when she advised you about men,' he mused.

Gina laughed as she dished up the meal. At one time she would have reacted defensively to that statement. But not now. Somehow things had changed within her. The change had come so subtly she hadn't even been aware of it. She replied in the same vein. 'You're treading on sensitive ground.'

'Just an observation,' he said lightly. 'No offence meant.'

'None taken.' She smiled.

As they ate, she decided to ask Rick more about his past. 'What about you? Why did you leave the police force? I thought cops look on it as a career for life.'

'It usually is.' His face turned serious. 'It was a combination of things. The deciding factor was Karen, my working partner. She was shot when we were out on night patrol. We were the first two on the scene of a robbery. When we entered the building the crims were still there. They opened fire. She was killed instantly.' He stared into space for a second. 'I didn't see one of them hiding behind the door. We fought. He stabbed me. I was in hospital for a month. After that, I decided to leave. I'd put in a few good years to the force, so I didn't feel too guilty about going.'

'Did Karen have a husband?' she asked, curiously.

'No, she didn't.' He hesitated, before adding, 'She wasn't married. We were dating at the time.'

Gina paused, surprised at his admission. Up to now, he hadn't opened up much about his personal life. 'I'm sorry.' She meant it.

He shrugged. 'It happens. I liked her a lot. But I wasn't in love with her,' he admitted, 'It never got to that stage and I guess I wasn't ready to settle down then. After she died, I became disillusioned with the force. Management have no idea what goes on in the front line. We needed new radios, new cars.' He sighed. 'And in my estimation, the focus on crime had been lost somewhere along the way. Some good men left around the time I did.' Rick paused in between mouthfuls. 'So when I left the police force I had to find another job. It wasn't easy. I figured the best thing I could do was to start a security business in my home town.'

'You don't mind you've given up a career in the police force?'

'Sometimes I do. But that's the way things have worked out.' He gave her a long, level look. 'And you?'

She wasn't sure how much to give away, although she had confided in him more about her past and her marriage than she had anyone else.

'Long ago, I made a big mistake. I paid for it as you know,' she explained. 'I won't pretend it's not altered my attitude to life. Knowing that it was Russo who killed Maria and that he will face charges does bring some justice to the whole thing.' She shook her head, puzzled. 'I'd like to have known why he did it . . . that still bothers me. We can only assume it was revenge.' She took another sip of her wine trying to stem the tightness in her throat which was only a moment away whenever she thought of Maria. She didn't want to spoil the mood of the evening. Rick had made an effort so she ought to do the same.

Rick had obviously sensed the change in her because he said lightly, 'Mmm . . . this tastes really good,' he remarked. 'Who taught you to cook?'

She laughed. 'My grandmother. That's one great thing about being Italian. We learn to appreciate food from an early age.'

'And we appreciate family, don't forget.' His next question completely threw her. 'Would you get married again?'

She fiddled with her wine glass, playing for time. 'I'm not sure. If you'd asked me that a few months ago, I would have said a definite no. After my marriage failed, I never wanted to commit myself to anyone again.'

'That doesn't answer my question.'

She held his gaze. 'You're right. It doesn't.'

Gina helped herself to another portion of pasta while she tried to think of an appropriate answer. Of course, she knew why she had changed her mind. But she couldn't tell him. Maria's death had made her realize that life was for living. And even if you made mistakes, there came a time when you got over them, and hopefully learned a valuable lesson. It was all about moving on. And now, here was Rick Caruso sitting right in front of her, having come into her life unexpectedly, penetrating her barriers. If she thought about it too deeply it really shook her, and yet, she couldn't help being increasingly drawn to him. She could imagine his type of wife. Someone who stayed at home with the kids and cooked good hearty meals. For a moment, she almost laughed out loud. That was what she had always wanted to do, wasn't it? But her marriage hadn't worked out like that. She didn't even know if she would ever get a second chance. And Rick had made it perfectly clear he didn't want to get involved. And so had she. So where would that leave her if she didn't put a stop to what was happening between them?

'I don't know if I'd get married again,' she finally said. 'It all depends.'

'On what?'

'Who asks me,' she teased. She picked up the tea towel and threw it at him. 'Since I cooked, you can dry.' She collected the plates and stacked them on the bench.

A ghost of a smile hovered on his lips. 'Looks like I can't talk myself out of this one.' The phone rang. 'Damn,' he muttered. His eyes met hers. 'I could ignore it.'

She shook her head. 'Might be important.'

It would be an opportunity to be on her own for a few minutes to compose her thoughts and extricate herself from having to answer more questions. She had never been afraid to answer anything or anyone in all of her life. It surprised her how she had reacted when he started touching on topics like marriage which were close to her heart. Then again, since Rick Caruso had come on the scene, she could expect anything.

He turned to face her, his expression serious. 'That was Brougham. Danni Russo has been refused bail.'

She breathed a sigh of relief. 'Thank God.'

She put the kettle on and made coffee while Rick selected some music. He connected a car battery to the CD player. 'Generator charges the batteries,' he explained. 'That way we don't have to listen to the generator while we try to enjoy the music.' They both sat around the fire listening to Billie Holiday just like she had imagined they would. 'Tomorrow I've got a surprise for you,' he told her.

'Oh. What?'

'Surfing.'

She raised her brows. 'Surfing? Isn't that a bit ambitious? After all, I'm a lie on the beach with a book in my hand kind of girl. The nearest I get to anything strenuous is putting the sun tan lotion on.'

His mouth twitched. 'We can soon change that.'

'You can?'

'Yeah. . . .'

'Are you sure you know what you're letting yourself in for?'

'Nope. But I have a lot of patience.'

That's what she liked about him, she thought. His patience. His understanding. There were starting to be too many good qualities she was noticing, she thought. The way he looked at her sometimes for a start. Could she dare think that he might be feeling the same about her? She pulled back abruptly, rising to her feet. 'I'm tired. I think I'll head to bed.'

'So soon?' He stood up. 'Have I said something wrong?'

My God, he was even starting to know how she thought. 'No . . . no . . . not at all. It's just that . . .' Her voice trailed off as she failed to find an excuse.

'Just what?' he prompted, his forehead creasing in puzzlement.

'I'm still feeling a little raw,' she said lamely.

He smiled. 'Sure. I can understand that. I'll be sleeping on the sofa, so just yell if there's anything you need. 'Take a candle with you.' Rick took one in an old-fashioned holder and lit it from the fire before handing it to Gina.

By the time she reached the bathroom she heaved a big sigh of relief. Now that she was alone, she could finally deal with the turbulence of her emotions. Had it been a good idea to come here, she wondered? Being with him like this in such an intimate setting wasn't something she had envisaged. Or had she been fooling herself? Was it what she had wanted all along?

She switched on the shower, letting the hot water spray across her skin. It refreshed her. When her head finally hit the pillow, Gina found she was exhausted. She was falling silently through the darkness. But it wasn't a restful sleep. Her breathing quickened, her hand clutched the sheet. She tried to claw at the large forms which danced around her but they were elusive, slippery. A face loomed into hers. It was Maria's. She was trying to tell Gina something. Her lips were moving but no sound came out. Gina couldn't stand it any more . . . she let out a scream.

CHAPTER EIGHT

When Gina woke to candlelight, Rick was sitting beside her, his hands curved around her shoulders. Shadows danced on the walls behind him.

'It's OK,' he said softly. 'You're safe. It was only a bad dream.'

She trembled as she pulled herself up. The duvet had slipped on to the floor. Her sheet was tangled in her legs and all that covered her was her silk nightdress. One thin green strap had fallen onto her arm. She hitched it up quickly.

When she met his blue eyes, they were full of compassion. She wanted to tell him how frightened she had been. How lonely. But somehow the words wouldn't come. Eventually she managed to say, 'I had a nightmare. It was so real. . . .' Her voice faltered, still shaking.

'It's over now,' he soothed, his hands seeking hers and pressing her fingers reassuringly. 'It's just the trauma you've been through. Sometimes the mind can play tricks like that.'

He was sitting close to her and she studied the strong planes of his face. His black hair was loose around his shoulders. It made him seem more physical in the dim light of the room. She saw his bare chest, tanned to a bronze shade, lift as he breathed. Conscious of his close proximity, she tried to concentrate on the carved bone cross that he wore on a leather thong around his neck. Seconds passed. Her gaze dropped further where she noted a trail of dark hair plunging from his belly button to the top of his jeans. He obviously hadn't had time to fasten the silver button on the waist band because with every breath he took the denim parted revealingly, showing smooth, taut muscles.

'When I heard you scream like that, I thought someone was in here.'

Her gaze shot upwards. 'I haven't had a nightmare like that since I was a kid,' she admitted. She gave a sigh. 'I'll be fine now, honestly.'

'Well, if you're sure. . . .' His hand reached out to caress her gently on the cheek. She didn't know why she did it, but her fingers caught his, pressing the palm of his hand to her face. His warmth was reassuring.

'Gina,' he started to say, 'I think I should go before—'

'No,' she cut in strongly, angling her chin upwards. 'Please, don't go. I want you to stay.'

The need between them set the air humming. Gina knew that it was too late to take back her words. Nor did she want to. It surprised her especially after what had happened the last time she let him get physically close. But somehow this time it was different. Put it down to the loneliness of the night, she thought fleetingly, but right at this moment in time she needed him to stay.

He stared at her. His hand moved caressingly to her neck and then slid downwards to her shoulder, in a caring gesture. She liked the feel of him, the tender way his fingertips skimmed over her skin.

He spoke softly, disturbing the stillness of the room. 'I want you real badly. I won't deny it, but I don't think it's a good idea.'

Hurt sliced through her. 'I thought you were into one-night stands.'

His mouth tightened. 'One-night stands are OK if both partners know the score,' he shot out, 'but in our case, I'm not about to take advantage of you because you've had a bad dream. You're upset. And emotional.'

'Emotional?' she repeated, stunned. 'You make me sound like

some sort of needy female.' No way. He was wrong about that.

His gaze locked onto hers. 'A one-night stand isn't what you need right now.'

'Huh, you haven't got a clue what I need,' she retaliated.

Rick groaned. 'Oh yeah? I've lived with you these past few weeks. I know exactly what you want. What you need.'

'Oh . . . you do, do you? That's just typical.' Tears seared her eyes. 'You say you know what I need. That I'm emotional. Then you back away.' Furiously, she wiped the tears away with her hands. She would not give into self pity.

'Just being sensible,' he growled.

'And that's what you're good at, isn't it? Common sense,' she said, unable to help herself. Hurt demanded hurt. 'Why can't you think from your heart for once? Or are you going to tell me you're a male and too logical for that?'

'No.' Then he surprised her. 'I'm sorry, I didn't mean to upset you,' he said softly. 'It's the last thing I'd ever want to do.'

Her heart ached at his apology. She cursed herself at her own desperation in asking him to stay and leaving her wide open to rejection. She felt humiliated.

'Show me,' she uttered.

'Show you what?'

'How sorry you are.'

She heard him groan, 'Gina. . . .' A deep sound emitted from his throat. 'You don't mean it.'

'I do.' She kept her gaze level and steady. She needed to convince him. She wouldn't back down. Not this time.

He pulled her roughly to him. Before she knew it, his mouth was on hers. Sensations slammed into her. This was what she wanted, wasn't it? And oh, he tasted so good.

Her hand slid to his chest, right above his heart. His skin felt hot, clammy. She could feel his heart pounding deep, just like the ocean outside. She knew her own heart danced to the same tempo.

'You sure you know what you're letting yourself in for?' he

whispered. He gave her a smile. The kind of smile that trebled her own heartbeat with no effort at all.

She jolted. 'No.'

He gave a low laugh. 'Guess that makes two of us.' She knew if she had any sense she should stop now. But something pushed her on. Unable to help herself, she reached up to press her lips against his, and when she found his mouth, she drowned. Her mind clawed desperately to make some sense of it all. But couldn't. Maybe it was better not to think, only feel. And feel she did. Like in a whirlpool, she spun, and spun, her thoughts tangled between need and want.

His kiss increased in urgency and she matched him with reckless abandon. He eased her down onto the rumpled covers. Desire claimed her, fast and furious. Now she wanted him more than she could have believed possible.

He slipped off the straps of her nightdress, and eased the silky material down further to her hips and ankles. He dropped her nightdress on the floor where it pooled beside the bed. Shivers of delight raced through her as her nipples brushed against his chest.

His mouth worked down her, across the hollows in her neck, to the curves of her breasts, his lips playing teasingly over her skin. The pleasure was pure and explosive.

He spoke in Italian, soft words of love, and she bathed in them. He was tender, she thought. Considerate too in so many ways. Instinctively, she knew he wouldn't just take what he wanted like some men she'd known.

Her fingertips stroked and caressed, smoothing over the hard muscles of his back and shoulders. It was when she touched the scar on his chest, her fingers gentling over the puckered skin that he stiffened. He pulled back, frowning. 'It looks ugly.'

'No, it doesn't,' she reassured him. 'It's a part of you. A brave part.' And to show she meant every word, her head went lower, lips and tongue exploring the white line across his chest which had long since healed. She reached out for the waist band of his jeans, tugging them lower, until he finally unzipped them and kicked them off.

'No going back, Gina,' he murmured.

She shook her head. In spite of his words, her eyes locked onto his, needing reassurance. She found it and more. Blue eyes, so deep, and so intense, started stripping her senses one by one.

His lips trailed down softly to her shoulders, and her arms, finding curves where he explored. 'If you're going to love me, then do it well,' she said, grateful at his tenderness and his patience.

His voice was quiet. 'I intend to. Perhaps more if you'll let me.'

Her heart began to thaw. Warmth slid through her body and she welcomed it. She was surrendering because she chose to she convinced herself, ignoring the desperate pull of need in her belly.

His mouth found one breast where his tongue teased and tantalized, then the other. Her nipples hardened. She grew hot with longing. And felt her hips surge against his. It was all the encouragement he needed. When his body finally slid over hers, she was more than ready. As he slipped inside her, she gasped.

Her world tilted. She clung harder, her arms circling his neck. The air around her became heavy while shadows on the wall danced wildly, sometimes blending into one. She ached for release. And for him a thousand times over.

She was near the edge. Her senses went into overdrive somewhere along with his.

When they crash landed, no words were said, or even needed. Fingers linked together, limbs tangled, their hearts were as one. And for those few precious moments, Gina revelled in the closeness, the intimacy, knowing the return to reality was only a breath away. And eventually one of them would have to take it.

'Did that really happen?' she asked, lying back against the pillow, still reeling.

'You'd better believe it, babe.'

'You're a surprise, Caruso,' she murmured, laughing. 'I guess there's more to you than you've let on.'

His voice deepened. 'Maybe, you just didn't look hard enough.'

'I thought I had, but maybe I wasn't ready to see.'

'I'm right in front of you,' he replied, seriously. 'Look harder.'

She did. And what she saw was the strength in his face. The determined angle of his jaw, and his well-defined mouth which had pleasured her. She saw the lethal calmness in his eyes. So calm, they bore straight into her as if he guessed all her secrets, all her longings, perhaps even her wildest dreams.

'Well?' he prompted.

'Well what?' she teased, basking in the afterglow.

'Do I pass?'

A smile tugged at her lips. 'Now, that would be telling. A woman has to keep some things to herself.' Her fingers brushed his unshaven jaw, saying softly, 'I feel like I've been to heaven and back.' It was true, she thought. She did.

'That's what every man likes to hear. Keep going.'

She wagged a finger at him. 'But . . .'

He winced. 'Damn. I knew it. There's always a *but*,' he mused.

She gave a pretend scowl. 'Sometimes you make me really mad.'

He chuckled. 'Yeah, that sounds about right in a healthy relationship.'

Stunned, she stared at him. 'Relationship? What are you saying?'

'Isn't that what we've just shared?' His eyes narrowed slightly. 'Or are you calling it something else?'

He was sounding her out. *Warning. He was getting too close. I want that yet I'm scared.*

Something slammed shut within her. 'That's kind of hard to answer right now.'

To her surprise, he put his fingers against her lips. 'Then don't.'

She shook her head, knowing it would be only fair to answer his question. And she needed to do it for herself, at least. Only how was she going to say it?

He lifted himself onto his elbow and looked down at her in puzzlement. 'OK. What's on your mind? I want the truth. Nothing less.'

She'd never been good at lying. But the lies tripped off her tongue like honey off a spoon. 'No promises have been made . . . no strings. I don't want marriage, if that's what you are thinking?' And because she didn't want him to know that it might have been nice to share her life with him, she added, 'If this is a one-night stand, I won't hold it against you.' She tried to get some semblance of order into the way she was feeling but failed miserably.

'Are you saying that this is as far as you want things to go?' he asked tightly.

Pain shot through her, keenly. She ignored it. 'Yes . . . yes, of course,' she answered, hating herself for saying it. It was better this way, she told herself. For both of them. No ties. No hurt. No commitment. And he would be free to walk away which she guessed was what he would want the following morning when normality returned.

His voice deepened. 'I'm not sure I want to let you go.'

Oh God, she couldn't believe he had said that. She clenched her fist at her side, conscious of her throat tightening. She hoped she wouldn't cry. No way could she let him see what his lovemaking had done to her. Or even those words he had just uttered. If she was honest and admitted now she had fallen for him, where would that leave her? She wasn't doing it, she decided. He might throw it back in her face. Hadn't he told her in the beginning that *he* was the one who didn't want commitment? And she had been adamant she didn't want another relationship after her disastrous marriage. So nothing had changed except they'd both made the most incredible love.

And now, the more freedom she gave him, the safer she was. Feigning the need to sleep she lay back against the pillow and closed her eyes.

'You're shutting me out,' he accused.

'I'm not.'

'Then look at me.'

She did. But wished she hadn't. Those deep blue eyes again. Damn. 'Stop it.'

He frowned. 'Stop what?'

'Looking at me like that.'

'I'm looking at the woman I've just made love to. What do you expect me to do?'

She lowered her gaze, feeling uncertain. 'I don't know.'

Exhaling, Rick fell back against the pillow. But he wasn't fooled. Tonight had brought them together. Only why did he have a feeling they were further apart than ever?

Thinking deeply, his gaze lifted across the room to the window. The moon had peeped out from behind dark clouds, throwing silver light onto the waves. Then, almost magically, a large schooner appeared out of nowhere, sailing through the light like a ghostly apparition until finally it disappeared into the deepness of the night.

He didn't know what tomorrow would bring but he'd be ready, he told himself. As far as he was concerned, there was a turning point in everything and he had a feeling they'd just reached it.

When Rick woke the next morning, he knew something was wrong with Gina but what he hadn't reckoned on was her quick change of mood.

'OK, what's wrong?' he finally asked.

Her hands balled together. 'We . . . we didn't use any protection last night.'

Rick froze, not sure he heard right. 'You mean you're not taking the pill?'

She shook her head. A worried frown etched between her forehead. 'Why should I? It's not like I sleep around. Last night was. . . .'

'Something unexpected,' he finished off for her. 'It's just as much my fault. I shouldn't have just assumed.' He raised his shoulders dismissively, then moved closer wanting to take her in his arms and chase the worry from her face.

'Don't,' she said, stepping away, out of reach. 'What if I get pregnant?'

In his experience what ifs didn't always happen. Again, he moved forward, reaching out for her wanting to reassure her. But this time she moved to the window, so instead his hands fell to his side. He watched her carefully from where he was standing. 'If you fall pregnant, we'll face that if it happens. It's no big deal, Gina.'

'No big deal. Huh, easy for you to say.' Her eyes were distant. 'It wouldn't affect you.'

A nerve tightened in his jaw, but he kept his voice calm and level. He could see she was strung up tight. 'You've got me wrong if you think I'm like that. I've never been afraid to face up to responsibility.'

'That's what they all say,' she shot out bitterly.

Anger shot through him. His voice came out hard. 'Don't compare me with your ex-husband.' Impatiently, he took two steps towards her. 'Do you trust me?'

'That's not the point.'

'Isn't it? I think that's exactly the point.'

She didn't answer. It wasn't good enough for Rick. He let out a disappointed sigh. 'For Christ's sake, I can't believe it.' Their sleeping together had crossed one barrier but infuriatingly had erected another. 'He certainly did a good job on you.'

She looked at him warily. 'What do you mean?'

'I'm talking about your ex-husband.'

Her voice rose. 'Jason has nothing to do with us.'

'Think again.'

She didn't answer. Then, 'Maybe we're just infatuated with each other—' she started to say, as if trying to justify what had happened.

'Infatuated? Last night was something we both couldn't control. Don't destroy it by trying to analyse it.' He sighed. 'We're both adults. I know the difference between infatuation and love.'

What was he trying to say to her? She felt confused. She took a deep breath and made for the kitchen to make coffee.

Rick was worried about what had happened too. While Gina made coffee, he walked outside to get some fresh air. Sure, he was in deep, but then he'd never been one to waste time when he wanted something. And he knew now he wanted Gina. Only he hadn't quite decided how to go about it because, as he saw it, there were a number of problems that only time could sort out. Her grief over losing Maria was one. Her wariness, stemming from an abusive marriage, had affected her in more ways than he knew how to handle. Too many hurts still lingered, putting her on the defensive whenever he got close. He had offered commitment if she was pregnant, but he had a feeling that after her first experience of marriage, things weren't going to be that straightforward. He could stand here and argue with her or he could let the matter rest. He had a feeling arguing would only make the situation worse. He needed to think carefully about what to do.

He turned to face the sea. Fishing boats were outlined against the horizon. He knew the boats belonged to Rosselini Fisheries. Seeing them gave him a sharp reminder of who Gina was. Yeah, there was that complication too.

His gaze shifted, focusing on the long stretch of white sand. Curling surf beckoned like fingers. He knew it would do them both good to have a swim and to take some of the heat out of their argument. It would put things back to the level they were before. He heard her footsteps behind him. He turned to find her standing there, looking uncertain. Worry still shadowed her eyes.

'I've made coffee.' She held out a mug to him as if it was a peace offering.

He took it. 'Thanks,' he murmured. He gave her a smile. 'I promised to teach you to surf, so here's your chance. Let's head down to the beach soon,' he said lightly.

He hadn't regretted what had happened the night before and he only hoped she hadn't either in spite of what she'd said earlier.

By the time they drove down the narrow track with the surf board on top of the wagon, it was nearing midday.

A strong wind blew with large rolling breakers. Conditions were excellent. Lying on the surfboard, Rick paddled out to deeper waters. He half-turned to face the shore keeping an eye on the oncoming waves. A few seconds later, a wave tubed and raced off. He'd catch the next one, he decided, as he started paddling again. It came before he knew it. It was the perfect wave to cut loose on. Soon he was skimming the water fast. Adrenaline pumped, making him clench his fists as he rode it through. More waves followed, thick and hollow with enough punch to severely hammer him should he make a mistake.

After an hour, his muscles were aching from the constant tension. He noticed Gina swimming in to meet him. Ready to take a break, he met her halfway. She stood up, the water nearly to her waist. She was wearing a black and gold bikini which when wet revealed more than it ought to. Desire shot through him, hot and sudden.

'Are you ready to have a go?' he asked hoarsely.

'Sure I am,' she answered, tossing back her hair. Her eyes met his in a challenging look.

'OK. Here's what you do. Paddle out lying flat and then turn with the oncoming waves. Try and gain your balance first before you stand up,' he instructed.

'You make it sound so easy,' she replied, laughing.

Gina did her best and managed to hang on for all five seconds before she lost her grip and fell backwards into the water as the surf ripped over her head. When she surfaced, she shook the water from her hair and climbed back on again. After a few attempts, she got the hang of it, though didn't stay for long on the board. He smiled at her determination not to give up.

About an hour later, Gina swam towards him. 'My arms are aching. I need a rest.'

'You did well for your first time,' he acknowledged, taking the board from her.

'Who said it was my first time?'

'So you have been out before?' he replied with a smile. 'I suspected as much.'

'Once or twice,' she admitted, 'but it was a long time ago.'

They walked out of the water side by side and Rick left the surf board on the edge of the beach.

When they reached their towels, Rick lifted one up and draped it over her shoulders, turning her around to face him. He tilted her chin up and kissed her squarely on the mouth, tasting the salt on her lips. Then he pulled back, his hands curving around her shoulders.

'Feeling better?' he asked. She gave a smile that made his heart flip.

She nodded. 'The sea always calms me. I really am sorry about before.'

'Forget it.'

He gathered up their things, and together they walked towards the car. A movement in a gully on the hillside caught her eye. She stared. 'Someone is watching us.'

He frowned. 'Where?' He scanned the gorse covered hills. 'I don't see anything, only native bush.'

She pointed. 'Over there. A man. He was standing there, staring straight at us.'

Rick scanned the area again but all he could see was a flock of seagulls wheeling high above the beach house, their screeches echoing along the cliff face. His arm slid around Gina's shoulders. 'There's no one there.'

Her forehead creased in puzzlement. 'That's odd, I was so sure. . . .'

Rick felt uneasy. Nothing he could put his finger on, but the feeling was still there, niggling away at him. It was probably the weather, he justified. Change was on its way. In spite of the sun beating down hotly on the sand, grey clouds were rolling in from the north.

As he walked beside her, he took her in. He'd seen beautiful women before but Gina was something else. Her dark hair hung in wet strands around her shoulders but that only seemed to emphasize the slant of her high cheekbones. The fresh air had heightened the colour in her cheeks, and brightened her eyes.

He had surprised himself by his strong response to her. But it wasn't just her physical looks he was drawn to, it was her mind as well. It irked him that she hadn't given her whole self, not even during their lovemaking the night before. He moved closer, his hand slipping around her waist. Without hesitation, he lifted her up into his arms.

'Hey, what are you doing?' she exclaimed.

'Wait and see.'

When he found a sandy private spot he put her down gently, and lay beside her. 'We've still got a few minutes. Let's talk for a while.'

'OK.'

'What you've told me about your marriage, it doesn't have to be like that between us. You need to give us a chance. You have to trust me. Don't you see that?' he said gently. He pushed her hair back from her face and brushed his lips over hers. The kiss deepened.

Eventually she pulled back, breathless. 'When you kiss me like that I can't even think straight.'

She didn't know a kiss could be so seductive. It promised more than she had ever imagined. Long ago she had convinced herself that she wouldn't feel like this again but she was wrong. So very wrong.

Neither of them knew exactly when the tempo changed. One moment, she was lying in his arms enjoying his mouth on hers, the next riotous sensations clawed through her, demanding release.

She couldn't believe she responded so readily to his touch. As his mouth found hers again, she let herself melt into his embrace.

'Now,' she urged. 'Let's make love here.'

'Making you wait will do us both good.'

'Damn you. You believe in making me suffer.'

His mouth slid to her throat where he tasted and savoured, then slipped lower to her breasts, which were straining against the silky material. With one quick movement, he unhooked the top of her bikini and dropped it beside her. Only within a moment of him touching her, he realized he'd underestimated himself badly. That control he'd always prided himself on having, disappeared in a flash.

He heard her breath come in short gasps as his hands slid down her hips, pressing her to him. When he stroked, he could almost swear she purred. Grains of golden sand fell between them, trickling down her abdomen, and rubbing harshly against her skin.

Her eyes told him what her voice refused to and for now he was heartened. He wanted all of her. But he knew he only had her body still. While some men would have been grateful for that, he wasn't. If this didn't work, nothing would.

'Marry me, Gina,' he shot out.

Shock floored her eyes. 'What? You can't mean it.'

'Why? Is it so hard to believe?'

'It's not that . . . it's just. . . .'

He waited a few seconds, his mouth twisting. 'Well?'

'It's unexpected,' she said lamely.

'You mean, I don't have the money the Rosselinis have?' he replied, coolly. He picked up her bikini top and handed it to her.

'What?' she exclaimed in disbelief. 'How can you think that?'

He laughed dryly. 'Well, what else am I to think?'

She shook her head. 'You make is all sound so simple. Marriage, love . . . but what happens if you get tired of me . . . will you play around? I had enough of that before.' She shook her head, trying to form the right words to make him understand her fears.

He sighed wearily, 'That's something you need to decide for yourself. It all comes back down to trust.'

He could see the tears she'd held at bay for so long, threatened again.

'Trust?' she repeated.

His voice deepened. 'Yeah, trust. Think about it.'

He softened when he saw the fight inside of her and wanted to reach out for her to tell her he'd be by her side always but he also knew realistically she had to make up her own mind about him. He needed her complete trust. He couldn't settle for anything less.

And because she still said nothing, only stared at him, he had no choice but to walk away.

Late afternoon, the rain hit. Softly at first, and then it came down in torrents, the sound deafening as it battered the iron roof of the beach house. Large pools of water formed in the driveway, mirroring the dark, grey sky. Gina knew that storms like this in summer were not unusual but they could be severe.

Gina flicked her wrist to look at her watch. It was early evening. Rick's sister still hadn't arrived and the weather was worsening. She turned up the radio, hoping to drown out the pounding of the waves against the cliff. Feeling restless, she stood at the French doors, looking out. The colour of the sea had changed from turquoise to an angry dirty green colour, churning and frothing, wild in its fury. Tension coiled in her stomach. A rift had opened up between her and Rick. It had been all her fault. Only she didn't know how to make things right again. Perhaps, later, when they were both alone, they could get over this hurdle. She hoped so. Right at the moment, she could see the worried look on Rick's face. She knew it was because of his sister. Not because of her.

'Still no answer from Elena?' asked Gina.

'I've left two messages on her mobile, but she hasn't returned my calls.' He looked thoughtful. 'I'll ring my mother. See if she's heard anything.'

He'd only just picked up his mobile, ready to dial, when it rang in his hand. He pressed the button and held it to his ear.

A voice said, 'I need you to come and pick me up.'

'Elena? Is that you?' Rick frowned as he detected a tearful note in her voice. 'What's wrong?'

'I skidded on the road, and hit a bridge. The car's a write-off.'

Rick swore under his breath. 'Are the kids all right?'

'Yes, they're OK although shaken up a bit. The cops wanted us to go to hospital to get checked out, but I decided the best thing we could do was to call you to come and get us. They'll be fine once they're tucked up in bed.'

'Where are you?'

She quickly gave him her whereabouts.

'I should be there in about an hour. Just stay put.' He hung up.

Gina, realizing something had happened, moved over to stand by his side. 'Trouble?'

'You could say that.' He explained what had happened.

'Shall I come with you?' she asked softly.

He hesitated for a moment. 'I don't want to leave you here on your own, but they've got a car full of luggage and there's not going to be enough room.'

'I'll be OK. I'll make dinner while you're away.' It was the least she could do.

Rick nodded. 'Thanks. The kids will be hungry when they get here.' He looked thoughtful. 'Have you got your mobile phone with you?'

'In my bag.'

'Let me see it.'

She took it out and handed it to him. He checked it, making sure the battery was charged.

'Good.' He handed it back to her. 'Promise me, you'll keep it close by you.'

She nodded.

He grabbed the car keys and gave her a hug which suddenly made her want to say, 'Don't leave me,' but, of course, she couldn't do that. His sister and her children needed him more right now.

'Make sure you lock the door behind me.'

She nodded.

After he left, she noticed how empty the place was. It unnerved her. To take her mind off things, she set about making an evening meal. Before long she had meatballs simmering which she would serve with spaghetti. Elena's children would love them. They were always a favourite with families. She settled down to read a magazine for a while, but she couldn't concentrate. Her thoughts returned to what had happened between them earlier in the day. How could she have been so stupid? She had made a complete mess of things.

It hit her. She was hopelessly in love with Rick whether she liked it or not. Only she was too damned scared to tell him. He wouldn't have offered marriage if he didn't love her, she justified. He had been testing her, waiting for her to meet him halfway. And she'd backtracked.

Her thoughts were disturbed by a noise at the window. She looked up, realizing she hadn't pulled the curtains closed. She hurried over to the window. Only now, the noise sounded like someone tapping on the front door. She turned.

She hadn't locked the door. Rick had told her to after he'd left, but she'd been distracted and forgot. She hadn't heard a car drive up, so what could it be? The handle started to turn. Someone was coming in. She rushed forward intending to slip the latch. Too late. The door swung open with a crash. Gina screamed. A dripping wet dark figure stood in front of her.

Oh God, it couldn't be. When she finally found her voice it was hardly more than a whisper.

'Jason, it's you. I . . . I thought you were dead?'

When she saw the firm set of his jaw and the violence in his face she knew she was in trouble.

'Not dead. But very, very angry with you, Gina.'

Gina felt the familiar fear grip her tightly. She had thought she'd never have to face him or his temper again, but here he was standing right in front of her and she was all alone.

Telling herself not to panic, she took a deep breath, and tried to keep her voice calm. 'What is it you want?'

He gave a low laugh. 'You Gina. It's you.'

When the first blow came, it caught her on the side of her face, stunning her. She heard herself cry out as she lost her balance and fell to the floor. He took her arm and hauled her up again. Then, he slapped her across the face again, making her eyes water.

'Did you think I wouldn't see you with lover boy?'

'You've no right to do this.' She tried to twist away, lashing out at him but he held on to her in a vice-like grip. Desperation gave her sudden strength so she kicked him hard on his shins. He grunted with surprise. Then he laughed out loud and Gina knew then he had gone completely over the edge. He made a move to grab her again but she fought hard, raking her nails over his face. Her movement incensed him. He grabbed her hair and yanked it, making her cry out loud.

'You're not going to get away from me this time,' he said harshly.

Gina let her body go limp. If she could fool him into thinking he had won, he might loosen his grip on her and when he did, she'd make a dash for the door. Maybe if she kept him talking it would even buy her some time.

'Why?' she managed to say through a haze of pain.

He smiled, making her shiver. 'Because you deserted me.'

'I didn't. I tried to help you. Please . . . let me go and we can forget this ever happened.'

'You think I would do that?' He released the pressure on her arm slightly while he was talking. 'Your boyfriend can't help you this time.'

'How did you find me?' she asked.

'Anthony's secretary.'

While he was talking, Gina's gaze slid over to her mobile phone sitting on the table. If only she could reach it in time.

He let her go while he bent to retrieve the rope he'd dropped at the doorway. Gina saw her chance. She grabbed her mobile phone and sprinted into the bedroom, slamming the door shut behind her. With a sinking heart she realized there was no lock on the door. She put her back up against it, digging her heels in and bracing herself.

Quickly punching in the number of the emergency department, she said, 'Help me, please. . . .'

The pressure behind the door increased as he rattled the door handle.

'Let me in, Gina. You can't escape,' he growled.

It was only a matter of seconds before his strength would get the better of hers and the door would finally be forced open. An unexpected heave from behind the door jolted her. She dropped the phone. It clattered onto the floor, just out of reach. If she bent forward to retrieve it, he'd be able to push the door inwards. She turned quickly and, with both hands, pressed hard against the door with all her strength. But it was no good. The door was inching open slowly, until finally Gallagher stuck his foot in the doorway, jamming it open. It was then Gina knew she had lost. She let the door go suddenly and made a grab for the phone lying on the floor. Her fingers had only just curled around the plastic casing when she felt him jerk her head back by her hair. He plucked the phone from her fingers and threw it against the wall where it shattered.

Jason's face contorted with fury. 'So you thought you could get away from me, did you?'

Fear slid up and down Gina's spine completely immobilizing her. He was going to kill her, she was sure of it. He slipped the ropes over her wrists and bound them tightly.

'Jason . . .' she pleaded again, this time sobbing. 'Please don't do this . . . please.'

He didn't answer her. Suddenly she leapt forward, surprising him, but he was fast and bolted after her. He caught her by the arm and whirled her around so quickly, she thought she had dislocated her shoulder. She jarred her back against the wooden dresser, knocking off a large vase of flowers. It smashed on to the floor with a loud crash, water spilling everywhere. She didn't see the blow coming to the side of her head and in the encroaching darkness sank slowly down to the ground, knowing there was no escape.

CHAPTER NINE

Rick drove in some of the worst road conditions he'd seen in years. The rain pelted down. Twice he had to pull over to the side of the road until it eased.

Large slips of brown mud and rocks had rolled down from the hillside, landing on the main highway. The road maintenance crew were clearing it and putting up large yellow warning signs for the traffic. Rick focused on the road ahead, the car radio a low murmur in between the rhythmic sound of the windscreen wipers. Thunder growled and flashes of lightning in the distance brightened the grey sky.

Rick glanced at the rear-view mirror noticing the long trail of traffic behind him. When the road curved around the corner, he saw the queue of cars stretched just as equally in front. It was going to take him longer than he thought to reach Elena. He grimaced.

The mobile phone rang unexpectedly. He flicked on the answer button. The voice came through the loudspeaker. It was Dave Brougham. 'Gina's mobile phone number has registered at the emergency services. The caller asked for the police and then the line went dead. Any idea what's going on?'

Rick tried to control the alarm that shot through him. 'No, but something must be wrong. I've just left her at my beach house.' He was in two minds whether to turn around and head back.

'Do you want us to send a patrol car?' offered Brougham. 'We can check things out.'

'No. I'm closer.' But what was he going to do about his sister and the children? He explained the position.

'We'll arrange for a patrol car to pick Elena up. We'll drop them off at your place.'

'Thanks, I'd appreciate that.'

'Rick, there's something else.'

'Yeah. What?'

'Recovery brought up Gallagher's car. They can't find the body. It's possible he was thrown from the car. We don't know yet. Divers have been searching the area, but with the storm hitting we've had to call the search off until conditions improve.'

Could that mean Gallagher's alive, thought Rick? His heart slammed against his chest.

'Maybe he was never in the car. The suicide note might have been a ruse.'

'That had occurred to me too. I'll keep you informed if anything turns up.'

Rick glanced again in his rear-view mirror. A big logging truck with a full load was travelling behind him, too close for his liking, so he signalled in plenty of time, indicating he was pulling in to the side of the road. He waited until there was a gap in the traffic and did a U-turn. His foot pressed down hard on the accelerator, picking up speed quickly. He knew he was taking a chance ignoring the speed warning signs especially with the wet, slippery road but he knew he had no choice. He had to reach Gina. Fast.

He'd only driven a few kilometres when he realized the cars ahead of him were slowing down. He braked. Ahead there had been a landslide. The road was blocked. He swore under his breath.

There was nothing he could do. He tapped his fingers on the steering wheel, thinking furiously. What if Gallagher had tracked Gina down? He dialled Gina's number. No answer. Only a disconnected tone. He swore again.

He threw the door open and climbed out. With quick strides, he started walking towards the road block. The rain had eased off slightly but there was a thin drizzle forming a mist around the hills. Cars were lined up behind each other on the main highway. A few horns honked impatiently. When he reached the road maintenance crew, he asked how long it would take to clear the road. The man dressed in yellow oilskins scratched his head and looked vague.

'Can't say. Maybe an hour at the most.'

Rick grimaced. 'That's an hour too long for me.' He was trying to keep calm but couldn't help the panic beginning to grip him. If he could get by the landslide, he could reach Gina faster than any patrol car. He saw a motorcyclist, dressed in black leather gear, parked nearby and headed over to speak with him.

'I need to borrow your motorbike,' Rick said quietly. 'I don't have time to explain now ... but I need to reach someone who's in danger.'

The black leather figure removed his helmet. Rick was surprised to see it was a woman, and an attractive one at that. She had copper-coloured hair and green eyes.

'Come on,' she drawled. 'You don't expect me to believe that, do you?'

Rick flashed his private investigator licence but knew perfectly well it didn't give him any more rights than an ordinary citizen.

'A private eye, huh?' she remarked, tossing back her head. Interest entered her eyes. 'Funny that, I'm married to a cop.'

'I was a cop too.'

'Then you might know my husband. McKenna's his name.'

'Mike McKenna?' asked Rick, surprised. When she nodded, he added, 'Yeah, we worked together a few times. He's based on the West Coast. A detective in the drugs squad, isn't he?'

She inclined her head, her face thoughtful. 'That's right. Seems like you might have just convinced me.'

Her voice was unmistakably Scottish, Rick realized. Then he remembered hearing that McKenna had married an undercover agent from Scotland. He'd also heard that they had a couple of kids.

While he would have been pleased to chat to her, he knew he was running out of time.

'Look, I really do need to borrow your motorbike,' he repeated urgently. He was ready to use force if necessary and be willing to face the consequences later. 'You can use my wagon over there.' He pointed to his vehicle sitting behind a line of cars. 'Here's my keys.'

She gave him a wide smile. 'My name is Kelly Anderson. Just you make sure you look after my motorbike. I want it back in one piece,' she told him, her hands on her hips. 'If you drop it off at the police station in Nelson, I'll collect it there later.'

'You're doing someone a favour,' he replied gratefully. 'I owe you.'

'I guess she must be someone special,' she answered, her teardrop greenstone ear-ring jangling against her cheek as she handed him the helmet.

It was Rick's turn to smile. 'Yeah, she is.'

He climbed on to the Triumph Tiger motorbike and revved it hard. It had been a while since he'd ridden a motorbike but he hadn't forgotten how. When he took off, he immediately headed along the white centre lane and whenever he saw debris, skirted round it. A large mound of mud and stones ahead posed a bigger problem but increasing speed he flew past the maintenance crew ignoring their shouts of warning. For a few seconds, when he peaked on the landfall, he thought he wasn't going to make it. The tyres were wheeling deeper as they slid backwards in the mud. He gripped the throttle hard and put his feet on the ground to keep his balance. Suddenly, the bike broke free with a lurch, the tyres gripping on some rocks. Before he knew it, he was zooming down the other side. When he glanced in the rear-view mirror, he saw the maintenance men shaking their heads at him, so he gave them a wave. He rolled back the throttle tight, the bike screaming as it sped along. Adrenaline shot through him. If he hadn't been so worried about Gina, he would have enjoyed the ride. A sharp corner loomed up. He leaned left, easing his speed. Before he knew it, he had reached the turning to Kokorua.

It took him half the time to reach the house than it would have done in a car. He pulled up outside. Something was wrong. The door was open, swinging back and forth with the wind. He switched off the engine and took the steps two at a time, drawing his Glock. When he entered the living room, his jaw dropped. A table had been overturned. The vase of wild flowers which Gina had so carefully picked that morning, were lying strewn on the tiled floor in a soggy mess. It was obvious there had been a scuffle.

'Gina, are you there?' he called out, even though he knew with a sinking heart she wouldn't be.

He approached the bedroom door carefully. When he stepped into the room he saw the shattered mobile phone lying on the bedroom floor. He bent down and, without touching it, peered at it closely. He froze when he saw the smear of blood on the back of the door. Was Gina hurt? She would have put up a good fight, he knew that instinctively. Was she lying hurt outside somewhere? If anything happened to her, he'd never forgive himself. His hands trembled at the thought. He had to keep calm and think. There wasn't much time. He had to find her.

An hour later, a patrol car pulled up outside. Rick went forward to meet it. Dave Brougham climbed out a grim look on his face.

'There's no sign of her,' said Rick. The words came out oddly like he had trouble saying them. Rick swallowed again carefully. He had to get a grip on himself if he was going to be of any use.

Once inside the beach house, Brougham took a look around. He gave instructions to the police officer standing next to him. 'Get a forensic team out. Make it urgent.'

Rick knew all about procedure. Seize, cordon and contain the scene. When the forensic team arrived they'd look for blood, fibres, hair, and fingerprints.

Rick started to make his way to the door. 'Did you touch anything?' asked Brougham.

Rick turned. 'No.'

Brougham caught his arm as he moved past. 'Where are you going?'

'Where do you think? To find her,' he said. 'She could be outside somewhere.'

'You'll never find her in this weather – it's pitch black out there. Whoever took her had a car. They'll be long gone now.'

Rick knew he was right but he had to try. Frustration consumed him. He bunched his fists together. 'Damn it. I should have been here. I shouldn't have left her by herself.'

Brougham's hand fell on his shoulder sympathetically. 'You weren't to know.' His face was regretful, his voice low. 'I'm sorry.'

He didn't admit the mistake outright, but Rick knew that was as good as an apology he would get from Brougham. The police had got it wrong. The killer was still out there, somewhere, and he had Gina. They had to work together to find her. He only hoped it wouldn't be too late.

Gina's hands were tied so tightly, the pain was excruciating. Her arms had gone numb and she was feeling queasy from the blow Jason had given her. But her physical condition was nothing compared to how she was feeling emotionally. She was terrified. He had gone completely crazy and he was going to kill her. She was sure of it.

She tried to move slightly but no matter which way she shifted, there was no comfortable position in the boot of the car. Two wooden boxes hemmed her in at each side, crushing her into the one position. The car finally slowed down and stopped. Jason opened the boot and shone a flashlight into her face. Her eyes closed painfully. Then he hauled her out and she half fell to her knees on the dirt track. It had stopped raining. Moonlight filtered through patchy clouds casting ominous shadows everywhere she looked. The fronds of a palm tree shivered above her.

Where was she, she wondered?

Jason led her like an unwilling animal down the track until they reached an old shack. He tied her to the veranda post. She couldn't stop shaking.

He left her alone for a few minutes while he drove the car into a shed part way down the track. She heard the sound of the doors being dragged over the rough, stony ground. Soon he was back. A set of lights flashed somewhere in the distance and that was the last thing Gina saw as he dragged her up the steps into the shack and slammed the door shut behind them.

If Gina could have yelled, she would have but her mouth was taped firmly shut. She started to pull away, but he pushed her and she fell to the floor with a thud. The impact winded her. Her face lay against the musty floorboards. If he was going to kill her, she only hoped he'd do it quickly. She stifled a sob in the back of her throat as she thought of Rick and how much he meant to her. Would she ever see him again?

After a few minutes of Gallagher moving around in the dark, he lit a candle. 'Get on your feet.'

She tried to stand, but her legs shook so much she had to lean against the wall.

With one quick swipe, he removed the tape across her mouth. 'You can yell all you like, but no one will hear you.'

'Why?' she asked hoarsely. 'Why are you doing this to me? Why didn't you take the money I gave you and leave? You said you would.'

'You cancelled the cheque,' he accused.

'I didn't.' She shook her head.

'If it wasn't you, who was it?'

'I don't know,' she lied. 'There must have been some mistake at the bank.'

'It doesn't matter now, anyway.' He laughed, an unpleasant sound.

'Jason let me go. This will only get you in worse trouble.'

His face hardened. 'Shut up. This time your family are going to pay big time. I wonder how much you are worth to them. After all, you're the only granddaughter left now.'

Gina's heart sank. The realization that he'd killed Maria struck her. 'You shot Maria, didn't you?'

He nodded. 'Now you know what it's like to lose someone you love. I want you to suffer as much as I did.' He stared at her for a few more seconds. 'You shouldn't have divorced me, Gina. By the time I've finished you'll be begging me to love you again.'

'You're despicable,' she spat out. She couldn't believe she had once been married to this man. It was the drugs, she reminded herself. Once he'd started taking methamphetamine, his personality had started to change. He hadn't always been like this, she thought sadly. 'You need help.' But deep inside, she knew she would be wasting her time.

He laughed out loud. 'Help? That's a big joke, Gina. This is what I need.' He then leaned forward, his mouth drawing closer. She turned her face to the side, shuddering.

'No . . . no . . . don't even touch me.'

Jason pulled back, his eyes glittering. He picked up the rope and tied it to the end of the bed. When he'd finished he stood over her. 'Let's see if a few hours on your own might change your mind.' He blew out the candle. The acrid smell of wax wafted over to her in the darkness, making her want to gag. 'Watch out for the rats,' he threw over his shoulder.

Rats? Oh God. No. She heard a scuffling noise in the corner and something running across the floor. A scream lodged in her throat. But screaming wouldn't get her anywhere. No one would hear. She had to think. Not panic.

She was still alive, she realized with a jolt, and she was going to try and stay that way. Even so, she didn't know if she'd see the sun rise.

CHAPTER TEN

The forensic team had finished. Rick stepped over the plastic yellow tape stretched across the front of the beach house and made his way down the driveway. Brougham was squatting beside a set of car tracks, a short distance away.

'What do you think?' asked Rick.

Brougham stood up. 'Whoever it was must have parked in that clearing, fifty metres back up the track so Gina wouldn't have heard the car engine. Then he'd crept towards the house.'

Rick exhaled. 'It has to be Gallagher. Everything points to him being the one. Dumping the car over the cliff and leaving the suicide note had to have been a ruse. All along he's been tailing her. Just waiting for the right moment.' And Rick had given him all the chance he needed when he'd left Gina on her own to pick up his sister.

He had to find her, Rick thought, over and over again. God damn it . . . he loved her. He just hadn't had a chance to tell her.

Brougham was sitting at his deck when a phone call came through from reception. Denise Thompson, Anthony Monopili's secretary, was at the front desk demanding to see him urgently. He drank the dregs of his cold coffee and made his way down the corridor to the interview room.

She was already seated at the Formica table when he entered. The detective sat down opposite her. 'Ms Thompson, what's this about?'

She shifted position, her gaze darting around the room. 'I . . . I need help.'

Brougham spoke calmly, taking in the pale, tear-stained face. 'Help? Why?'

'Jason Gallagher is going to kill me. He's crazy.' She pulled out her handkerchief and dabbed at her eyes. 'He killed Maria and now he's threatened me. He phoned up last night and said he wanted me to deliver a message. He said he had Gina, and that the Rosselini family were to give him fifty million dollars or he will kill her. He wanted them to pay for treating him the way they did.' Her voice was almost hysterical as she added, 'You have to understand. I didn't want to be part of this. But everything's got out of hand.'

Brougham leaned forward, his eyes narrowing. 'How do you know Gallagher?'

She took another breath. 'After he got out of rehab he came to me, asking for help. He promised that if I did, Anthony would come back to me.' She gave a sob. 'I guess I fell for it. I was just so angry that Anthony dumped me to marry Maria I went along with Jason's plans. I was the one who wrote the anonymous letter to Gina under his instructions. He wanted to scare her a little.'

'Any idea where Jason might be hiding out?' demanded Brougham.

Her voice shook as she twisted her handkerchief round and round in her hand. 'No, I don't. He left the flat he'd rented. He said he was heading for the bush.'

'Where is his flat?'

Denise gave him the address. 'I told him that I didn't want any more to do with him. He was furious. Said if I didn't do as I was told, he'd come after me as well. Please, you have to help me. I've not been well.' She leaned forward. 'I need police protection.'

Denise was crying uncontrollably and Brougham, although he had a million questions still to ask her, decided he had to give her a break. The last thing he wanted was the police being accused of harassing a sick woman. But he also knew when her lawyer got here, she might not be so helpful. Brougham looked up at the woman police officer standing near the door. 'Make her a cup of tea, will you?' He turned to another police officer. 'Get me Rick Caruso on the phone. I need to speak to him urgently.'

Later that night, Rick was sitting in the bar of the Club Italia when a news flash came over the television. The news reader announced that one of the wealthy Rosselinis had been abducted. Rick's stomach clenched tightly, souring the brandy he had just drunk. Gina's photo flashed across the screen. His hand curved tightly around his glass, almost crushing it. He felt so helpless. He had to find her, but he didn't know where to look. He'd spent hours scouring the hillside near the beach house but there had been no sign. No clues. Nothing.

He paid for another drink, downing it in one go, then checked his watch. Time to get going. He'd only called in briefly to question some of the patrons to see if he could get any leads on Gallagher. No one knew anything. He was just about to leave when his mobile rang. It was Brougham. 'We've got something. Get down here as quick as you can.'

'On my way.'

Twenty minutes later, he sat opposite the detective.

'Looks like Denise Thompson's been in on this all along,' said Brougham. 'But says she didn't know Gallagher was going to shoot Maria.'

'You believe her?'

'I'm not sure.'

Rick's grimaced. 'If anything happens to Gina, I'll find Gallagher myself and kill him.'

'You do that and you'll be breaking the law,' replied Brougham quickly.

His reminder didn't sit well with Rick.

Brougham stood up. 'Denise has given us the address of a flat in town where Gallagher has been hiding out. We've sent someone round to check it out now and I'm heading down there in a few minutes.'

'I'll come with you,' offered Rick.

They reached Gallagher's flat accompanied by two squad cars. When the officers piled out, the neighbours stood looking over the fence at what was going on. They were used to the police turning up in this part of town but seeing this many at once was a little unusual. Statements were taken, but no one had seen their elusive neighbour for some time.

Inside the flat, Rick had a good look in the bedroom. There were no clues, nothing that would indicate where Gallagher had gone. There was an unmade bed, a rumpled towel lying on the floor and some worn trousers hanging in the wardrobe. Rick was just about to walk out when he saw a bit of paper lying on the ground. It had caught underneath the door. He kneeled down and pulled it out. Unfurling it, he saw it was a receipt from a local outdoor and mountaineering shop in town. Gallagher had bought candles, a small camping stove and a length of rope.

Rick shouted through to Brougham. 'This could mean he's got a hideout in the bush somewhere.' He showed him the receipt. The name of the shop was printed at the top.

Luckily, Rick had done the shop owner a favour in the past when they'd had a problem with shoplifting and the owner was only too pleased to help. Rick spoke to all the staff asking if they remembered anyone coming in recently to buy some camping gear, in particular the items listed on the receipt.

'I remember that customer,' one sales assistant said. 'The guy was a bit creepy if you ask me. He wanted a map of the Nelson coast. He mentioned something about Kokorua.'

'Did he say anything to you about where he was going?' Rick asked hopefully.

'Yeah, he said he was living rough for a few days. That was why he needed the candles.' She thought again. 'When I asked him what the rope was for, he clammed up. Then he paid his money and left.'

They were still no further forward, Rick thought, disheartened. Kokorua stretched for many kilometres along the coast and the thick native forest of pungas and palm trees could hide anything since it was so dense. Still, at least it was a start.

'We'll get search and rescue on to it,' Brougham said.

Rick knew it was a slim chance of finding her but anything was worth a try.

The darkness lasted for hours. The cold silence made it worse as Gina wondered when Jason was going to return and what he would do to her. Sometime during the night, she had heard the unmistakable sound of a car and had thought someone had arrived, but quickly realized Jason must have gone out. She tried to move to a better position as she lay on the bed, but it was impossible. Her legs were tied so tightly.

Her mouth was dry and it was painful to swallow. She licked her lips to try and moisten them but all she could taste was the salt from her tears. She glanced upwards, towards the window, seeing a welcome shaft of morning light filtering through the dark green wooden shutters. Odd patterns shifted upon the water-stained walls. She watched the movement for a while, because there wasn't anything else she could do.

She thought of Rick and wondered if he was looking for her. His strong image appeared, lingering for a few seconds in her mind, and giving her much needed courage. More memories flooded back as she remembered the strong feel of his hands as they caressed her body and those blue eyes of his as they looked at her.

She loved him. Oh God, she loved him so much. She didn't want to die like this without him even knowing how she felt. Her breath caught in a sob. Rick would find her. He was a private investigator and an ex-cop, and he was clever, she told herself. She just had to buy herself enough time until he did.

It took Gallagher an hour to reach his flat from the shack. He'd wanted to pick up a couple of things he'd left there. But when he saw the police cars parked out front, he didn't stop. He increased speed, cruising on by hoping no one would recognize him with his cropped blond hair. The fake suicide note should have thrown them off the track for a while but he should have guessed that Denise would have proved difficult. In the beginning, she'd been only too keen to help him. Anything to get Maria out the way and get Anthony to come back to her. But she'd panicked, especially when he'd told her he'd abducted Gina. So he'd threatened her and, under duress, she had gone to the police just like he had planned with his ransom threat. They didn't know where to find him though. And he had Gina, he thought, smiling. And very soon he'd have the fifty million dollars as well. He smiled. The Rosselinis would only be too willing to pay up.

Rick looked up at his sister as she entered his office. She was always so calm. That's probably why she made such a good nurse, he thought.

'Ben and Sam are playing outside,' she told him. 'Has there been any word?'

He grimaced. 'None.' He glanced out the window at the two children, sitting outside in the morning sun beside his father in his wheelchair. They were giggling and playing cards, oblivious to the drama playing out in real life. Innocence, thought Rick. There was a lot to be said for it. Seeing them sitting there, Rick realized it was at times like this he appreciated his family around him.

Elena put her arms around her brother's shoulders. 'You should eat, or at least get some sleep,' she told him. 'You were up all last night.'

He swung around in his swivel chair still holding the map of Kokorua in his hands. 'I can't. I've just got to keep going,' he said, his voice breaking. He laid the map down on a desk already cluttered with a heap of paper. He tried to concentrate, but couldn't.

'Come and have something to eat,' she said gently. 'It will make you feel better.'

'The only thing that will make me feel better is finding her,' Rick replied wearily. He leaned forward, then slumped back again. 'All I can hear is her voice. See her face. I keep imagining what must have happened to her after I left the beach house. She would have been terrified.'

'Stop torturing yourself. No one could have known what was going to happen. As far as everyone was concerned the man responsible for Maria's death was dead. And from the sound of it,' she added, 'he's been harbouring a grudge for a long time. Didn't the psychiatrist at the rehab clinic mention that in his medical report?'

'They should have warned her what he might have intended doing.'

'He could have fooled them,' she replied.

He got up and opened the cupboard in front of him. He took out his gun and knife. Elena put her hand on his arm. 'Don't take those . . . it could leave you wide open.'

Rick ignored her and took out an orange and black packet. He opened it and pushed the brass .9mm into a spare magazine for his Glock.

'Elena, we're dealing with a psychopath: he'll stop at nothing.' He flashed her a determined look. 'And neither will I.'

Ellen nodded as she sighed. 'You love her, don't you?' One quick nod from him confirmed her question. 'For Christ's sake, be careful. I don't want to lose a brother.' She gave a worried frown and then a smile, as she touched him reassuringly again on the arm.

A knock at the door interrupted them. It was his mother. 'There's a police car waiting for you.'

Rick nodded. 'Good. Right on time.' He grabbed an iced can of Coke from the fridge as he passed. 'I don't know when I'll be back.' He shut the door behind him and made his way down the steps. In exactly fifteen minutes, they'd be flying in an Iroquois helicopter and begin searching the Nelson coast.

Gina heard a car pull up. Daylight filtered through the shutters. She was desperate to use the bathroom and just hoped Jason would let her. When he opened the door and entered the room, she asked him. He untied the rope binding her to the bed and freed her feet but didn't untie her hands.

'The bathroom is through there,' he said, indicating a door off the hallway. Jason had a broody look on his face and Gina wondered what had happened to make him so withdrawn compared to his arrogant state he was in last night. Even so, she knew any mood of his could be dangerous. He was so volatile, anything could set him off.

She lowered her gaze as she walked in front, hoping nothing she did would antagonize him. After entering the bathroom, she tried to shut the door.

'Leave it ajar,' he demanded.

Humiliated, she did as he said and, as she stood in the small bathroom, she spied a small piece of broken glass lying on the floor. It had obviously come from the cracked window above her. If she could get it, she might be able to saw through her ropes. Bending down, she tried to pick it up.

When she almost had it within her grasp, he opened the door and peered in.

'What are you doing?' he asked suspiciously. He leaned forward, pushed the door open wider. His hand clamped on her shoulder, digging in painfully.

Gina's fingers curled around the glass shard quickly as she twisted around to look at him. 'I was dizzy. I lost my balance.' She put her elbow on the toilet and hoisted herself up slowly.

He gave one quick look around as if to make sure she was telling the truth and then went back out again.

Her hands were tied in front, so at least she didn't have the indignity of asking him to remove her clothes. He didn't give her long before he came in again and hauled her out by the arm. This time she did lose her balance and fell forward against the wall. Determined to say nothing in case a beating ensued, she righted herself as quick as she could. Then she shuffled back to the room, where she sat down on the bed while he retied the ropes around her feet.

'I'm so thirsty. I need a drink,' she said, pleading. 'Please. . . .'

For a moment, she thought he was going to ignore her, but when he finished what he was doing he left the room. Gina let the small piece of glass fall under her body to hide it when he tied her hands to the top of the bed. He brought in a bottle of water and let her drink through a straw. When she had enough, her head fell backwards onto the bed and she closed her eyes, pretending to be too weak to do anything else.

Jason checked the ropes were secure and then went out the room locking the door behind him.

Gina had intended using the shard of glass straight away, but she felt as if she was going to black out. She must have drifted off to sleep and wasn't sure what time it was when she finally woke. Her back was sticky with sweat and her limbs were stiff. She glanced upwards at the shutters across the windows and realized it must be early evening from the light filtering into the room. A bell bird sang nearby in a tree outside the window, and she listened for a few seconds to its haunting bell-like sound which unexpectedly soothed her. As the light faded, her hopes did as well. They would never find her, she realized, dully. There were hundreds of kilometres of native bush all around them and no one would think to look in an abandoned shack in the middle of nowhere.

She pulled her arms towards her abdomen, stretching the rope. The glass shard was lodged near her back. She twisted around but couldn't reach it. She tried repeatedly. Frustrated at her efforts, tears ran down her cheeks as she realized how helpless she was. Then she had a thought. Maybe if she was to bounce on the bed it might move the shard to where she could reach it. After a couple of movements, all she succeeded in doing was making a thumping noise as the ancient bed springs protested at her weight. She hoped Jason couldn't hear her although she wondered if he had possibly gone out. He could have come back while she had been asleep and she hadn't heard him. But there was nothing to lose, she thought. She had to try.

For another half-hour, the glass shard bounced around the bed until finally it fell off the bed on to the floor. Gina sobbed. When no tears were left, anger shot through her. He wasn't going to get away with this. She wouldn't let him. She wrenched the ropes really hard, again and again, knowing what she was doing would have no effect at all. Her arms ached. She cried again. Then gave one last heave. To her surprise, there was a cracking sound and the post at the top of the bed came away. Gina couldn't believe it. The thin post had split in two. For a few seconds, she stared at it, knowing that if Jason came in and found what had happened, he'd be furious.

Although her hands were still tied, she was now free to sit up, but her legs were tied to the bottom post. Leaning over the bed, she reached out for the glass. With one swoop it was in her hands and she began sawing. Half an hour later she had her hands free and then she started on the ropes on her feet.

The sound of a car again made her start. It was Jason. He had returned. He'd find her any minute. Hurriedly, she unwound the rope, dropped it from her ankles and stood up. Her legs were stiff. Moving to the window quickly, she tried to unbolt the shutters. The bolts were rusty and difficult to slide back. She beat at them with her hands but they refused to budge. She needed a lever. But there was nothing in the room apart from the broken bed post, so she picked it up. Using all her strength, she started to beat at the bolts, forcing them to slide along. All of a sudden, one of the shutters swung open into the night and crashed against the outside wooden wall. Fresh air hit her face. The sweet fragrance of the native forest at night overwhelmed her. The moon was high in the sky, its brilliant white glow bathing her in light. She climbed up to the window ledge. It wasn't too far to jump. She tensed. Then she heard the door swing open in the room. Her heart catapaulted. She glanced over her shoulder briefly at Jason's surprised face and with one leap was sailing through the air. She fell to the ground heavily. Winded, she lost valuable seconds. When she heard Jason climbing out of the window after her, fear gave her extra strength and she pushed herself up and started to run.

If only she could reach the bush, she could hide. Sharp branches scraped her face as she fought her way through the thick foliage. Finally the bush cleared a little. She increased speed, not knowing in what direction to head. It was only when she stopped, her chest heaving from the exertion, she realized she was completely lost. But at least she was safe and away from Jason. Her legs finally gave way and she sank to the ground amongst the ferns and the soft leaves. And she thanked God she was alive.

At first light, on the second day, the Iroquois helicopter hovered at points along the coast, the pilot pointing out various abandoned dwellings dotted below. Rick peered out the window. He could see trackers and search dogs. He adjusted the headphones and microphone before he spoke. 'What do you think, Dave?'

'We need to find out who owns all this coastal property on this stretch of the coast. The City Council should have that information.'

Rick pointed to the map. 'It's possible he could have hidden for a while in the bush, then doubled back to any one of these deserted dwellings.'

'We have to consider every possibility. This guy knows what he is doing.'

Brougham talked through the radio. Then he hung up, and turned to Rick. 'Sounds like someone rented out an old shack to a guy who fits Gallagher's description. It's further up the coast. About here.' He pointed to an area on the map, quite a distance away from Rick's beach house. 'Let's check it out.'

It didn't take long for them to reach the place by helicopter. The pilot managed to land in a clearing though it was tight. Rick made a quick check of the shed. Brougham came up behind him. 'Any luck?'

'A car. No number plates. Probably stolen,' Rick remarked.

Brougham went to have a look. 'We'll get the tyres checked. See if they match the ones in your driveway.'

Both men made their way to the shack nearby. Brougham ordered two men to watch the front of the place while Rick offered to check out the back.

'I'm going inside,' Rick informed Brougham.

'No. We'll wait for more men to arrive,' Brougham said firmly. 'We'll surround the place. It would be safer.'

'Forget it, we haven't got time. Chances are high he heard the chopper overhead.' Rick pulled out his Glock, a determined look on his face and continued to make his way around the corner of the wooden building. An opened shutter banged against the wall. Ducking underneath, he crept around to the back door, noticing it was wide open. Entering quietly, his feet making no noise on the wooden floorboards, he crept down the hallway.

In the kitchen he found a camping stove and tins of food sitting on a table. Obviously someone had been living here. He swung the torch light around. No sign of movement. His heart hammered in his chest as he approached another room, just off the hallway. Pushing the door open slowly with his foot, he peered inside. It had no furnishings apart from a bed. Ropes were tied to the bed. One part had broken off and was lying on the floor. His chest tightened at the implications.

A silver *cornicello* lay on the bed, the chain broken. He picked it up, and studied it in the palm of his hand. It was the amulet her grandmother had given her. So Gina had been here, after all. He slipped it into his pocket. With quick strides, he crossed the room to the open window and looked out. Had she jumped out in a bid to escape, he wondered? Without a moment to lose, he sprinted outside to find Brougham. The Armed Offender Squad had just arrived. Two vanloads of officers were parked nearby and weapons were being allocated. Rick briefly told Brougham what he'd found.

'She's been here but she's gone now. No sign of Gallagher anywhere. If she did get away, he might have gone after her. His car is still here so that tells us something.'

Rick knew realistically the search was going to take some time. If Gina had managed to escape she was out there in the bush somewhere. And the question was, would they find her before Gallagher did?

His heart heavy, Rick walked over to join the briefing.

Gina nestled amongst some leaves and fallen branches, listening carefully. The events of the past few hours came hurtling back, almost paralysing her. She knew Jason would be searching for her and he wouldn't give up.

Daylight started to filter through the branches of the palm tree high above, the warm rays of the sun caressing her face as if offering some comfort. Hope shot through her. She was free and she had to stay that way. She was just about to move when she heard a twig crack. Her breathing shallowed.

He was there. Somewhere near. Gina could sense it. She had to do something and quickly. Her hand curved around a small stone and she threw it, as far away as she could, in the opposite direction. Her suspicions were soon confirmed when she caught a glimpse of Jason's blue T-shirt as he stepped out from behind a tree. With slow movements, she started to crawl away through the undergrowth. Behind her, she could hear him swearing profusely.

'Gina, I know you're around here,' he said in menacing tones.

Gina's heart pounded so frantically, she thought he would hear her. She stopped, waited for what seemed like an eternity, then when she peeped out from behind the fallen log, she realized he had disappeared. He must have gone the other way. Her gaze slowly skimmed the thick forest around her but there was no trace of him.

She had to keep moving. There wasn't a minute to lose. Keeping her body low, she again crawled forward on her hands and knees as quietly as she could. When she was sure she was far enough away to be safe, she stood up in a small clearing and leaned against the tree to catch her breath. Suddenly, an arm came swiftly from behind, grabbing her. Her scream came out as a muffled cry as a hand clamped over her mouth. She struggled furiously, kicking and scratching, but he was too strong. He grabbed her by the throat and slammed her up against the tree, winding her. The cold steel of a knife pressed hard into her neck as his face leered into hers.

This time she knew she was going to pay heavily. Her mouth trembled as her legs threatened to buckle. Gina screamed as loudly as she could.

CHAPTER ELEVEN

'Did you hear that?' said Rick.

The search and rescue team had been battling their way through the bush for hours. Brougham finally called a halt. 'It's getting too dark. The last thing we need is to get lost ourselves.'

Rick shook his head. 'Just a few more minutes.' He pointed to a grove of palm trees and continued walking. When he reached the grove he stood and listened. His radio came on. It was Brougham requesting the search and rescue squad return to base. He knew Brougham would consider searching in darkness using night vision goggles and a heat-sensing camera.

Rick sighed with frustration. Damn it. Another day had gone. Rick was just about to turn around and head back the way he came when he thought he heard something again.

He swopped glances with Brougham. 'That was no seagull.'

Then they both heard it. It sounded like a loud, high-pitched scream, true and distinct.

Gun in hand, Rick started running in the direction he thought the scream came from.

When he burst through to a clearing, he saw them. Gallagher was towering over Gina. She was fighting him off. Rick ran forward and tried to grapple him, but Jason swung round, a knife in his hand. The blade caught Rick, slicing him across the chest. Pain shot through him. Gallagher lunged again and Rick jumped back, avoiding the knife by centimeters. He raised the Glock but Gallagher moved behind Gina.

'Put the knife down. You're surrounded,' growled Rick.

Jason glared insolently. 'No chance,' he said, lifting the knife so it rested against Gina's throat.

A shot rang out from behind Rick. The bullet missed him but slammed into Gallagher's shoulder. He gave a grunt and staggered backwards away from Gina. Then he whirled around and charged into dense bush. Rick chased after him. He tackled him from behind. Both men fell, landing heavily. Rick's head slammed against a tree trunk, stunning him. With desperate strength, Gallagher shoved Rick off and rolled away. He scrambled to his feet, knife raised.

Another shot pierced the air, missing Gallagher and hitting a tree. Rick pulled himself up and retrieved the Glock from the ground. He sat slightly dazed as several officers yelled at him to keep down as they sprinted past.

A barrage of shots rang out.

Rick was tempted to go after Gallagher as well, but he heard Gina call out. He turned, saw her huddled against a tree, ashen-faced. He had to go to her. He holstered his gun, got slowly to his feet and went to her. Gently, he helped her up and hugged her.

'He was going to kill me . . .' she muttered.

Rick held her tightly. 'You're safe now. You're going to be just fine.' He wiped the tears from her face with his hand, noting the yellow bruised cheekbone and the bleak look in her eyes.

'We'll find him. I promise. He won't get away,' said Rick. He wasn't sure if she really had heard him, so he added softly, 'Come on, let's get you out of here. We'll have plenty of time to talk later, OK?'

She nodded.

The Iroquois flew them straight to Nelson Hospital. Medical personnel were waiting near the landing pad and they moved forward as soon as Gina stepped out of the helicopter escorted by a crew member. Rick helped her towards the gurney.

'Don't leave me,' she whispered, holding his hand.

'I won't. I'm right here.'

Rick waited in the corridor in the Emergency Department. A nurse brought him a chair.

'Thanks,' he murmured, and sat down. Half an hour later, the doctor came out. 'We'd like to keep Ms Rosselini in for a few days. Take a few x-rays, just in case.'

Rick nodded.

'You'd best get those wounds seen to,' the doctor added. 'You've taken a nasty blow to the head.'

Rick followed the nurse to another room where he took a seat on the bed. After removing his shirt, the nurse bathed his cuts and bandaged his chest and arm and cleansed around the heavy bruise on his forehead. He didn't need stitches.

'You're lucky it wasn't worse,' she commented.

'Don't I know it?' replied Rick drily.

The nurse slipped him a couple of strong painkillers swilled down with a strong cup of coffee.

'They should help,' she said sympathetically. 'Just take it easy, or that wound on your chest will open up again. Any sign of delayed concussion come straight back here. OK?'

'OK. Thanks!'

Rick returned to see Gina who had already been taken up to the medical unit. Her mind and body had taken a battering and it was going to take some time before she'd be well again. She'd been through so much, he thought. It wrenched his gut to think what Gallagher had done to her. Meanwhile, his resolve hardened. He had to find Gallagher. He knew Gina would never know any peace until he did.

Morning came. Rick woke, feeling stiff and sore. The painkillers had worn off. He'd slept in the soft chair beside Gina even though he'd been offered a room next door. He sat up, and looked over at her. Her face was as white as the sheets which covered her. He hated to leave her but he'd be back, he promised, and he told her that even though she was fast asleep, under sedation. He'd make sure she'd never have to worry about Gallagher again.

Outside the room, two police officers stood guard at each side of the door and Rick acknowledged them as he passed. 'I'm heading out to see Brougham. If Gina happens to wake, call me. The doctor said she'd be out for a while.'

The officers nodded.

Twenty minutes later he was at the station sitting in front of his former boss.

'Didn't think I'd see you so soon,' said Brougham. 'How are you feeling?'

Rick winced. 'Sore but I'll live.'

'And Gina?'

'Battered and bruised and upset. But she'll be OK. She just needs to rest.'

'We'll need to interview her again. As soon as she's awake.' Brougham got to his feet. 'Need a coffee?'

'Thanks. Make it strong. One sugar.' Brougham came back within a few minutes carrying two mugs of steaming liquid. He handed one to Rick.

'Have you eaten?' asked the detective.

Rick shook his head. 'Haven't had time. Figured I'd better get down here and see what's happening.'

Brougham opened a plastic box of sandwiches and shoved it across the table. 'Here. Help yourself.'

Rick gave a grin. 'Looks like your wife's still looking after you.'

'How did you guess?'

'No male I know cuts sandwiches that cute.' He bit into one and chewed. 'Hmm . . . tuna. Not bad.' He swallowed. 'Any word on Gallagher?'

'Not a damned thing. We were that close. . . .' The Detective swore softly. 'We've put out road blocks, the airport is covered heavily and we've got our helicopters searching the area constantly. It's just a matter of time before we pick him up.'

'You won't find him. We're going to have to wait for him to come to us. He's determined to get Gina. I think he'll make another attempt.'

Brougham scoffed. 'He wouldn't dare. We've got cops swarming all over the hospital.'

Rick leaned forward. 'All the same, I'm going to be staying there to keep a close eye on things.'

Brougham looked thoughtful. 'Don't forget he's wounded, so he's not going to be able to move very far.' He leaned back tiredly. 'It's been a hectic few days. Let's hope we get this wrapped up soon.'

'I wouldn't count on it. Gallagher will come when he's ready. Not before.'

Rick wolfed down another couple of sandwiches and drained his coffee cup. He glanced at his watch, then stood up. 'Time to get back to the hospital. Keep me posted, will you?'

Brougham nodded as he picked up the phone. 'I'll do just that. But remember what I said: don't take the law into your own hands. If you see Gallagher, or anything suspicious, call me.'

'I'll do what I have to,' Rick replied firmly, as he left Brougham staring after him with a frown on his face.

Rick called in to his office where he changed his clothes, and picked up an ordinance survey map. He estimated that Jason had gone bush. But he was injured, so he wouldn't last long without some medical help. Rick spread the map out on the table. Rick suspected that he would head for the nearest settlement where he would force someone to help him. The residents would have been warned that Gallagher was on the loose and that he was armed and dangerous. But realistically the police couldn't be everywhere. No matter how efficient they were.

Rick was right. Within seconds Brougham rang him. 'We've had a report Gallagher broke into a doctor's surgery and took some drugs and needles.'

'Once he's patched himself up, my guess is he'll head for the hospital.'

Brougham didn't agree. 'Now that he's got away, he's hardly going to walk back into a town where every cop knows what he looks like.'

'He wants Gina Rosselini and I'd say he'd be prepared to die doing it,' Rick stated firmly. 'We're dealing with a psychopath.'

'That much is obvious,' added Brougham, 'By the way, two other rifles were taken in the sports shop burglary so we can consider he stashed them so he's armed. So let's not take any chances. He fooled us before with the fake suicide. So we'll double the guard around Gina just in case.'

Rick grimaced. He didn't tell him he was wasting his time. And he also didn't tell him, when Gallagher came calling, he had every intention of being the one to face him. 'Just make sure the officers are armed.'

'They already are,' replied Brougham.

It was early evening when Rick arrived back at the hospital. Gina had only woken briefly and had then gone back to sleep. He went into her room and sat on the chair next to the bed, and stared at her pale face. Again, he leaned forward and kissed her lightly on the forehead.

'He'll never touch you again. I promise.'

Her eyes fluttered open. 'Rick. . . .'

'I'm right here.'

'Are you OK?'

He smiled. 'I'm fine. Just a few scratches. Nothing serious.'

'Have they found him?' she murmured.

He hated to tell her. 'No, but they will. And when they do, he'll be going to jail for a very long time.'

'Will he come after me again?'

He hesitated. He didn't want to worry her, and yet, he needed her to be on her guard, just in case.

'He might do. But he'd have trouble getting through all the protection around you. And he'll have trouble getting past me.'

'I'm glad you're there.'

His voice lowered. 'Yeah, me too.'

As if his words comforted her, her eyes fluttered, and closed. He could see by the rising of her chest she had fallen into a deep sleep again. Maybe that was for the best, he considered. Keeping Gina in one place, with one door to the room, made protecting her a lot easier. His mind ticked over. The first thing he needed to know was the layout of the hospital. A nurse came in and he asked her for a schematic of the place.

'It's just a general one, marking out the different floors and departments,' she answered. 'We give it out to our patients. I'll just get one for you.'

'When does the nursing staff change around here?' Rick enquired, following her to reception.

'Not until eleven o'clock tonight.' she informed him. 'And then again at seven in the morning.'

Rick thanked her. Gina's grandparents came in soon afterwards and Rick had a quick chat to them, and left them to sit with Gina. He waited outside, respecting their privacy. Later, when they had finished, Luigi came out to speak to him. 'I want Gallagher dead. Name your price.'

'A generous offer,' replied Rick. 'But that would be murder.'

'You're telling me it is murder? He killed my granddaughter Maria, and he almost killed Gina. I call that a vendetta. You're Italian, damn you.' He thumped his chest, right across his heart. 'What do you feel in here?'

Rick didn't need anyone to remind him who or what he was. 'Point taken. But the law will deal with him.'

Luigi shook his head. 'The law will put him away again and he'll be released in a few years on good behaviour. Then he'll come looking for Gina again.' He took a deep breath, his eyes stony hard. 'I don't want her living in fear all the time. Kill him . . . it's the only way.'

This time Rick said nothing and Luigi Rosselini taking his silence for refusal left. Thinking deeply about what Luigi had said, Rick settled down in the chair opposite Gina with a blanket and tried to get some sleep. Only he couldn't still his mind. He tried to put himself in Gallagher's place.

What would his next move be?

CHAPTER TWELVE

When Rick woke it was six in the morning and the clatter of a trolley could be heard somewhere along the tiled corridor. Jesus, he'd been in the hospital for two days. Didn't time fly, he thought? He glanced over at Gina, still sleeping. Stretching his cramped muscles, he got up to speak to the police officers, standing guard outside the room.

'Just heading to the hospital café to get some breakfast. On no account let anyone in the room, OK? Only nursing staff. Make sure you see their ID first.'

Twenty minutes later, after buying a croissant and a hot coffee, he made his way back to the ward. As he turned the corner on the second level, he caught a glimpse of a man dressed in a white coat, wearing a surgical mask and going into the elevator. Rick's forehead creased. The man was carrying a long black sports bag. There was something about the way he moved which attracted Rick's attention. Rick dropped the food and started to run. By the time he got to the elevator, the doors had already closed and it was going upwards fast.

Frantically, he looked around for the stairs and bounded up the steps until he reached the next level. He did a quick check to see if the elevator had stopped but it was still on its way up.

Rick charged back into the stairwell until he reached the next floor again stopping again to see if the elevator had halted. It continued to climb. He checked every level until finally the elevator stopped on the sixth floor, two floors up from Gina's ward. If it had been Gallagher, why hadn't he stopped sooner to get out? By the time he reached the top floor, and rushed through the doors, the elevator door was already open. No one was there.

'Damn it.' Rick swung around looking both ways down the corridor. The man had disappeared. Rick sprinted down the steps until he reached the fourth floor.

Once he reached Gina's room, he noticed the two officers guarding her were no longer at the door. His heart started to pound. He entered the room. Gina had gone and a nurse was busy changing the bed. She gave him a bright smile. 'If you're looking for Gina, an orderly came for her. She's gone to x-ray.'

Rick grabbed the nurse's arm. 'Where's the X-ray department? I need to find her urgently.'

'On the second floor.'

Rick hoped the cops had stayed with her as Brougham had instructed them. He couldn't believe he had stayed right beside her for twenty-four hours a day and, for only twenty minutes he'd been away, she'd left the hospital room.

Rick raced toward the stairwell and, taking two steps at a time, he reached the second floor. A quick glance at the sign, told him the X-ray department was further along the corridor. He sprinted. The receptionist sat at the front desk. 'Where's Gina Rosselini?'

'I think she's gone back to the ward.'

That was possible, thought Rick, if they had used the elevator. The only way to check was to phone the ward. Rick reached over for the phone. Once he got through, he found out Gina had returned. 'Is she in her room?' asked Rick. His fingers tapped on the reception counter.

'Just a minute, I'll check,' said the nurse. Within seconds she came back on the phone. 'Ms Rosselini is having a shower. The two officers are still there, standing guard outside. All's well.'

Rick heaved a sigh of relief. 'Good. Tell the police I'll be back in a few minutes.'

As he walked out the X-ray department, Rick thought about the man he had seen. An uneasy feeling came over him. It just didn't gel. The man dressed was dressed in white, but he carried a black bag. And where had the man disappeared to so quickly?

Rick decided to retrace his steps but found nothing. The pharmacy was situated on the top floor, the door locked. He rang the intercom and someone came to the door. But no one, of the description he gave them, worked in the pharmacy.

When he'd returned to Gina's room, she was sitting up in bed drinking a cup of tea. Her bright smile warmed him. 'Hello.'

'Hello yourself. Feeling better?'

She nodded, then winced. 'Oh, apart from my head. It won't stop pounding.'

'That's to be expected.' He sat down on the bed, and took her hand in his. 'It's going to take time.'

'I know.' She frowned. 'Is something wrong?'

'No . . . nothing.' He said it too quickly and he had a feeling she didn't believe him. He didn't want to tell her about the man he'd seen earlier. It would only worry her and that was the last thing he wanted.

She sank back onto the pillows as her hand in his tightened. 'You can't be here twenty-four hours a day. I'll be fine if you want to take a break. Go home, get changed. See your family. They'll be worried about you.'

'I will. Soon,' he promised.

'Now,' she countered firmly.

He gave a grin. 'You feel like arguing? You must be feeling better.'

She gave a smile. 'I do have two officers outside. And in case you hadn't noticed, they've got muscles like wrestlers.'

He knew she was right. He needed to get another change of clothes at least. If he went home, he could be back to the hospital within the hour.

After several days, Gina felt much better. A quick look out the hospital window convinced her that a short walk around the gardens below would lift her spirits. But when she suggested it to Rick, he refused immediately.

A worried frown etched his forehead. 'Not yet. It's still not safe.'

'You can't keep me locked up forever.'

But he still refused. 'Maybe tomorrow. We'll see.'

The feeling of being caged in didn't sit well. A claustrophobic feeling swamped over her. If she didn't get out of the hospital room soon, even for a short while, she'd go crazy.

The opportunity came when Rick went down to the café to buy lunch. 'I won't be long,' he said.

'Why can't I come?'

He shook his head. 'No. Best stay here. Fancy anything from the café?'

'Uh-huh. Chocolate. Dark and rich with lots of nuts,' she emphasized. 'I have this craving—'

He stared at her. 'You're not. . . ?'

She went forward, gave a chuckle, and reached up to kiss him on the cheek. 'Just teasing.' She didn't tell him it could still be a remote possibility.

He breathed a sigh of relief. 'For a moment, I thought—'

'Don't think. Just go eat.' She gently pushed him out the door. Then when he was halfway down the corridor she shouted, 'Better make that two bars of chocolate. Just in case.'

'Gina,' he growled, but she could see the amusement on his face.

'It will give me energy,' she added wickedly.

Once he'd gone, Gina went back into the room and sat down on the bed. She didn't feel like reading, and there was nothing on television. She stood up, looked out the window again. The gardens were right below. If only she could go for a little walk. Surely there wouldn't be any harm in that? She made a quick decision. Reaching for her silk dressing-gown, she put it on, and slipped on her sandals.

The two officers were outside the door talking when she approached. 'Please, can you take me downstairs into the gardens? Just for some fresh air.'

'Sorry but we've got orders for you to stay here,' answered Constable Lowe.

Her chin lifted. 'A short walk won't do any harm. And I've got you two with me. Come on,' she pleaded. 'If you don't, I'll just go out myself. And you'll have no choice but to follow me.'

Lowe swopped glances with his colleague, looking unsure. The other constable spoke up. 'A short walk should be OK, I guess.'

Gina smiled. 'Thank you. I knew you'd see it my way.'

Within minutes, she was outside breathing in the fresh air. It felt so good to see the blue sky. Sunshine belted down, warming her skin. The gardens were well kept, she noticed, with native shrubs and ferns. It was a peaceful place. Somewhere you could gather your thoughts. She needed that. Near the cabbage tree a garden seat beckoned. Gina made for it and sat down. The two armed uniformed officers stood nearby conversing amongst themselves. She leaned back against the seat and closed her eyes. Her thoughts drifted. She had to try to put the nightmare of her abduction behind her.

'We ought to be heading back upstairs, ma'am,' said Constable Lowe. 'We've already been away longer than we should have.' He gave a worried frown.

'Just another few minutes, please,' she pleaded. She reckoned she had a few minutes more before Rick returned to the hospital room. And who could possibly get to her in the hospital gardens?

Rick cut short his lunch when one of the nurses, who was on her break from the ward came over to his table and said Gina had left the room.

'Where did she go?' he asked.

'For a walk. I think she headed downstairs. The two uniforms were with her.'

Rick cursed. He should have guessed what she'd get up to. Dumping the rest of his lunch in the bin, he made for the windows where he could survey the gardens below. Gina sat quietly on a seat talking to the two officers. He breathed a sigh of relief. She was safe. All the same, it would be better if she came back inside where she wasn't so vulnerable. He took out his mobile phone intending to phone Lowe, but then pocketed it. He'd head down there himself and talk to her. Chances were high she wouldn't take any notice of him by phone anyway. If it came to it, he'd carry her inside.

He was just about to turn away when Rick caught the flash of something white at a window in the building opposite. A man wearing a white medical mask, stood there staring down at Gina. Something about the way he was looking at her sent alarm shooting up his spine. He took out his phone again and punched in a number. Lowe answered.

'Get Gina inside, quick,' urged Rick.

'What's up?' came back the reply.

'Never mind, just get inside. Now.'

Rick watched them. The officer bent over and said something to Gina. A stubborn look crossed her face.

'Let me speak to her,' added Rick.

Lowe handed her the phone. But Rick never got a chance to speak. A shot rang out. He glanced upwards. The white figure held a rifle resting on the window ledge. Rick's eyes widened. He swore in Italian.

Lowe swung around, pulling his gun from his holster. Rick heard him utter the words, 'What the hell . . .' and then another shot rang out. The bullet hit Lowe who was standing behind Gina. He staggered and fell forward. The other officer also whipped out his gun and grabbed Gina's arm and pulled her down, trying to gain some protection from the wooden bench. Another shot was fired by the rifleman.

Rick heard Gina sobbing for help into the mobile phone.

'Stay down,' urged Rick. 'I'm on my way.' He had to get there and fast. It would take him five minutes at least to get to the bottom floor. Not bothering to wait for the lift, he barged through the swinging doors to the stairwell. Once he reached the ground floor, he shouldered open the fire doors and charged outside. He glanced upwards. The man in white had gone.

Gina shouted out to him, got to her feet and ran into his arms. He pulled her safely inside and held her tightly.

'Are you hurt?' he asked, his heart pounding.

'No,' she said trembling. 'Just shaken up. Where was he shooting from?'

Rick pointed. 'Up there. On the third floor.'

Within seconds, the medics arrived to see to the injured police officer. Rick turned to an orderly standing nearby. 'How do I get across to the building over there?'

'I'll take you. I know a shortcut.'

Rick knew by the time he got there, Gallagher was likely to have moved on and he was right. The room where Gallagher had been was empty. It looked like a storeroom. Rick ran back out to the corridor, and then down the stairwell to the next floor. He peered over the railing to see if he could see anyone descending the stairs. He saw a flash of white. Rick started after him. He'd almost caught up with him on the basement level and jumped the last remaining steps. He gave a tackle which would have impressed a rugby team but Jason twisted round and lashed out with the butt of the rifle catching Rick on the side of the head. The blow stunned him. Rick let Gallagher go as he dealt with the pain. He staggered to the side, clutching the railing with one hand and his forehead with the other. He watched furiously as Gallagher disappeared through a set of swinging doors to yet another corridor.

Rick stood gasping, trying to ignore the pain thundering through his temples. He straightened up, took a few steps forward. No way could he let Gallagher get away now, not when he was so close. He drew his Glock, and peered carefully through the small window of the swinging doors in front of him. The first thing he saw was the sign of the morgue. Loath to enter with all lights blaring and knowing he'd be a target the minute he walked through the door,

Rick found the light switch and flicked it upwards. An emergency light came on, giving out an eerie amber glow.

Although he knew the actual corpses would probably be in one of the refrigerators in the back room, he couldn't help the unease which crawled up and down his spine as he made his way past some empty trolleys, parked side by side, obviously ready for use at a minute's notice.

With the Glock held in front of him, he lowered himself to the floor and squatting down he made his way along the green marbled floor until he reached a large desk in the reception area. A noise like a bottle clinking had him swinging around but he couldn't see anything. His gaze roved along the line of tall cupboards and shelves opposite, stacked full of black folders. Nothing moved. He crawled around to the other side, checking out the room fully from behind the rim of the desk. Still no sign. Gallagher had to be hiding but it was obvious it wasn't in here. That meant he had to have gone through one of the four doors in front of him. But which one? Taking a gamble, he chose one that said the laboratory. He moved forward slowly and tried the door handle. It opened. He pushed it ajar slightly. Then kicked it open fast. Nothing happened. He stepped inside. An emergency light glowed in the corner of the room. Shadows from the trolleys threw dark thick lines across the polished floor. Rick gripped the automatic tighter, sweat pouring down his temples. Another noise. He swung round quickly, both hands holding the gun steady. Then he realized where the noise had come from. Pipes ran across the ceiling making gurgling sounds. Gallagher had to be in one of the other three rooms.

Rick tried the door handle of another room but it was locked. Had Gallagher locked it behind him? He moved across to the next one. It was only a large cupboard. Finally, he faced the fourth door. It opened with a slight creak.

The first thing that hit him was the smell of the place. An odd odour wafted nearby, making him want to hold his breath. He saw the stainless steel sink and the opened bottles sitting on the bench.

Medical instruments lay side by side, along with some cameras on tripods as if some sort of macabre movie was about to take place.

He jolted. A body lay on the trolley. He stared at it for a few seconds, his gaze taking in the length of it. A label hung from the big toe. He wasn't easily perturbed, having seen death many times before, but there was something pretty horrible about a body lying so still with a pure, white sheet draped over it. He went closer to have a look. A quick glance at the label said it was a female. He stood for a few seconds looking around, wondering if there might have been an exit he might have missed. But no, there was nothing. He was just about to leave, when his gaze was drawn back to the body again. There was something strange about it. He went closer and flicked the tag. One dead female. He looked curiously at the feet. They were big for a female, he noticed. He would have sworn they belonged to a male.

He stepped forward intending to whip off the sheet. Before he had a chance, the body leapt upwards. Two hands grabbed him by the throat. The move was so violent, Rick dropped the Glock and it clattered onto the floor. Staggering back, he swung his arms upwards dislodging Gallagher's deathlike grip. It worked. As soon as Gallagher let go, Rick swung his fist round and caught Gallagher on the jaw, snapping his head back. Gallagher fell backwards hitting the trolley. He didn't go down. Instead, when he righted himself, he grabbed the trolley and swung it round hard in Rick's direction. Rick caught it with his left hand and deflected it, where it crashed heavily against a cupboard. A whole line of dark-coloured bottles toppled over smashing heavily onto the floor. Liquid pooled near his feet, making the floor slippery. Fumes choked his throat, making Rick cough and his eyes water.

When Gallagher saw the automatic lying on the floor, he made a dive for it but misjudged the distance. Rick leapt forward, kicking the gun away, out of reach. While Gallagher tried to scramble to his feet, Rick tackled him, wrenching the man's arms behind his back. Now, he had him in an arm lock.

'Move and I'll break your arm,' said Rick, roughly.

The door swung open and Dave Brougham stood there, his mouth agape, as he took in the chaos before him.

'About time,' Rick said, gasping. 'Where the hell have you been?'

Brougham gave a smile. 'Why rush? I knew you would take care of it.'

Gina hadn't seen Rick yet since he was still at police headquarters giving his statement. The only thing worrying her now was facing Rick after what he had done for her. She'd heard all about it, in great detail, from the police officers on duty outside her room. How he had tackled Jason in the morgue. Put his own life at risk. Good people had been brought into this whole horrible episode. All because Jason had gone stark raving mad determined to have his revenge on her and her family.

The nurse, seeing her packing her belongings, called the doctor. He arrived within a few minutes, casting her a disapproving look.

'What's all this about Ms Rosselini?'

'I'm leaving.'

'I think you should stay in longer,' he reasoned. 'Besides, we have strict instructions you were to wait for Mr Caruso to pick you up.'

She said adamantly. 'I'm going down to the police station to find him.' She calmly finished packing her things and lifted her bag, before turning around to face the doctor again. 'I don't want to make a fuss, but I really do feel OK.'

It was obvious the doctor still didn't believe her. 'You've been through a lot. I don't think you should leave the hospital alone. Let me call your grandparents first. They can come and collect you.'

'No,' she said sharply. 'I don't need them to come and get me. I'll make my own way.'

Thankfully, two police officers escorted her to a waiting squad car and offered to give her a lift. She had just thrown her handbag into the back seat, when to her surprise Rick drew up in his wagon. She paused, her hand on the door. She watched him climb out and make his way over to her.

'Going somewhere?' he asked softly.

'Rick,' she murmured, moving forward. She stopped, unsure what to do next.

He stood there, within an arm's length, just watching her. She noticed he had showered recently, his hair slightly damp. He wore faded jeans that clad his thighs, emphasizing strong, muscled legs. His shirt, a soft white cotton, offset his tanned skin.

Her gaze lowered fractionally as she tried to think what she was going to say, but instead her gaze kept being drawn back to his eyes looking at her so intensely.

'Gina. Don't be afraid.'

And the more she looked, the more the doubts faded and she knew that she loved him. She saw the fresh cut on his forehead and before she realized what she was doing, her fingertips touched it ever so softly. 'You're hurt.'

'It's only a scratch,' he said reassuringly, 'nothing to worry about.'

'I want to thank you,' she said simply. 'I know you went after Jason singlehanded and I know in doing so, you risked your life for me. It's something I can never repay.'

His finger tilted her chin upwards. 'Gina, you owe me nothing. Forget the past now. There's a whole new future out there waiting for us both. It's up to you to take that chance.'

'Do you really think we can?' she asked. 'You don't think what has happened with Jason will taint everything? Maybe even us eventually?'

'No, I don't believe that.' He paused slightly as if searching for the right thing to say. 'As far as I'm concerned I'm in love with you. Nothing can ever alter that.'

She moved closer to him. A soft breeze blew gently, cooling her skin, and blowing back the tendrils of her hair. It cleared her thoughts, chasing away the last remnants of doubt. Her heart suddenly soared.

'Oh, Rick,' she murmured. This was a chance for happiness,

wasn't it? And oh . . . it felt so right.

He lifted his hand again, skimming his knuckles over her cheekbone.

'I've been thinking, Gina Rosselini.' His voice had dropped an octave as he said her name caressingly. Then his arm slid casually around her shoulders, drawing her away to a secluded corner, out of sight of the police officers. His lips found hers. The kiss was all she ever dreamed it could be and more.

When she pulled away to take a breath, he said, 'I've got us a flight booked on the first plane out in the morning. We'll head to Sicily for our honeymoon.'

Surprised, she stared at him, noticing his smile filled with promise. She only had to say yes. He was waiting for her, ever so patiently, and for that she was grateful.

'We'll have lots of kids,' he carried on teasingly.

She gave a smile. 'You mean we'll have fun trying.' She couldn't resist a little teasing herself.

He chuckled. 'I'm Italian, don't forget. Kids and marriage go together,' he added softly, with a glint in his blue eyes.

As if she could ever forget *that*, she thought. 'Know something? I've always wanted to go to Sicily . . . and lots of kids sound just fine,' she replied, the lump in her throat growing. 'Besides, I've already decided that I can't live without you.'

He raised a brow. 'You have?'

'Uh-huh. I love you, Rick Caruso. I love you now. And I'll love you forever.'

As they both climbed into his car, Gina realized how lucky she really was. Sure they had both faced adversity, but they'd both come through it. And in doing so, it made their love even stronger. Nothing would ever break it. Or them.

'No regrets?' he asked.

'None,' she replied firmly.

And she knew then, there never would be.